Help us Rate this book...
Put your initials on the
Left side and your rating
on the right side.
1 = Didn't care for
2 = It was O.K.
3 = It was <u>great</u>

	DATE DUE	8/19	
m/c 1 (2) 3	SEP 0 3 2019		
_____ 1 2 3	NOV 1 2 2020		
_____ 1 2 3			
_____ 1 2 3			
_____ 1 2 3			
_____ 1 2 3			
_____ 1 2 3			
_____ 1 2 3			
_____ 1 2 3			
_____ 1 2 3		DISCARDED	
_____ 1 2 3			
_____ 1 2 3			
_____ 1 2 3			
_____ 1 2 3			
_____ 1 2 3			

PRINTED IN U.S.A.

Wooing Cadie McCaffrey

Center Point
Large Print

Also by Bethany Turner and available
from Center Point Large Print:

The Secret Life of Sarah Hollenbeck

**This Large Print Book carries the
Seal of Approval of N.A.V.H.**

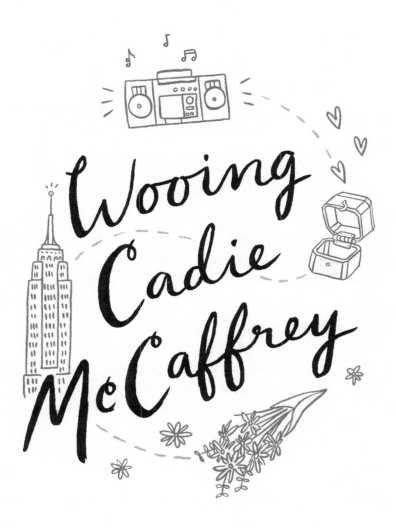

Wooing Cadie McCaffrey

BETHANY TURNER

CENTER POINT LARGE PRINT
THORNDIKE, MAINE

This Center Point Large Print edition
is published in the year 2019 by arrangement with
Revell, a division of Baker Publishing Group.

The text of this Large Print edition is unabridged.
In other aspects, this book may vary
from the original edition.
Printed in the United States of America
on permanent paper.
Set in 16-point Times New Roman type.
ISBN: 978-1-64358-261-0

Library of Congress Cataloging-in-Publication Data

Names: Turner, Bethany, 1979- author.
Title: Wooing Cadie McCaffrey / Bethany Turner.
Description: Center Point Large Print edition. | Thorndike, Maine :
    Center Point Large Print, 2019.
Identifiers: LCCN 2019016453 | ISBN 9781643582610 (hardcover :
    alk. paper)
Subjects: LCSH: Large type books.
Classification: LCC PS3620.U76 W66 2019b | DDC 813/.6—dc23
LC record available at https://lccn.loc.gov/2019016453

Dedicated to the memory of Nora Ephron,
Who taught me that you always
need someone to kiss on New Year's,
That daisies are indeed the friendliest flower,
And that sometimes people don't
just want to be in love.
They want to be in love in a movie.

Prologue

Four years ago, on my thirtieth birthday, I had two very important realizations.

1) I didn't need a man in my life in order to be happy or fulfilled.

2) My chances of meeting and falling in love with a man—and having him fall in love with me—would increase exponentially if I lowered my standards.

Not my standards for the man, of course. No, with the introduction of realization number one, the standards for the man had never been higher. If I didn't *need* a man, then there was no harm in being very picky and waiting for the right one to come along. But with the introduction of realization number two, I could no longer deny that I did very much want to be in love . . . whether I needed to be or not.

In my heart of hearts, I knew I had no desire to settle for anything less than a man who would make at least one of the Bronte sisters proud. But there wasn't much chance of falling in love with any man at all if I stayed hung up on the idea of my romantic life playing out like the classic novels and films I loved so much.

Cary Grant does not exist in my Millennial world.

Of course, I wasn't expecting Will Whitaker to show up, or for him to burst onto the scene as if acting out a storybook meet-cute.

You know what a meet-cute is, right? It's that charming first encounter between two characters that leads to a romantic relationship between them. Suffice it to say, with realization number two, I had given up on ever experiencing a true meet-cute. Actually, I was pretty convinced that I wouldn't know a true meet-cute if it fell on me. I'd spent most of my life trying to force the meet-cute. Trust me . . . that doesn't work. Intentionally bumping into guys and dropping your books rarely results in them saying, "Hey, let me help you with that." I've found that "Hey, watch where you're going!" is more common.

So by the time I turned thirty, I was absolutely convinced that meet-cutes were a thing of legend.

Enter Will, stage left.

It was a day like any other at ASN, the American Sports Network. That's where I worked. ASN. But not like in *sports* or anything. Heavens, no. All I know of basketball, football, lacrosse, or any other sport is how much money is generated in advertising dollars as a result of our coverage of said sport, and how much all of those on-air sports people get paid. My office is in the part of the ASN complex that the sports people call The Bench. They come to our stark wasteland of blah concrete walls for marketing and accounting needs. Perhaps the occasional human resources disaster. But then they happily return to the glitz and glamour that they refer to as The Field.

"Gotta get back on The Field," they love to say. *On* The Field? That sounds so stupid. But when I say "I'm heading over *to* The Field for a bit," I am invariably met with questions that they think are hilarious. "Got some plowing to do, McCaffrey?" Sure.

So there I was, in The Bench—or *on* The Bench, as they continually correct me—when I heard the most dreaded of all birthday sounds: about twenty tone-deaf sports experts and about half as many barbershop quartet wannabes from The Bench, all singing "Happy Birthday." To me, presumably.

"Oh, wow. You shouldn't have," I managed to say in a way that I'm pretty sure sounded grateful, as they made their way into my office—holding a monstrous cake ablaze with thirty giant candles.

"Happy birthday, dear Cadie," they belted. "Happy birthday to you!"

I waited for Kevin Lamont, who was carrying the cake, to set it down on my desk so I could blow out the candles, but he just kept holding it. Kevin, of course, is now the host and executive

producer of *The Daily Dribble*, the most successful show on ASN. He's also the vice president
over all prime-time programming for the network, which makes him my boss. But back then
he was simply *The Daily Dribble*'s host and one
of my absolute favorite people around the ASN
offices. And though he's gone a bit gray and put
on a little around his midsection, he certainly
hasn't lost a centimeter of height from his NBA
days.

"Make a wish and blow out the candles,"
Kevin teased as he held the cake at his shoulder
height—which is still at least an inch above my
head.

"Well, I'd love to, but—"

"Here, Cadie," Max Post, resident sound
engineer extraordinaire, chimed in as he pulled a
chair over to my desk. "Climb up here."

"Very funny, guys," I replied with a smile.
"C'mon, Kevin. All of the wax is going to melt
down onto the cake."

"You'd better do something about it then!" he
insisted as he jutted out his chin toward a couple
of former linebackers.

In an instant, the linebackers had grabbed my
arms and hoisted me up—not onto the chair by
the desk, but onto the desk itself.

I was so grateful that after six years at ASN, I
knew better than to wear a skirt to the office.

"Very funny," I repeated, as I did all I could

to remind myself that I loved my job—and that it wasn't my coworkers' fault that they were savages. They meant well, and I knew that everything they were doing was an attempt to show me that they cared. They just happened to be from a culture in which you showed someone you cared by snapping them with a wet towel in the locker room.

I was ready to end the spectacle, so I took in a deep breath and prepared to use every bit of power my lungs could muster to blow out those thirty massive candles in one fell swoop. But just as I released the pressure of air, Lindy Mason called out from the hallway.

"Hey, everyone. Montana's here."

Kevin turned his 6'9" frame toward the door—and my cake went with him.

"Happy birthday, Cadie!" scattered voices called out as they left me in favor of Joe Montana, who was on The Field for an interview. An interview that they'd been waiting months for—but that only about eight of them were actually required to be present for. The others were just going as fans who happened to get paid to gawk at their heroes.

"Sorry, McCaffrey," Kevin said as he shrugged and handed me the cake.

"Et tu, Kevin Lamont?"

He smiled and winked as he said, "Next time, don't have your birthday on a day a legend is scheduled to be in the studio." And then he ran out after everyone else.

Perfect.

I held the ridiculously large cake in my arms and tried to figure out how to get down. I had learned not to wear skirts to work, but unfortunately I still insisted on wearing heels.

"Now what?" I asked, of absolutely no one.

I sighed and looked at the chair next to the desk. I wouldn't be able to see where I was stepping, due to the sheer magnitude of the cake, so stepping down onto the chair was out. I decided instead to squat down and place the cake on the desk, but the combination of the weight of the cake and balancing on heels made me very wobbly. I felt myself losing my grip on the cake as I teetered forward—the cake that still burned with the light and heat of three decades' worth of candles.

"Whoa, whoa, whoa," a voice called out from behind me.

Before I knew what was happening, he had one arm around my waist and the other under my cake. He gently lowered the cake onto the desk and then looped his arm under my knees. Pretty instantly I was back on the ground, on my feet, but there was a brief second when he was carrying me in a manner of which I knew Charlotte, Emily, and Anne would all approve.

"Sorry about that," I muttered, the heat of my

cheeks undeniable, even before I had looked at him. And then I *did* look at him.

He was taller than me, but not as tall as most of the guys from The Field, who regularly made me feel like a Hobbit. No, he was just the perfect amount of tall. Okay . . . probably not an athlete. Although he was fit and muscular. At least not a star athlete. A golfer, maybe? His face drew me in—with its crinkly eyes and perfectly shaped mouth. But it was also just the tiniest bit . . . goofy. His nose was a little too big, as were his ears, and while he was handsome—without question—he was also blatantly imperfect. So probably not an on-air personality.

"Um, is your cake from Madame Tussaud's bakery?" His eyes darted with humor back and forth from my eyes to the cake.

"What?" I turned to face the cake on the desk, and my mouth and eyes flew open as I took in the sight of candles, which had become nothing more than melted wax nubs barely standing between the fire and the frosting. "Oh my goodness!" I exclaimed, and then I huffed and puffed—and hardly made a dent.

"These must be those hard-to-extinguish candles," he astutely observed as he began huffing and puffing alongside me.

I wheezed. "You think?"

"Just a hunch." He shrugged, and I laughed.

We kept blowing, and the sparks kept

reigniting. We could have doused the flames, or suffocated them, but that didn't seem to occur to us just then. All we knew to do was use all the air our lungs could generate, over and over again. Finally—one by one—sparks faded, as there was nothing left but little bits of wick swallowed by extremely waxy frosting.

Neither of us said a word for several seconds. He backed away to provide a comfortable distance between two people who had just met. Yes, he had very recently carried me in his arms, but that had been a cake emergency. Now, the proximity would just be awkward. But I barely even took note of any of that. I just stared at my once beautiful cake. Well, at least it had given the appearance of being beautiful, when it had been lit up like a friskier version of the Olympic torch. Once the dazzling spectacle was gone, I was able to see what was written on it, in black icing.

"Happy 50th Birthday, Cadie!"

"Happy 50th," I said aloud. "Lovely." I shook my head and laughed. "Kevin Lamont is a punk."

"Oh! You know Kevin Lamont? I'm supposed to be meeting with him today. In about—" He glanced at his watch, and then his eyes flew open. "Oh, man. About five minutes ago!"

I scooped some icing onto my finger and then licked it off as I said, "Don't worry about it. The whole Field is in a Joe Montana haze right now. No one knows you're missing."

14

His eyes opened even wider. "Joe . . . Joe Montana? Is he . . . is he here?"

I turned away from him so he wouldn't see me roll my eyes. "He is. Kevin's interviewing him for *The Daily Dribble*. I'm sure if you hurry, you can still catch him."

"Am I allowed? I mean . . . I have an interview—"

"Oh yeah?" I interrupted, not meaning to show interest but unable to stop myself. "For what position?"

"Well, hang on a second," he said as he crossed his arms and leaned against the doorframe. "What makes you so sure it's a job interview? Maybe Kevin Lamont is interviewing *me* on *The Daily Dribble*. Did you ever think of that?"

I turned his direction once again—increasingly charmed by him. "No. I didn't."

"Oh, come on." He stood up taller and puffed out his chest. "I've played some ball in my day."

I laughed. "I'm sure you have. You are very clearly a fine athletic specimen." I felt the heat rise back up to my cheeks. *Please let him know I'm teasing.*

"Why, yes. Yes, I am." He knew. "In fact, it's probably best I wait a few minutes before going out there. Montana's not quite the well-tuned machine he once was, so—"

"You wouldn't want to make him feel insecure or anything . . ."

"Exactly."

The corner of his mouth crept slowly upwards, but there was nothing gradual about the appearance of the twinkle in his eyes.

"Researcher on *The Daily Dribble*," he finally said. "I'm not sure what gave me away."

"It was mostly the fact that you called Kevin by his real name. His close friends—you know, pretty much all the major athletes in the world—call him—"

"Swoosh."

I tilted my head, trying to figure out if the cute, imperfect, charming guy was as much of a sports fan as the rest of them, or if he just knew things because he was a researcher. I was really hoping it was option B, but I wasn't optimistic. I mean, do people really become sports researchers if they aren't obsessed with sports? I just didn't know if I could allow myself to be interested in another sports guy.

But the fact of the matter was that most people didn't come to work at ASN if they weren't governed by their love of the game. Whichever game. At least *one* of the games. I knew I was an exception to the rule, and always had been, and that worked just fine for me. Spreadsheets don't need color commentary, and they don't go into overtime. What *did* go into overtime, however, pretty much every single day, was my work schedule. And when you work all the time, work is the best place to meet guys.

It would be nice if once—just once—the guys weren't *sports guys.*

"Yeah." I sighed. "Swoosh. Well, thanks for your help with the cake and, you know . . . that whole embarrassing birthday debacle."

"Anytime," he replied with a smile. "I guess I should get to this interview."

"Definitely. And if you hurry, maybe you can still catch Joe Montana."

He nodded appreciatively and made his way out the door and into the hallway. "This way?" he asked, pointing toward The Field.

"Yep. Good luck."

I smiled at him and then turned back to my mess of a cake. A girl can't afford to be a cake snob on her thirtieth birthday, so I began the arduous task of scraping the wax onto a paper plate, salvaging as much of the frosting as possible. It took several minutes, but I tackled it with the precision of a neurosurgeon, sucking on wax chunks as necessary so nothing went to waste. Of course it was just as I had stuffed another giant dollop of icing into my mouth that he showed up at my door again.

"So, I'm going to venture a guess and say you're not really turning fifty years old today. Correct?"

I gulped down my glob of sugary indulgence as quickly as I could and turned to face him. "That is correct."

He was in the doorframe, leaning against one side of it, one leg crossed in front of the other, his arms mirroring the position. He really was cute, my second viewing confirmed. And he got even cuter as a wide grin overtook his entire face.

"What?" I asked, my own smile growing by leaps and bounds at the sight of his.

"Black frosting," he replied as he took one step back into my office.

I still didn't understand what he found so amusing, but as long as his amusement kept resulting in that smile, no one would hear me complain. Finally, he realized that I had no clue why we were staring at each other with goofy expressions on our faces.

"Black frosting," he repeated. And then he took yet another step. "It's . . . well . . ." He chuckled softly and then said, one more time, "Black frosting." But this time the words were accompanied by a general sweeping motion across his own mouth and pearly whites, and I understood.

"What's your point?" I asked, hoping that my self-assured demeanor was at least somewhat believable. "I refuse to allow the world's prejudice against food coloring–stained teeth and lips to stand in the way of my birthday celebration.

After all, a thirty-year-old only turns fifty once. Or twice potentially, I suppose."

"Very true." He nodded and smiled and then stepped farther into the room—closer to me, and then closer still. It had been quite a while since I had felt any sort of chemistry with any guy, or even been somewhat attracted to one, so to be attracted *and* feel a spark was almost enough to make me wonder if my two important birthday realizations from earlier in the day had just been the sad, pathetic musings of a woman desperately grasping at straws upon waking to discover she was no longer in her twenties.

But then the cute stranger with the slightly too-big nose and the slightly asymmetrical eyes—and the absolutely bewitching smile—walked straight over to my cake and used his fingers to dig into the thickest patch of black icing he could find. He turned to face me and grinned the toothiest grin you can imagine—and his teeth were the stuff of Halloween legend, just like mine. Then I knew—or at least I suspected, or at least I really, really hoped—that those two realizations had been rendered obsolete. My smitten brain was already working on the revisions.

1) I didn't need a man in my life in order to be happy or fulfilled. But having the *right* man in my life certainly wouldn't stand in the way of happiness or fulfillment.

2) My chances of meeting and falling in love

with a man—and having him fall in love with me—would increase exponentially if I lowered my standards. But that didn't mean that I couldn't be pleasantly surprised by someone actually raising the standard. And it didn't mean that someone who raised the standard wouldn't be . . . better.

"So, you're thirty?" he asked, not taking his eyes off of me as his icing-stained fingers went back for seconds. I laughed and nodded. "What other lies has this cake told? I bet your name isn't really Palie at all, is it?"

My eyebrow rose. "No, it isn't." I peeked at the smeared, waxy icing, which now said, "Harpy soy Birdbay, Palie!" and started cracking up. "You think my name is Palie? And . . . today is my thirtieth birdbay?"

"Well, it doesn't seem quite right, I confess," he said. "But really, your name . . . how old you are . . . none of that matters. What really matters is that you have a harpy soy birdbay. So . . . *has* it been a harpy birdbay, Palie?"

It's getting better all the time. "Yes, thank you. It's been pretty harpy."

"Good." He smiled and looked down at his shuffling feet. Once he looked down, he realized he was fidgeting and put a stop to it. "I'm Will Whitaker, by the way," he said, raising his eyes to meet mine once more. He began to stretch out his arm to shake my hand but quickly realized the staining was not just reserved for his face. With a laugh he stuck out his left hand instead. I would have met it with *my* left hand, but I was even more untouchable than he was, so I awkwardly shook his hand with the pinky finger and thumb of my right hand.

I finally told him my name as I laughed and shook my head at the absurdity of it all. "Cadie. Cadie McCaffrey."

"Ah yes." He nodded. "That suits you so much more than Palie."

I would have gladly stood there, being amused by each other, all day long, but the thought suddenly occurred that I had work to do—and he was supposed to be in an interview.

"Oh my gosh." My eyes flew open as his had earlier when he'd realized he was running late. And now he was *very* late. "Aren't you supposed to be meeting with Kevin?"

"He was busy with Joe Cool. We're meeting in a few minutes."

"Joe Cool?" I repeated, my men-who-love-sports trepidation rising back to the surface.

"You know . . . Joe Cool. Joe Montana."

"Yeah." I sighed. "I figured."

"You're not a Montana fan?" When I didn't reply and just shrugged my shoulders, he pushed further. "Not a football fan?" I bit my lip and still said nothing. "Not a *sports* fan?" he asked incredulously.

"No, I'm really not."

That was it. I knew that was it. See ya, Will Whitaker—ye of the shaggy head full of hair and the tiny little dimples that had already presented themselves as an added benefit of making him laugh. If there was one thing I knew from experience, it was that I wasn't nearly as opposed to dating sports guys as they were opposed to dating someone who didn't understand the first thing about their greatest passion.

"Okay." He shrugged, the intensity of his eye contact and the sparkle in his eyes not fading one little bit.

Hang on. What?

"But listen," he continued. "You don't have to like sports to still appreciate Joe Cool. Montana was the best of all time. It didn't matter what was happening on the field all around him—his head was always exactly where it needed to be. He could size up fifty yards of chaos in an instant, and zero in on exactly the right play at exactly the right moment. He's the reason I fell in love with football. He made me realize that sports— when done right—isn't just about strength and speed and agility and all of that. Yeah, Montana had an arm like no one else, but he's in the Hall of Fame because of his brain."

I have to admit, Will Whitaker had found a way to make sports talk somewhat interesting to me. And a little bit of that may have even had something to do with Joe Montana.

A very little bit.

"Will?" I began with a smile.

"Yes?"

"It sounds like Joe Montana is a hero of yours."

He nodded. "Absolutely."

"Okay, so you need to get over to The Field. Run to the men's room, splash some water on your teeth, and go meet your hero! What are you doing standing around here?"

The corner of his mouth rose once again, and the shuffling feet returned—but this time, he didn't look down at them. His eyes never left mine.

"I needed to see if you have plans tonight. Because, if not, I'd love to take you out for your birdbay." He leaned in slightly and added, in a near whisper, "That would make me very harpy."

Ladies and gentlemen: the meet-cute.

1

Four Years Later. To the Day.

W hat a difference four years can make.
   I sniffed and dabbed at my eyes as I scrolled through the countless photos on my phone. Selfies on roller coasters; shots of beautiful scenery, taken on weekends when we got out of the city and drove upstate; Central Park, covered in snow—serving its premiere purpose as a worthy backdrop in every picture I could manage to sneak of him.

Those were always my favorites. The sneak attack photos. When he knew I was taking his picture, it was as if his face wasn't capable of a non-goofy expression. And I liked those too. But when I caught him taking in his surroundings, delighting in . . . anything? Well, that was when Will Whitaker was the most photogenic man on the planet.

I hadn't taken a sneak attack photo of him in almost a year. Actually, I had to go back six months to even find any photo of him at all.

If no longer feeling compelled to snap adoring photos of the person you're supposed to be in love with isn't a sign that the relationship's in trouble, I don't know what is.

I threw my phone against the cushions of the couch and stood—finally resolved. That phone call had pushed me as far as I was willing to go. I crossed to the mirror beside the front door.

"Okay, that won't do," I told myself upon witnessing the brown-black mascara circles underneath my eyes. I hurried to the bathroom and grabbed a washcloth. "What's your rush, Cadie?" I muttered. "It's not like you have anywhere to be for 'A day or two. Three at the most.' " I groaned as I repeated his completely noncommittal brush-off.

I couldn't remember the last time he'd been on time. At least not for a date with me. For work? Sure. Kickoff? You bet. He'd never so much as missed a performance of the national anthem. Punctuality was, apparently, completely unnecessary for evenings with his girlfriend. But cancelling altogether? That hadn't happened very often at all before tonight.

Four years.

The number seemed to magnify and expand each time it entered my thoughts. The number of years had felt like a huge, wonderful accomplishment back when I thought Will and I were building toward something—and a huge, disastrous waste of time now that I finally accepted that we weren't. And if we weren't building toward something, it had to end. That was all there was to it.

Work would be awkward, of course. I wasn't looking forward to that. But it wasn't as if either of us ever had much reason to visit the area where the other worked—and we'd have even less reason now. In fact, I'd be perfectly content if I never had to step on The Field again, whether Will worked there or not.

I dropped the white washcloth covered in dark smudges into the sink. "Who cares?" I groaned.

I stared into the mirror, but I wasn't looking at the remnants of makeup, or the angry red hue of my fair skin, splotchy from crying and agitated further by my careless use of the wash-cloth. I wasn't even looking at the constellation of freckles across my nose, which had once made me self-conscious until Will convinced me they were one of his favorite things.

I was trying to see deeper than that. What was it about me that would never be enough for him? I knew my flaws, and *of course* Will knew my flaws. But he still called me his girlfriend. He still professed his love for me. Nothing had ever made him run. Nothing had ever caused him to seek comfort in the arms of another woman or to grow bitter with me.

Nothing had ever caused him to ask me to be his forever, either.

I could play it tough all day long and put up

the defenses that had to be in place in order to keep from being destroyed by him, but staring in the mirror, with only my doubts and fears and fragile heart to guide me, I knew I was in very real danger. My heart had been claimed long ago. It belonged to Will Whitaker for as long as it was beating. And I didn't know how it would survive the final, painful realization that he didn't love me quite enough to give me his in return.

I stopped in my tracks, midway between the bathroom and the kitchen, where the cold, congealed marinara sat in its pan and unlit candles sat on the table, taunting me.

Am I actually going to end things?

Tears pooled in my eyes as I thought of it all as an inevitability for the first time. No more trying to figure out how to keep things fresh. No more wondering if something had caused him to lose interest—if something had caused *me* to lose interest—or if our ho-hum monotony was normal for couples who had been together as long as we had. No more dropping hints about marriage. No more disappointment each time another significant date or special occasion concluded without a proposal.

No more walking through doors that he held open for me. No more laughing together at four years' worth of inside jokes, lost in a language that only he and I understood. No more of that bewitching smile, reserved just for me.

Stop it, Cadie. I couldn't afford to spend time thinking about all I would lose by ending my relationship with Will—not when there was so much to gain. After all, I had had two very important realizations.

1) I didn't need to get married in order to be happy or fulfilled.

2) My chances of convincing myself I actually believed realization number one would increase exponentially if Will Whitaker was out of my life.

2

About Twenty-five Minutes Earlier . . .

"A re you absolutely sure, Will?" Kevin asked—all eyes on the guy at the table who *really* needed to be sure.

"Yes. Of course I'm sure," Will replied, *almost* as sure as he was trying to convey that he was.

If there were two things Will had learned in his four years at ASN, they were that Kevin loved it when *The Daily Dribble* staff stuck their necks out and made bold assertions, and that he hated it when their bold assertions proved to be incorrect.

"You can trust me on this," Will continued. "There's going to be a doping story break, some of baseball's biggest names are going to be at the center of it, and it's going to break before the World Series."

"Who's your source?" Lorenzo Bateman asked from across the table.

Will raised his eyebrow. "I think you know I'm not going to tell you that, Enzo."

Enzo sat up taller in his seat in an attempt to intimidate, but he always seemed to be the one person who forgot he wasn't the least bit intimidating, in any way. Lorenzo Bateman worked in legal and sported less of an imposing presence than even Will, the only other person in the room who had never been a professional athlete.

"Okay then," Enzo pushed with a sigh. "How big are we talking?"

Will took a deep breath, ready to put it all on the line. "Big enough that, if my source is correct, we may not *have* a World Series this year."

"Oh, come on!" Enzo retorted through his laughter.

His deep chortles seemed strangely out of place considering everyone else in the room had been consumed by completely silent shock.

Kevin cleared his throat. "Hey, everyone, can you please give us the room for a few minutes?"

This can't be good, Will thought, though he refused to back down. He was sure about this. Absolutely positive. His source was ironclad, the intel was indisputable, and most importantly, his gut told him he was right.

"That means you too, Enzo," Kevin boomed, and the lawyer made his way out into the hallway along with everyone else. Suddenly, Kevin and Will were alone, and Will was completely aware that his career was on the line.

"Okay, Kev . . . listen. I'm sure about this. If I'm wrong, fire me. But if I'm right, I just can't stand the thought of any of the other networks getting the exclusive. Can you?"

"Will—"

"Besides, wouldn't it really be more surprising if it *weren't* true?"

Kevin did a double take. "You think it would be more surprising if we *weren't* about to encounter the biggest scandal in baseball since 1919?"

"Yes." Will nodded and remained resolute, though he couldn't help but realize that maybe he'd overshot somewhat. "Surprising" was difficult to defend. But he hadn't come this far to not even try. "We've been hearing the stories coming down the pipeline for years, Kev. And then the stories have magically disappeared. And if they're magically disappearing, someone must be *making* them magically disappear."

"Sure. Yes. You bet." Kevin lifted his giant frame from the chair at the head of the conference table and began pacing the room. "I'm with you on all of that. I guess what I don't understand is why you're so sure they aren't going to magically disappear this time."

"Because . . ." Will took a deep breath and glanced around the room cautiously. No one else was present and the door was shut, but it still didn't feel secure enough. He walked to the windows and drew the blinds before facing his boss and saying, "Because my source is the Magician."

A proud, surreal disposition overtook Will as he reflected on how perfectly he had managed that moment. He felt like Kevin Costner confronting James Earl Jones in *Field of Dreams*, and Robert Redford and Dustin Hoffman taking on Nixon in *All the President's Men*—all at once.

"What magician?" Kevin asked, shattering the perfection of the moment.

Will groaned and threw his hands up in the air. "You know! The Magician. The guy who has been magically making things disappear."

Kevin's deep, booming laughter filled the room. "I'd bet a month's salary that you've spent every bit as much time coming up with the best way to set all of that up as you have actually working on the story."

"And you would win that bet." Will nodded, undeterred. "It was perfect. Seriously, how did you not get it right away? Should I have worked 'magically' into the setup a little more?"

"I don't know that you *could* have worked it in more than you did." He sat back down in his chair. "So, walk me through it."

Will sat in the chair next to him. "We protect his identity and he's ready to talk."

"Money?"

"He just wants to go away."

Kevin leaned back in the chair and laced his fingers behind his head. "I bet he does. So, what? We put him on a plane and send him to Tahiti?"

"Papua New Guinea, but yeah . . . you get the idea. We get his story, and he's on a plane before we run it. That's the deal. He won't negotiate."

"And then we're left to clean up the mess, and we're left with the burden of proof, and it's as if our source no longer exists."

Will smiled. "Simple, right?"

"Simple was when my job was to get a ball through a basket. Or, actually, simple was before I hired you. We used to talk about the joy of the game, and the thrill of competition. And then I hired this researcher—"

"To research, presumably . . ."

"Who seems to think we should be covering hard-hitting news."

"Only part of the time," Will replied with a shrug.

Kevin shook his head and then buried it in his hands. It was from that posture that he muttered, "I trust you. You know that. I've got your back on this. But I also need to make sure you understand that if you're wrong, I won't have any choice but to fire you. You know that, right?"

"I do."

"All right then." Kevin sighed. "Set it up. Let's talk to the Magician."

"I knew it!" Will exclaimed as he pushed his rolling office chair back from the table and pumped his fist in the air. "You like it. I knew you would. I really think every reference we make, we need to call him the Magician. We might actually want to talk to legal and see if we can get a trademark on that—"

"Will?"

"Yeah, boss?"

"Don't make me every bit as likely to fire you for being right as for being wrong."

Will nodded. "Got it."

Kevin put his hands on the table as he stood. "Okay, I'm heading home."

Will glanced at his watch and then slapped his forehead. "Oh, man. Yeah, me too."

Just as he began to stand from his chair, Kevin put his hand on Will's shoulder and pushed him back into his seat. "I don't think so. I want a full preliminary report on my desk before I get here in the morning. Timeline, expenses, backup sources—"

"Okay. No problem. I'll get in here early and get it done. But it's Cadie's birthday, Kev. She's making dinner, and—"

"She's making her own birthday dinner?"

Will shrugged. "It's also our anniversary. She wanted to. I'm already late, so—"

"Sorry, man." Kevin's firm grip became a kind pat. "And please tell Cadie I'm *really* sorry. But I think you're going to have to make it up to her later. It's not just your career on the line here. You've got an entire program—an entire network—counting on you. If we miss a single step, it will be disastrous."

Will sighed deeply and nodded. "I know. You're right."

"But seriously, tell Cadie happy birthday from Larinda and me. Maybe you can both take some time off and get away for a little while once we're finished with . . . The Magic Show?" They both scrunched up their noses and shook their heads. "Well, whatever. You'll make it up to her. And if this all goes down as quickly as you seem to think it's going to, you should have some free time in a day or two. Three at the most."

"Sure thing," Will said, though all he was thinking was, *It would be difficult to make up for missing a birthday dinner. A birthday dinner* and *an anniversary?* That's *where we're going to need some magic.*

"And tell her I miss the days of having time to get her Over the Hill cakes. Of course that's *your* fault, Whitaker." He grabbed the door handle and grumbled, "This job used to be simple . . ." as he walked out of the conference room.

3

A Day or Two Later.
Three at the Most . . .

I just wasn't sure how much longer I could
avoid him. Thankfully, he was busy and
I was busy—Will on The Field, me on The
Bench—so it wasn't as if we kept running into
each other. Quite the opposite. I hadn't been in
the same room with him since the afternoon of
my birthday. But I hated the feeling of knowing
he might peek around the corner at any moment.
Worse, I knew he could peek around the corner
and think that everything was okay between
us.

I used to love waiting for him to peek around
the corner. It was like this glorious anguish,
knowing that he was just about fifty yards away,
doing his thing, and that he could possibly be in
need of something administrative at any moment.
Knowing that at any moment he could pop his
head into my office and sternly say, "McCaffrey.
Lunch. Let's go." He could never remain stern for
more than a second or two before an enormous
smile would break out on his face, and I would

grab my purse and kiss him in the doorway. Whoever was walking by would whistle or clear their throat and then he would throw his arm over my shoulder and we would escape to our own little world for an hour or so.

For so long, for *years,* I couldn't imagine ever growing tired of that.

But for a day or two, maybe three, I had lived in absolute dread that I would hear his voice. "McCaffrey. Lunch. Let's go." And how would I respond? I had no idea. All I knew for sure was that I wouldn't grab my purse and kiss him in the doorway. I couldn't allow myself to act as if we were still *us.*

I was absolutely dreading that, and so ready to just end things. I mean, I was dreading that too, of course. But I was ready for it to be over. I was ready to stop waiting for the moment when he thought everything was normal, and I had to tell him it wasn't.

But it would be really difficult to end things without talking to him.

Apart from a couple of texts, we'd exchanged no communication with each other since he called me to cancel our plans—if you don't count interoffice memos, which were also shared by sixty of our co-workers.

"Maybe *he's* breaking up with *me!*" I suddenly exclaimed in a hushed tone to my best friend, Darby, as we stood at the copier.

"What?" she asked as she shut the copy room door behind us. "Not possible."

"Why is it not possible? Why wouldn't he? That would totally explain it. That would explain why he's been avoiding me, and why he ditched me on my birthday, and why he hasn't bothered to call. That's it, Darby. He's dumping me."

She pulled the stack of budget reports from the copier output tray and began sorting. "Nope. No way. Will wouldn't do that."

"He wouldn't break up with me? How can you say that for sure? Something's been going on with him for a very long time, and maybe he's finally realizing that he doesn't love me like he used to." My breath caught in my chest as I heard the words that I'd been turning over and over in my head for a year. I cleared my throat and attempted to force all of my insecurities to the back of my mind, where they'd grown quite comfortable and invested in beachfront property. "But, um . . . you really don't think he'd break up with me?"

She sighed and placed a comforting hand on my shoulder. "I meant he wouldn't break up with you like *that,*" she clarified. "He wouldn't just avoid you. You know he wouldn't. After all you guys have been through, after all this time? No way."

I nodded and acknowledged to myself that I knew she was right. Maybe the spark was gone, and maybe I was no longer certain that I wanted to be with him for the rest of my life—which was a good thing, when you think about it, since he'd never given me any real indication that he'd thought about our relationship past the dating stage. But Will Whitaker was still a good guy.

And of course, I wouldn't break up with *him* like that, either. Which was why I was desperately hoping we weren't on such completely different channels that he really did think everything was okay. The idea that he was preparing to break up with me was actually easier to swallow.

"He's got to know things aren't good anymore. Right?" I asked Darby—though I'm not sure why I thought she'd have any more of an idea about that than I did.

"I don't know," she replied with a shrug. "You've always said Will isn't the most intuitive of men."

My face scrunched up. "That's true. But *this?* This one is pretty obvious, don't you think?"

"Maybe. But do you remember when you guys had that whole awkward sex talk last year?"

"Oh, good grief. It wasn't an 'awkward sex talk.' It was an awkward *talk.* Period." I grabbed half of her sorted papers and began 3-hole punching. "Besides, I thought we agreed never to speak of that again."

"I'm just saying, he wasn't exactly picking

up the clues that day. That one seemed pretty obvious too. You even pulled out your womanly charms."

I laughed, though when I thought back on that night, I realized I hadn't gotten to the "someday we'll look back on this and chuckle" stage, nor could I imagine that I ever would. All I really felt was embarrassment and regret. In so many ways, that conversation had been the beginning of the end for me, but I didn't blame him for that. At least not entirely.

"My womanly charms? You make it sound like I tried to seduce him."

She continued calmly sorting. "Well, I mean, you kind of—"

"I did not!" I exclaimed. She giggled at my reaction as I took a deep breath and then repeated, much more quietly, "I did not. Did I use the *intimation* of sex in an ill-conceived attempt to make a statement and get my point across? Yes, I did. I'm not proud of it. But I most *certainly* did not try to seduce him. Nothing about any of it was actually about sex. It was about commitment. Taking the next steps." I shrugged and added, with great emphasis, "Marriage."

Darby nodded and smiled. "And how if the two of you didn't take those next steps and get married, you'd never have sex. Like I said. An awkward sex talk."

Embarrassment washed over me anew. There

was no point in continuing the debate. Ultimately it *was* about marriage and not just sex, but I couldn't honestly deny the fact that sex had, regrettably, made its way into the conversation. I wished I could undo it. I wished I had never steered us down that path.

Actually, I just wished I could go back in time and coach myself to not get my hopes up that night. It was all in the expectations.

Of course it would be really nice if someone else could go back in time and coach Will to not drop clues that he was ready to commit to spending his life with me if that wasn't his intent at all. It had all begun so well—a romantic dinner in SoHo, a leisurely walk through an art gallery, time on a park bench spent talking and laughing and people-watching at a level you can only find in Manhattan. He'd designed the evening just for me, and it was perfect.

And then I'd ruined it by getting the idea in my head that he was going to propose.

When it finally became clear that he had no intention of asking me to marry him that night, I'd become the type of woman I couldn't stand in romantic films: manipulative and catty to try to force his hand. But I didn't get what I wanted that night. He didn't ask me to marry him. In fact, that was the night I began losing my last shred of certainty that he ever would.

And he had probably walked away fairly

certain that he was in a relationship with a crazy woman.

I shook off memories of that horrible conversation and forced myself back to the present. "Do you really think he's happy with how things are, Darby? Really?"

Yet another shrug, this time accompanied by a dramatic sigh. Darby could always be counted on for a dramatic sigh when it was exactly what was needed in order to sum up the complex emotions of the moment.

"I really don't know, Cadie. Happy? Yeah . . . I don't know. But he does seem fairly content. Don't you think?"

"I do. And that's the problem. It's like we've both lost sight of the idea of *more*."

Darby took our stacks of reports and spreadsheets and expertly sorted them into their appropriate file folders, as we had so many times throughout our years working in the ASN accounting office. It was a boring, statistical dance we had long ago perfected.

"So how long are you going to avoid him?" she finally asked.

"*Avoid* him? I'm not avoiding him. That's the point. I really think he's avoiding me. I don't think he's left The Field in three days—"

"Just like you haven't left The Bench?"

"And we haven't talked since he called to stand me up on my birthday."

She chuckled. "Okay, Cadie. That's not fair. You don't call someone to stand them up. You just . . . stand them up."

"Whose side are you on?" I asked indignantly.

The smile remained on her face as she said, "Yours. Always yours."

"You better be," I muttered with a smirk.

Thirty seconds later I was opening the door to exit the copy room, only to find Will standing just outside, preparing to open the door and come in.

"Hey," I greeted him—a calm exterior betraying the fluster within. *Well, crap.*

"Boy, have I missed you," he said softly as he leaned down and wrapped his arms around my waist.

His hug pulled me upward onto my tiptoes, and I instinctively threw my arms around his neck. *Okay, Cadie . . . what are you doing? Don't hug him back!* Yep. My brain knew that I wasn't making anything any easier by embracing him as if nothing was any different, but for whatever reason, my arms didn't seem to be listening to my brain.

Old habits die hard. That was all there was to it. It didn't have anything to do with missing him, or being glad that he missed me. And it certainly didn't have anything to do with an unexplainable sense of relief coming from feeling wanted by him for the first time in far too long. Right? It was just a hug from my longtime boyfriend. It was instinct.

"Excuse me," Darby muttered from behind me, mercifully ending the introspective moment—and ending the embrace.

"Oh, hey, Darb," Will said, releasing me and scooting himself out of her way, and pulling me with him. "Sorry about that."

"No problem." She studied me for a moment—no doubt trying to read my mind and determine if I wanted her to stick around or leave us alone. I'm sure my flushed cheeks and silence weren't the easiest clues to interpret. "Well, okay, um . . ." She was stretching for time, but I wasn't giving her any cues at all as to what I wanted. Probably because I had no idea *what* I wanted.

"So has it been a busy day over here?" Will asked, seemingly oblivious to the silent conversation my best friend and I were attempting—and butchering.

"It has," Darby spoke up. "In fact, I'd say it's been a very busy several days. You know, really since Cadie's birthday. And, I mean, obviously you've been *super* busy too . . ."

"Um, Darby," I hastily interjected. "If you want to go disperse the reports, I'll be there in just a minute."

"Yep. Got it." She nodded and scurried away, relieved to finally receive a clear message from me.

And then we were alone, and I wasn't sure which was worse—hoping Darby didn't say anything I didn't want her to, or hoping I didn't say anything I shouldn't.

Of course, I had no idea what I shouldn't say. Or what I should, for that matter. It was one thing to be absolutely resolute that it was time for Will and me to end our relationship, and another thing altogether to finally get around to doing it. But I wasn't going to do it at work, so I needed to hold on to that tiny little shred of salvation.

"So, what's up?" I asked him nonchalantly. Probably a little bit *too* nonchalantly.

He laughed gently. "Well, a lot, actually. There's a lot happening on The Field. In fact, I've got to get back over there, but—"

"Oh, are you needing a budget report? Darby has them, but I can—"

He grabbed my hand as I began rushing away from him, and I was stopped in my tracks.

"Cadie, stop," he commanded gently.

I turned back to face him again, so afraid that all of my resolve was going to give way to thoughts of happier times and memories of being madly in love. I was in such a precarious situation, and I knew it. The look in his eyes, the sound of his laughter, the feel of his hand touching mine . . . it all had the potential to either push me further over the edge toward life without him or pull me closer back toward what was safe and familiar.

Back toward what had once been very nearly everything.

Back toward what was no longer enough.

I sighed and diverted my eyes. "I need to get back to work, Will."

His one hand holding mine made its way up my arm and rested on my shoulder. "Hey, are you mad at me?"

Maybe he was more intuitive than I gave him credit for. Sure, it had taken him three days—or more accurately, maybe about a year—to realize something was bothering me, but he'd gotten there.

I sighed again. "Not mad, no." I took a quick breath, still determined not to break up with him at work—especially not standing outside the copy room. Four years deserved better. *The commissary?* I briefly pondered before shaking off the thought. I couldn't deny that with this minor opening of the entryway, it was somewhat tempting to just go ahead and kick the door wide open. No. I couldn't. But it would have been foolish to not at least give him a completely unveiled, unmistakable indication that all was not well in the world of Cadie and Will. I opened my mouth to speak, but he beat me to it.

"Good." He exhaled in relief and pulled me to him. "I felt so bad about having to cancel on you the other night. But I think when you hear—"

"Whitaker!" Kevin's booming voice abruptly

cut off whatever Will was about to say, and I didn't know whether to be frustrated or relieved. "Oh, hey, Cadie," he said much less aggressively once he saw that Will was not alone. "I'm afraid I'm going to have to steal him from you."

Will's hand dropped from my shoulder as he rushed to meet Kevin at the end of the hallway. They began speaking in hushed tones—something about a phone call and, if my ears didn't deceive me, something about a pigeon. At one point they both glanced at me, at the exact same time, and they both smiled cheesily—making me acutely aware that I had been mentioned in the conversation. Completely lacking subtlety, they turned back to face each other and spoke even more quietly.

"Yeah. Okay, I'm there in one minute," Will concluded before hurrying back over to me and kissing my cheek. "I have to run, but I'll be able to explain everything tonight."

"Tonight?" I asked, trying to remember if we had plans.

"Dinner? I'll pick you up at 7:00, and I promise you nothing will get in the way tonight." He smiled a very charming smile before leaning in and kissing me tenderly on the lips.

"Yeah." I nodded and did my best to smile a little bit. "Sure."

I knew I should be counting my blessings. I couldn't ask for much better, really. An end to this uncomfortable exchange, and a promise that I could finally begin moving Will Whitaker to my life's archive folder, in just a few hours? Great.

But he really needed to stop kissing me. It had been a very long time since he'd kissed me like he was kissing me right then—as if there were the promise, or at least the potential, of something more. When he kissed me like that, I was ready to put the past year behind us and start over.

"Did you say something about a pigeon?" I asked as I breathlessly put some separation between us.

He began walking backward away from me, toward The Field, and as he did he tilted his head in confusion. "I don't think so . . ."

"To Kevin. He said, 'He's on the phone,' and you said, 'The pigeon?'"

There was one more brief moment of confusion on his face, and then recognition registered and he burst out laughing. "You didn't hear anything else I said, did you? Maybe about the pope's nose, or chromosomes, perhaps?"

"No . . ."

"Good. I wouldn't want the surprise to be ruined." He winked and then rushed back toward me. Before I could register what was happening, or brace myself in any way whatsoever, one of his arms was wrapped around the back of my neck and the other was around my waist, and I was being dipped for a sexy, straight-out-of-the-movies kiss.

"Surprise?" I asked—whimpered, maybe?—once he let me up for air.

He ran his fingers down my jawline and said, "I think tonight will be a really special night for us, Cadie. Thanks for being patient with me. I promise to try and make it worth the wait."

Darby peeked her head around the corner and interrupted the romance of the moment—romance I didn't understand at all, mind you—by saying, "Hey, Will . . . Kevin is calling out your name from The Field, in increasing levels of irritation, it seems."

He shook his head while simultaneously straightening his tie. "Thanks, Darb. I'll see *you* tonight." He pointed at me and winked again as he backed away. When he reached Darby's location at the end of the hall, he stopped long enough to exchange some ridiculous secret handshake they had made up and then turned and began running toward The Field.

"What in the world was that about?" Darby asked with a laugh, making her way toward me.

I shook my head and muttered, "I have no idea."

"Are you okay? You're all flushed—"

"He kissed me. Like, *kissed* me."

"Was that *after* you broke up with him, or . . .?"

I groaned and spun on my heel to walk away

from The Field, toward my office. Or anyone's office, really. I just had to get away from an open space where Will could potentially interrupt all of my well thought out intentions and once again call an entire year into question.

"It isn't funny," I asserted as we walked into my office and I closed the door. "I don't know what that was all about, but I can't let it affect anything. I just can't."

"Okay, Cadie, seriously. What in the world happened? He just kissed you? I mean, it's not like it's the first time he's kissed you. What's the big deal?"

That was a very good question.

"There was just . . . I don't know. An energy. He was kind of playful and sexy and mysterious. I don't know how else to describe it."

She chuckled as she slipped off her heels and plopped down in my desk chair. "Mysterious? Look, Will is a lot of things, but mysterious? I think you're just processing a whole lot of different emotions, which makes sense. *Total* sense. So don't let it get to you, just—"

"He said tonight is going to be special. He said . . ." My voice trailed off.

I knew there was a very good chance she was right, and I knew the best thing I could do was brush it all off and resume practicing my "We've just grown apart" speech, so that by 7:00 I could deliver it in the cold and detached—but not unsympathetic—way it needed to be done. But I knew Will Whitaker better than I knew anyone. I knew him better than anyone else knew him. And I knew that something different was happening.

I needed to talk it out with Darby, but I didn't even want to acknowledge the questions racing through my head. I was overwhelmed by a suspicion that absolutely nothing good would come from that acknowledgment.

But of course Darby wouldn't accept that.

"What? He said what, Cadie?"

"He said he promises to try and make it worth the wait."

She sat up straight in the chair. "Make *what* worth the wait?"

"He didn't say." I thought back through the conversation to make sure I wasn't missing a clue. "He thanked me for being patient—"

"Patient *how?*"

Darby's pestering shook me out of my stupor somewhat, and I laughed as I sat in the chair across the desk from her.

"I don't know. That was pretty much it. Patient with *him.* Just that and some nonsensical gibberish about pigeons and popes. And chromosomes, I think." She opened her mouth to, no doubt, ask the very necessary questions, but before she could proceed I added, "And he said he has a surprise for me. Tonight."

Darby jumped up from the chair and circumnavigated the desk. As she hoisted herself up to sit on it, right in front of me, she asked, "What are you going to do?"

"What do you mean?"

"What are you going to say?"

"About what?"

My best friend sighed. "Cadie . . ."

"Don't say it, Darby. Seriously, don't say it. I don't think I could bear it if you said it. I know what you're thinking, and *of course* I'm thinking it too. But I can't afford to be wrong again. I can't afford to set myself up for disappointment again. I can't. I just . . . can't."

"Okay," she said softly as she grabbed my hand in hers. "So, um . . ." She cleared her throat. "Can you explain the pigeon and the pope and the . . . chromosomes, was it? Sounds like the setup for a *really* bad joke."

I laughed and wiped away the tears that had begun pooling in my eyes. "I misheard him. When he was talking to Kevin. I'm not sure what he really said, but I could have sworn he said something about a pigeon being on the phone. When I asked him about it, he asked me if I overheard anything else. Like, something about a pope's nose or chromosomes. He was just teasing me."

And I didn't want to admit how much I had enjoyed being teased by him. What had once been a staple of our relationship had been mostly missing for a very long time.

"Then what?" Darby asked, all of the color gone from her face.

"What is it, Darb?"

"What did he say after that? What did *you* say? And then, yeah . . . what did he say?"

I shrugged. "I don't know. I just said that I hadn't heard that, and he said that was good, because he wouldn't have wanted the surprise to be ruined."

She leapt off of the desk as if she'd been electrocuted, and her hands flew to cover her mouth—which I could only assume was as wide open as her eyes.

"What?" I laughed, though it was a laugh I was forcing in order to hide my nervousness. I didn't even know why I was nervous, but I knew that nervousness was the proper emotion.

"He's going to propose," she muttered through her fingers.

I groaned and stood from the chair and began pacing. "I told you not to say it!"

"I know. I know! But 'pope's nose'? 'Chromosomes'? Clearly he was teasing you about whatever he said that you thought sounded like 'pigeon'—so he was dropping a hint. And maybe also making sure you actually didn't hear something? I don't know. But don't you see? Pope's nose. Chromosomes. *Propose!*"

"Oh, come on. That's stretching things at the very least. Don't you think?"

"Well, yeah . . . I *would,* if he hadn't also talked about surprises and patience and special nights."

Oh my goodness. She was right. She had to be right.

"So," she continued, "now that we're not just talking about obscure gut feelings and such, I'll ask again. What are you going to do?"

What *was* I going to do?

"I have no idea!" I exclaimed, a little more loudly than I meant to. I looked toward the door and verified that it was still closed. The speed of my steps back and forth across the room increased as I followed Darby's example and kicked off my own high heels. "It's, I mean . . . it doesn't change a thing. It doesn't change a thing, right?"

She threw her hands up in the air. "Beats me! On one hand, yes, you're right. It doesn't change a thing. It doesn't change the fact that it's been four years, and that all of the romance and consideration and, you know, having a clue for the past year has been pretty much—"

"Nonexistent," I interjected.

"Yeah. It doesn't change that. But suddenly today he's playful and sexy?"

"And mysterious."

"And mysterious," she repeated. "I mean, maybe he woke up. Maybe he was worried he was going to lose you—"

"Which was *totally* going to happen tonight."

"And he decided to pull it together. Maybe you're wrong. Maybe he *is* the most intuitive of guys."

I was with her until then. I really was. I was growing increasingly certain that he'd finally decided he wanted to spend his life with me, and increasingly uncertain that I didn't still feel the same way. But then reality reappeared.

"He hasn't seen me, Darby. He hasn't spoken to me. What in the world could have made him wake up? What could have possibly changed from the time he stood me up—"

"He didn't stand you up."

"To now?" I completed the sentence, choosing to ignore her constant beating of the "you weren't stood up" drum.

She shrugged. "I don't know. But for all we know, he was planning to do it the other day, and whatever made him cancel your date truly was out of his control. I don't know, Cadie. But I know he loves you. And I know that *if* he's finally gotten it all figured out, I want you to be with him. Because I've seen the two of you at your best, and at your best, you make each other happy. I know that. And you know it too." She paused as she made her way across the room to me, and then she planted her feet right in front of me and forced me to look straight at her as she said, "And I know that you still love him. I also know—and fully understand—that you can't keep going with him the way things are. But I'm also pretty doggone sure that if he could get his stuff together, you'd rather be with him than anywhere else, with anyone else in the world."

I couldn't deny that.

I stopped in front of my desk chair and plopped down as she had a few minutes prior. "I don't know what I'm going to do," I muttered as I buried my face in my hands.

She sighed. "Look, you know I'm no love expert—"

I raised my head slightly to peer at her over my fingers, eyebrow raised. "You've been on three dates this week . . ."

"Exactly. Three first dates with three different guys. I didn't say I wasn't a first date expert. I *am* that. But love?" She scrunched up her nose and shook her head. "But I really think you need to just live in the moment on this one. Trust your gut."

My eyes were drawn to the charts and spreadsheets that were placed all around me, wherever I looked. *My life* was charts and spreadsheets, quotas and budgets. There wasn't a single aspect of my job that required anything less than meticulous planning and consideration of all the variables. Trusting my gut never really came into play.

"I think I trusted my gut a year ago—"

"I know," she agreed with a nod.

"And all I've had to show for it is that whole awkward sex talk—"

She boastfully laughed at my use of her phrase.

"And a year of missing the good old days. I can't go through that again."

"And you won't." She crossed the room to stand behind my chair, wrapped her arms around my shoulders, and rested her cheek on the top of my head. "Because this time, if it's time to end it, you'll know. You'll be ready."

4

A Year Earlier
(AKA "That Whole Awkward Sex Talk")

"Thanks for walking me home," Cadie said with a smile as she unlocked the door of her West Village brownstone. "It was a really great birthday and anniversary."

"It was, wasn't it?" Will pushed the door open for her and then followed her inside. "Of course, when the birthday girl is as venerated as you are . . ."

Cadie laughed freely as she carefully hung her keys on the hook on the wall, above the tiny kitchen counter. Meanwhile, Will was locking the door and the additional dead bolts and chains that were a fixture in the home of any cautious New Yorker—even those who lived in the West Village. He had yet to give Cadie her birthday gift, but one of her anniversary gifts had been a Word of the Day app that Will had downloaded for himself—in reference to an inside joke they shared about his limited vocabulary. In fact, his vocabulary was perfectly sufficient, and they both knew it, but if he could make Cadie laugh by using new words—such as *venerated*—each day, he'd gladly play into the joke.

"I don't think I've heard that word as many times in my whole life as I've heard it today," she said, her laughter continuing.

"Well, it's only the first day. Give it some time." He took off his jacket and hung it on a hook by the door—as carefully as she had hung up her keys. "Will talk more good words soon," he added in his best caveman voice.

He crossed the limited square footage of Cadie's co-op and helped her off with her jacket, and then hung it up as well. In his apartment, throwing outerwear—and, let's face it, the occasional dirty sock—over the back of the couch was good enough, but for Cadie, he always strove to honor her meticulous habits.

"Want some coffee?" she asked.

He was suddenly just behind her, his much longer arm beating hers to the coffee maker. "Here. Let me."

Cadie pivoted where she stood and faced him, their bodies and faces only inches apart. "I need to have birthdays more often," she said with a smile, before quickly shaking her head. "No, I take that back. Forget I said that."

He set the carafe back down on the base, the desire for caffeine momentarily forgotten by them both. "Or maybe I just need to treat every day like it's your birthday."

He wrapped his arms around her waist and she rose slightly on her tiptoes as she threw her arms around his neck.

"I could live with that. You have made me feel *very* venerated today." She winked and planted a quick kiss on his lips.

"Maybe I should have gotten *you* that app. You need to learn some new words. That one's kind of overused."

She giggled and leaned her forehead onto his chest, and he pulled her closer. She turned her head so that her cheek rested on him instead, and he felt as if he had no control over the sigh of contentment that escaped from his mouth. She was so fond of her high heels, always a bit self-conscious of her slight 5'4" stature, but he personally loved it when she wore flats, as she did tonight. Maybe because it represented how comfortable she was with him. Maybe because she seemed to fit against him even more perfectly that way.

"I love you, you know," he whispered into her ear. A gratified smile overtook his face as he felt her shudder slightly in his arms, presumably a reaction to his breath against her skin.

"I do know that, yes," she replied, her voice nonchalant and seemingly unaware that when he was holding her as closely as he was, she couldn't fool him. He knew how affected she was by him.

"And . . . ?" His cheek rested against the top of

her head, and her chuckle let him know that she had felt his smile increase against her hair.

"And . . . I'm glad."

He pulled away from her in mock horror. "You're glad I love you?"

"Yes," she replied simply, as her smile widened despite her best efforts.

"That's all you have to say?"

Cadie shook her head. "No, of course not. I also want to say that I think you're very nice as well."

He laughed for a moment before capturing her lips with his. He'd really intended to prepare a witty comeback, to continue the repartee. But, as it turned out, his lips hadn't been privy to the plan.

He grew increasingly lost in her as his looped arms inched lower on her back, drawing her closer to him and helping her take some of the pressure off of her tiptoes. It was a familiar dance they shared. Familiar, yet every bit as exciting as the first time they'd kissed, so long ago.

Of course, every bit as familiar—and much, *much* less exciting—was what came next.

He loosened his hold on her and lowered her back down to flat footing. His hand left her back and waist and instead tenderly embraced her face as their kisses became less deep and more segmented. And then, the inevitable sigh.

Actually, in the easiest situations, there was an inevitable sigh. When separating was trickier and a little more dreaded—as it was tonight—there was an inevitable groan, from one or the other of them.

Tonight it was both.

Will pulled her back to their earlier posture—her cheek against his chest. That was better, but only slightly. She was still close enough to impact every single one of his senses, which made it so difficult to remember why they continued to repeat this dance, time after time.

Because you love her, he lectured himself. *Because you told her you would. Because it's the right thing to do. Because she's worth it. Because you didn't just promise her, you promised God.*

That was the one that always did the trick and brought him back to reality. He hadn't been with many women before making that promise. Before giving his life to God. But if he could go back and change that number from "not many" to "none" he would. In a heartbeat. God had forgiven him and Will had made his peace with it, but there was no way he was going to repeat the same mistakes—and there was certainly no way he was going to let Cadie get tangled up in the regret.

Her groan intensified as he put some space between them. "Don't go."

Well, that wasn't going to help.

He cleared his throat. "I'm not going anywhere. But, um . . ." He looked around, urgently grasping for something concrete to focus on. "Coffee!"

She laughed as he spun her around. She was instantly a few feet away from the coffee maker, and he was standing beside it, preparing their black, caffeinated salvation.

"I love you too, by the way," she whispered as she looped her arms around him from behind and rested her cheek on his back.

He wasn't convinced that coffee was going to be enough of a distraction.

"Your birthday gift!" he exclaimed, pulling away from her abruptly as soon as he had turned on the coffeepot.

"What?" she asked through her laughter. "There can't possibly be more, Will! This whole day has been perfect, and you already gave me the earrings—"

"That was anniversary. Doesn't count."

"And you gave me the gift of *venerated,*" she added with a sly smile. "And dinner and the gallery, and, well . . . that kiss a minute ago. That was a pretty special kiss, certainly reserved for a special occasion . . ."

She was crossing the room back toward him, and he knew he couldn't allow her to reach him. Not yet. He needed a little more time before he would possess the fortitude to dance the dance again. They were usually more disciplined, and he feared he wasn't skilled enough to handle more that night.

"Well, be that as it may, there's one more gift."

He returned to his jacket on the hook by the door and reached into the inside pocket. He glanced up at her and was relieved to see that she had ceased her advance into what he knew was very dangerous territory. Still, he was worried it wasn't enough. Cadie had the benefit of wealthy parents who had helped her get established on her own in Manhattan, and there were times, such as now, when he wished she had chosen square footage over location with the amount of money she had at her disposal. Sure, there's something to be said for a safe neighborhood and her shared English Tudor garden courtyard, not to mention being steps away from the Christopher Street Station—and therefore, effectively, steps away from all of Manhattan—and the Magnolia Bakery on the corner. But at least in, say, East Harlem, he'd be able to go to a different room to cool down a little.

"So, before I give you this—"

"Oh, Will." She was frozen in place, her hands clasped over her mouth.

He chuckled as he looked down at the tiny box in his hands, with its unmistakable signature Astor & DeLancey style, and then back up at her. "Of course you know," he said softly, gratified by how well he knew her. And how well she knew him. There he'd been, prepared to deliver the speech he'd begun practicing on the train back from Long Island, days earlier, after his initially promising but ultimately disheartening visit with her parents. But the expression on her face made it clear to him that she already understood.

He'd been worried that it wasn't enough. That it would seem like he was just grasping at straws—despite the fact that the box represented more than two years of planning and saving. He'd worried she wouldn't understand, even upon hearing the speech he had prepared, that the gift was a beginning. Step one. A down payment on forever. Most of all he'd been worried she wouldn't remember the obscure conversation from two years earlier—and that the memory had meant more to him than it had to her. Now he felt foolish for not giving her, and their bond, enough credit.

"Sorry," she said through her laughter and the joyful tears that were overtaking her. She began trying to wipe them away, but it was useless. "I didn't mean to interrupt you. I don't want to ruin whatever you had planned."

"Are you kidding?" he whispered as he decided to take his chances on the status of their familiar dance and make his way back to her. The need to share the moment with her was stronger than the need to keep a safe distance between them for a little bit longer. The fingers of one of his hands attempted to dry the tears from her cheeks, as the other hand clasped the tiny, antique ring box.

"All I had planned—all I've *ever* planned—was doing all I could to make you happy. And since I'm pretty sure these aren't sad tears . . ."

She laughed. "No."

"Then I guess everything's going according to plan."

Cadie wrapped her arms around him as she tilted her chin as far as it could go in order to kiss him. Will grew worried once again—one more kiss, one more touch, one more exquisite moment of her body melded against his, and he knew he could very well lose whatever restraint he had left.

Nevertheless, he was overwhelmingly disappointed when she pulled away from him.

"Okay, so forget I said anything," she gushed as she hurriedly grabbed a tissue from the box on the coffee table, blew her nose, and threw the tissue in the trash. "You said, 'Before I give you this . . .'" She laughed, and he smiled in response. "You can pick up from there."

He'd been preparing to make a purchase at Astor & DeLancey ever since they'd walked in on a lark one night while window shopping on Fifth Avenue, more than two years earlier. They'd each spent most of their adult lives in the city, but neither had ever dared to walk into the snobby, exclusive, ridiculously luxurious jewelry store before. Once they entered, they immediately wanted to exit. All eyes were on them. They were both moderately successful, independent adults—and Cadie even came from an affluent family—but they were inordinately out of place at Astor & DeLancey.

Cadie had begun to respond to the patronizing "May I help you?" request of the store's clerk with, "Just looking, thanks." Or maybe by acting as if they had wandered in by mistake. But Will was more used to life on the scrappy side of the income bracket and had no patience for the snobbery.

"I'm Lord Marbury," he'd said in a haughty British accent, not so much as putting out his hand for a handshake, but only bowing his head slightly. "Lady Marbury is looking for a retire-ment gift for the neighbor's gardener. What can you suggest?"

On it had gone for a solid ten minutes. Cadie didn't speak the entire time, and she'd later told him she'd been unable to open her mouth for fear that either laughter or horror would escape. At the very least she suspected her attempt at a British accent would give her away as a Cockney flower girl, at best. But Lord Marbury had carried on. Finally, they left the store, much to the chagrin of the convinced clerk, with a declaration that the neighbor's gardener—whose name he claimed he couldn't remember—deserved better than Astor & DeLancey had to offer.

"All I want," Cadie had said then, as they'd

laughed their way down Fifth Avenue, "is *something* from there. Or even just the box that something would normally come in—if I could even afford that! Just something to remember that by, because that was *us,* you know."

He glanced down at the ring box he now held, and the ostentatiously engraved Astor & DeLancey logo it sported.

"That was the first time we told each other, 'I love you,' " he said aloud as his thoughts brought him back to the present. He fiddled with the tiny wooden box, turning it over and over nervously. "I don't know what had taken us so long. At least I don't know what had taken *me* so long. I think I began falling in love with you as soon as I met you. Certainly by the time I saw your teeth covered in icing. But that night at Astor & DeLancey, for some reason, I knew it. I knew I wanted to make you laugh forever, and if I had to be Lord Marbury to make that happen, then I'd be Lord Marbury for the rest of my life." Cadie giggled as her tears began again, and her laughter made him smile, as it always did. It put him at ease and took away every doubt and question. "The fact that you like me even without my lordship? Well . . . even better."

He waited as she grabbed another tissue and blew her nose once again, and then he handed her the box as he said, "Harpy birdbay, Palie," as he had every year since the first.

He watched her with delight. On the train home from Long Island, he'd gone through so many options in his mind of how to salvage the romance of his original plan, while laying the groundwork for the new plan. To honor their past and their future, at the same time. Her reaction made it clear that by celebrating their time as Lord and Lady Marbury, he had hit it out of the park. He knew he'd made the right decision to present her with the wooden box—an antique from 1894, the sixth year the store was open.

"Should I open it?" she asked, an effervescent grin taking over her lips.

"Sure," he answered with a shrug. "I tested it out. It's old, but it's not overly delicate."

Cadie took a deep breath and then opened the box. Confusion immediately spread across her face.

"It doesn't have the original lining," Will rushed into his explanation as he took a step to stand beside her and point out what he had memorized about the very expensive box. "That's kind of obvious, isn't it? This one is kind of messed up. Sorry. But, here's the thing: in 1912, they had decided to start using silk interior instead of velvet. They pulled all of the velvet out of their existing inventory of boxes because they were expecting a shipment of silk. The silk was coming over on the Titanic. Isn't that crazy? When they, obviously, didn't get that shipment, they switched to Vicuña wool, which I guess switched to cashmere at some point. But anyway, that's why it doesn't have the original lining. Not sure why it doesn't have *any* lining, but that's probably why this was the one I could afford, honestly, so—"

He stopped rambling on about his endless research findings long enough to notice that her smile had faded and the tears in her eyes no longer seemed joyful. His confidence began to falter, and he once again began questioning the plan.

"It's an empty box," she muttered, bewildered.

She seemed to quickly pull herself together as she plastered a smile on her face.

"Thank you," she said softly. Her smile didn't appear insincere, but it also didn't seem as warm. "I really love it. Thank you, Lord Marbury." She tipped her imaginary hat to him and then placed her hand on his shoulder and kissed his cheek.

"Um . . . you're welcome?" He hadn't meant to phrase it as a question, but he was pretty sure it had come out that way. "Look, Cadie, I'm sorry it's not more, I just—"

"No, really. I love it." She took a deep breath. "I think the coffee's done."

"I'm sorry," he repeated softly. "I did think you'd like it."

"I do. I *do* like it, Will. Really. Thank you." She poured herself a cup of coffee, held it for a moment, and then set it down. "I think I'm just tired. It's been a long day. A *good* day!" She smiled that not-insincere but not-warm smile again. "I think maybe I should just—"

"Okay. Sure." He nodded and walked to grab his jacket.

He heard her laugh behind him, but it wasn't the laugh from before. It wasn't the laugh that had reminded him that it was worth dancing whatever dance was necessary in order to be in her presence. No, this laugh was bitter. Cold.

"Wow. Just like that," she mumbled—though he heard every painful syllable.

He threw his hands up in the air. "What is happening, Cadie? I get it—you don't like the gift. I'm sorry. I thought you would. But I don't understand why you're mad at—"

That was as far as he got before she threw her petite frame at him—with enough force to make him lose his footing—and kissed him like she had never kissed him before. It was rough and urgent. Sexy, without a doubt, but not in her usual way. He sensed that her kiss was some sort of battle cry, though he was so confused as to when they had gone to war. He couldn't even be sure they were battling the same opponent. Everything in him was telling him to tenderly pull away and hold her. He knew that she needed to talk. He understood that there was something she wasn't saying—even if he understood nothing else.

But the fact of the matter was that the woman he loved, the only woman he wanted, was throwing herself at him, and clarity was giving way to clouds with each touch.

"Have you ever even thought about the two of us being together?" she asked, her lips the smallest of margins from his.

"You know I have," he whispered as his lips bridged the distance between them.

His arms finally relented, unable to resist her, and prepared to pull her as close as he possibly could. But she was gone, as far across the room as she could manage—and he took back everything he had ever thought about wishing she had more square footage in East Harlem. He couldn't bear the thought of her being any farther away.

"Come here," he whispered.

"See, I can't. That's the problem. You know how important it is to wait until marriage—"

He cleared his throat and attempted to clear his brain, but that was proving to be a bit tougher. "Uh, yeah." He cleared his throat again. "I know. I wasn't suggesting—"

"But that's where it's going to go, right?" She picked up her coffee and took a sip. How was she calm enough to sip coffee? He was a wreck. "I mean, at some point. It's always like this."

He would have to beg to differ. "No. Sorry, but no. In three years, I think I can safely say it's never been like this . . ."

"Maybe not *just* like this, but . . . *this*. We have to stop before we go too far. We have to walk a line. We have to respect the boundaries we set."

He ran his hand through his hair and then used both hands to rub his face. He wasn't sure if he needed to wake up or focus. All he knew was that he was confused and consumed by a feeling of whiplash.

Also, he really wanted a cup of coffee. But he was afraid to move from his spot, in case it'd be another wrong move.

"Aren't you tired of it, Will? Don't you want *more?*"

His chest deflated as all of the air in his lungs rushed out, as if he'd been thrown up against a wall. Was that really what all this was about? Did she really doubt how much he wanted to be with her? If so, he knew he was going to have a very difficult time ignoring the expression on her face and the uncertainty in her voice, staying focused on the new plan he'd concocted on the train. As he left Long Island, he'd been consumed by frustration and disappointment, but he'd arrived back at Penn Station buoyed by determination. Now that determination seemed absurd and inadequate as she looked at him like she wasn't sure she knew him at all.

"Of course I do, Cadie. But—"

"What?" she asked sharply.

He sighed. "Are we really talking about this? I

mean, do you really want me to say this stuff? I know it's not the most comfortable—"

"I think we have to. Because I don't know what you want, Will. I don't."

"Look, it's—" He ran his hand through his hair again. "Can we sit?"

She stood up straighter and crossed her arms at the suggestion. "You go ahead."

Well, he couldn't very well sit after that answer. Instead he shifted his weight onto his other foot and racked his brain. He still came up empty.

Somewhere along the line he had apparently ruined the romance of this particular evening, but he knew that if he were to tell her the *why* behind it all, he would ruin the *potential* romance of the new plan. He would also undoubtedly say something he shouldn't. His conversation with her parents was still too fresh, and he couldn't be sure he had complete control of his emotions yet. Especially where *they* were concerned. And he couldn't, even unintentionally, ask Cadie to choose sides. So what were his options?

He sighed. "You're right. It's been a long day. Let's just . . . let's talk tomorrow."

He turned his back to her and went over to his jacket, pretty certain he wouldn't have to worry about being stopped by an unexpected kiss this time. He threw it on hastily and turned toward her, wanting to say so much but afraid to say anything.

But it was all forgotten at the sight of her huddled on the floor, sobbing. He took a deep breath—this time not in preparation for battle but in surrender.

"I'm sorry," he whispered as he approached her cautiously. *Cautiously.* He'd never felt the need to be cautious around her before, and it was a strange sensation. He'd been cautious *with* her, but that was something very different.

"No, *I'm* sorry," she cried.

With those words he was pretty sure a cease-fire had been drafted between them, and he had permission to approach the enemy, who could maybe once more become an ally. He sat beside her on the floor and pulled her to him. She cried into his shirt and he held her, and though no words were spoken between them, he was pretty sure he was beginning to understand.

He understood that after tonight, he would have to commit fully to the new plan. No more intentions, only action. He would do what her parents had asked of him, and he'd become the man Cadie needed him to be. No more wavering, no second guessing, no letting his frustration rise to the surface. All of that only stood to make it take longer, and it had taken too long already.

He also understood that he would do what he had to in order to remove all the passion and temptation from their relationship for now. Hearing it from her lips had opened his eyes. The constant awareness of the need to stop before they went too far. Walking the line. Working so hard to respect the boundaries they had set. He'd always looked at it all as *his* burden. He'd never imagined that resisting the temptation of being together was as difficult for her as it was for him, but clearly he'd been shortsighted.

Well, no more. He was willing to do whatever it took, as long as it meant they never had to go to war again.

5

⁓

7:00 (Back in the Time of Pigeons and Chromosomes)

I couldn't remember a time when I had ever been nervous sitting alone in my own home—apart from the occasional finale of *The Bachelor*, of course. It wasn't giddy anticipation causing the nerves, and they certainly weren't the result of a sense of dread or fear that I wouldn't receive my desired outcome. That was the thing. If I had a desired outcome, I sure didn't know what it was, so I was going to do all I could to follow Darby's advice and trust my gut.

But if I'm being honest, my gut was doing very little to elicit any sense of confidence.

I'd taken to my closet about an hour earlier and had attempted to trust my gut when it came to picking out an outfit. I figured that was an easy place to start.

Nope. I'd figured wrong.

I'm pretty sure I pulled every single item of clothing from my closet—apart from my old denim overalls, which even my conflicted, indecisive gut knew had no business being worn by a woman in her thirties, or any woman at all, really, outside of some sort of agricultural event, or 1994. All I knew for sure was that when Will showed up, I couldn't allow whatever I was wearing to give him the wrong impression.

It's awfully difficult to avoid the wrong impression when you're not sure what the right impression should be.

Finally, after I had stood in front of the mirror modeling my best "It's not you, it's me" attire, along with a smattering of outfits that cried out "Kiss me again like you did outside the copy room," I landed on the perfect compromise. I changed right back into the jade-colored blouse, black slacks, and black high heels I'd worn all day at work. Jade was definitely my color, so I knew I looked good. Good enough that he had actually dipped me when he kissed me—and surely that wasn't an everyday occurrence for any woman who didn't live in a Hollywood musical. But it was also obvious that I hadn't put in any special effort or tried to impress him.

Maybe my gut knew what it was doing after all.

When the doorbell rang at 6:59, which debunked Will's recently acquired reputation for being late for every date, I jumped up from the couch and then quickly sat back down—not wanting to give the impression of being eager. No one was present to witness my restraint, of course, and I did feel more than a little silly, sitting there alone, waiting for my gut to tell me it was time to open the door. Nevertheless, my gut appreciated the consideration and soon seemed to whisper, *Okay, Cadie. Go ahead. I promise to try not to send you down the wrong path if you promise to never again wear that paisley vest in your closet, unless you're asked to appear on a* Blossom *reunion.*

I opened the door just as Will's finger was making its way back to the doorbell for a second attempt.

My gut's tiny streak of confidence was broken when I saw him. I couldn't remember exactly what he'd been wearing at the office that day, but I was certain it hadn't been the perfectly tailored three-piece suit I saw in my doorway. A suit? Maybe I *did* live in a Hollywood musical. I couldn't remember ever hearing Will Whitaker sing—the occasional "bum bum bum" when "Sweet Caroline" broke out during a Red Sox game, and maybe a little karaoke sing-along here and there—but at that moment I wouldn't have been surprised if he'd found a lamppost to swing around as he serenaded me.

"Wow," I breathed, accidentally.

Cadie! What are you doing? I could almost audibly detect my gut crying out. *Do you know how difficult it is to break up with a guy after you've said "Wow" at the sight of him?*

Fair point. But Will deserved that wow.

"I feel really underdressed," I added, hoping to redeem myself.

"This old thing?" he asked with a wink as he walked past me into my apartment, kissing me as he passed.

I shut the door behind him and locked us in. "No, seriously, Will. I didn't know that I needed to dress up. I thought we were just having dinner."

"We are," he assured me. "And don't worry. I'll take off the jacket and tie before we go, if you want me to. I just wanted to see what you thought. Do you like it?"

Did I like it? Did I like the way the bluish-gray somehow brought out both the blue and the gray in his eyes, simultaneously? Did I like the way it was so perfectly tailored to fit his frame that I was flooded with memories—and more dangerously, daydreams—of how it felt to be held by him? Did I like how the sight of him made me want to run back to my closet and pull out the fanciest thing I could find in hopes that he would take me dancing, so that time could pass much too quickly, in that way it only does when you want it to stand still?

"Not bad, Whitaker," I finally said, forcing myself to sound nonchalant as I attempted to convince both of us that I was complimenting the perfect suit and not the man who wore it oh-so-perfectly.

Then my eyes finally made their way down from his eyes, his lips, his chest, and landed on his shoes. Attempts at a different brand of composure gave way to choking down giggles, and at *that* attempt, I failed disastrously.

"I know," he said with a laugh. "I haven't had a chance to shop for shoes yet. But don't let that get in the way of the overall impression. Pretend I'm wearing something, I don't know . . . leather and designer-y, I guess. And not quite so canvas and Converse-y."

"It almost works. I mean, you can totally pull off the look of a celebrity walking down the red carpet in a carefully constructed style that is meant to appear breezy. Next time, I'd probably go with red or white, to really stand out against the suit. If you're going to do it, do it all the way."

"And maybe I should add a fedora to the mix?" He grinned slyly as he crossed the room with more swagger than he ever sported when he wore his usual attire of wrinkled, baggy khakis. It was ridiculous swagger, but it was swagger nonetheless.

"No," I quickly replied as I shook my head and laughed. "No fedora. But the suit is very nice. Now, are you going to tell me the *reason* for the suit?"

"Well, I haven't spent any time with my girl-friend in far too long. So there's that."

That swagger that had so innocuously been making its way across the hardwood floor of my apartment was suddenly focused intently on me. Not all that many steps are required to cross from one side of the space to the other, but each one he took was laced with trouble. Danger, even. Not that Will has a dangerous bone in his body, of course. Nonetheless, my gut could sense that it was at risk.

"That's true," I responded as I took a small and uncertain step back. "But I thought that football jerseys were more in line with the traditional dress code for midweek dates. Or track suits, maybe?" I had a feeling that I would have been much more able to focus on breaking up with him if he had been wearing a track suit.

One corner of his mouth crept upwards. "Is that so? Well then, I'm afraid I may have received some faulty intel."

"How many times have I told you that the guys on The Field are not reliable romance sources?"

"Not even Ellis?" he asked as the other corner of his mouth rose to complete the grin.

Ellis Haywood. Former nose tackle for the Dallas Cowboys and current funniest guy in the studio on Sunday afternoons. Ellis is every bit as giant as you can apparently expect a nose tackle to be, but he also boasts the dance moves of Bruno Mars, the intellectual comedic chops that could have earned him a place in Monty Python, and a smooth, soulful singing voice that evokes thoughts of Luther Vandross.

Ellis is also a renowned ladies' man.

"*Especially* not Ellis." I laughed.

"But the guy knows everything, Cadie. I mean, he's been married four times. If I can't trust Ellis, who *can* I trust?"

"I don't know. Just definitely not Ellis."

I was so busy laughing that I had somehow lost track of how much closer he was getting to where I stood. Then, there he was. Right in front of me. Close enough to communicate with a whisper.

When that whisper spoke of work and sports instead of love and attraction, I didn't know whether to feel relieved or disappointed.

"A big story is going to break tomorrow. Baseball." When I said nothing he tagged on, "You know . . . the one with the bases and the innings. And Yankee Stadium has that rib joint you like with the amazing cheese curds."

Again, he teased. Again, I swooned.

"Oh, baseball!" I laughed and put my hand on his bicep before I thought about it. It was a move that would seem flirty at the beginning of a relationship but which after four years could only be described as natural. At least, I would *usually* describe it as natural.

On this night, it felt flirty.

"So, yeah . . . a big story is going to break in the sport with the cheese curds. And guess what?

It's my story. Not a story I did some work on, or a story I wrote some copy for. It's not even a story that I brought to Kevin, who handed it off to someone else. It's *my* story, Cadie."

"That's fantastic!" I squealed as I threw my arms around his neck. He was so proud, and I was proud of him. For a moment—a moment that I suspected would be willing to stick around longer if I asked nicely—I forgot that it was an evening that held the promise of either becoming engaged or becoming single. I was just proud of him. Happy for him. I felt as if I were sharing in his success, because I was the one he *wanted* to share it with. I broke from his embrace but immediately grabbed his hand and pulled him with me to the couch. As we sat, I insisted, "Tell me all about it."

"Okay, so, a few weeks ago, I was riding into work. I got on at 110th Street, like usual, and then at 86th, this guy gets on. He looked—I don't know how to describe it, really. He looked nervous, I guess, but also like he was in the middle of a breakdown or something. Whatever. This is New York. I didn't think too much of it. But then he says to me, 'Hey, buddy. You like baseball?' Just like that. And I knew I shouldn't engage, since I figured he was probably not exactly right, if you know what I mean, but—"

"Baseball," I said, completing his thought with a laugh.

"Yeah. I mean, what if he was in the middle of a breakdown because he had tickets to the World Series, and he wasn't going to be able to make it or something? What if he decided to give me the tickets just because I was nice to him?"

"Well, that's definitely reason to do the right thing and be nice to someone."

He laughed. "Right? So I said, 'Yeah. I like baseball.' And that was it. He switched seats so that he was next to me, and he started talking. Just talking and talking, Cadie. He threw out all of these dates and names and dollar amounts . . . none of it made any sense. Until I heard one name. Gael Cuarón."

Recognition dawned in my mind. "Didn't he direct *Gravity*? And one of the Harry Potter movies, I think . . ."

Will tilted his head in confusion and then chuckled. "Strangely enough—given the context of the story and all—Gael Cuarón is a baseball player. Actually, he's kind of *the* baseball player right now. Pitcher for the Cubs. More no-hitters than anyone else in the last fifty years."

"That's what I meant," I responded sheepishly.

"I promise I'm getting to the interesting part soon." He smiled and wrapped an arm around me to pull me closer to him. "So anyway, that caught my attention, and I started thinking back through all of the names he'd said. And the dates. Dates when records had been broken, or when

Cuarón had pitched a no-hitter. Wild card games, division series games . . . I could place almost every single date."

I didn't question that, but I couldn't help but be more than a little bewildered by it. Will is undoubtedly good at what he does, and a huge asset to ASN. And more than once I'd enjoyed eating buffalo wings and reading a book while Will singlehandedly won for our "team" at sports trivia night at Batter Batter Sports Bar in Chelsea. But I was still bewildered. There wasn't *anything* that I had committed to memory as expertly as Will had sports facts—with the possible exception of all the dialogue from every Garry Marshall film.

"So the guy knows as much as you do?" I asked.

"The guy knows *more* than I do. The guy is the story. He has personally covered up about sixty *major* performance-enhancing drug incidents in Major League Baseball."

He wasn't kidding about getting to the interesting part soon. I sat up straight and pulled away so that I could look at him.

"He told you that?"

"He did," Will answered with a laugh. "I can still hardly believe it myself. It was like he just needed to clear it from his conscience. He kept talking and talking—"

"You didn't tell him where you work?"

"At first, I couldn't get a word in edgewise! Finally, once he started telling me the details on Cuarón, and he mentioned the World Series, I stopped him. I said, 'Look, man. I work for ASN. I won't tell anyone else a single thing you've told me without your permission, but it seems like you're ready to tell your story. And if you are—' "

"Oh my gosh, Will!" My hands clasped over my mouth.

"I know! I just knew it was my story. Sure enough, the guy wanted to talk, and I convinced him to talk to me. I checked everything out, got the go-ahead from Kev, and have been working on it nonstop over the past few days. We just filmed, and it airs tomorrow!"

I jumped up from the couch in excitement. "Are you telling me *you* just filmed? They put you on-air?"

"That's why the network bought the suit. I mean, I certainly couldn't afford this thing. And it was a sit-down, so—"

"So they never show your feet." I laughed and threw my arms open. In a flash, he was standing along with me, his arms around my waist. "I'm so proud of you," I said softly as we held each other.

"Thank you," he whispered. "I'm sorry it's kept me so busy over the past few days."

"No! Of course. I completely understand."

Suddenly I was back in the single-or-engaged headspace as I realized I meant that. Once I knew why he cancelled our date, I did completely understand. The only thing left was to figure out whether or not that really made a difference. After all, it wasn't as if that proverbial straw could be removed and the camel's back unbroken.

"You've been so patient with me," he said into my ear before planting a gentle kiss on my neck, just below my earlobe.

There it was. The alarm once again began blaring in my ears and pounding in my heart. And my gut? Well, my gut didn't have any clue what it was supposed to do. It all made sense. It made sense why he would be ready to propose. I knew what had changed.

A higher-profile job and a substantial jump in income could very well be the enticement Will needed to finally take a step toward a wife and family.

"So, can I assume that after this story airs tomorrow, you may be on-camera again?" I asked.

He pulled back slightly, though he didn't release me. An excited smile overtook his face as he said, "Well, as Kevin so articulately put it, 'Tomorrow will either bring a promotion or a pink slip,' so . . ."

I gasped. "A pink slip?"

Will shook his head and brushed off my

concern. "Only if something leaks and the base-ball commissioner has a chance to . . . oh, I don't know. I don't even want to talk about that. Really. It's not going to happen. I was more thorough on this than I've ever been on anything else in my life. It won't be a pink slip. The Magician is going to make my career, Cadie. I'm sure of it."

"The Magician?"

He laughed. "Yeah. That's what we call him. My source. Because he made so many things magically disappear. Of course, you know him better as the Pigeon . . ."

"Oh!"

He smiled as he watched me laugh, but the smile grew more subdued as one of his hands made its way from my waist to my hair. He tucked a strand behind my ear and then traced the strand with his fingers as it fell—across my temple, brushing my ear, gently down my jaw-bone and neck. When his palm reached my collarbone, the strand of hair ended, but his hand lingered. Eventually—too soon, too late—his fingers made their way upward on my throat, finally resting on my chin, which he directed his way as his lips made their approach.

"I feel like I owe you an apology for more than just the past few days," he muttered as he placed soft kisses up and down my jawline. "It's kind of been a whole year of misfires and miscommuni-cation, I think."

Tears sprang to my eyes. "You knew that? I mean . . . you *know?*"

He sighed. "Of course I know." His lips ceased their onslaught and he held my face in both of his hands. "And I know things haven't been the same between us for so long. I just . . . I just haven't known what to do about it. I know that it's not just about being ready. It needs to be *right.* So every second of every day for the past year, I've tried to do what's right. Sometimes that's really difficult. Sometimes, like right now. When something big happens in life and there is literally no one else I need to tell about it, and then I'm looking at you, and you're so beautiful. And it's just tough to remember that there is anything that matters more than you." His fingers made their way through my hair. "I am madly in love with you, Cadie McCaffrey, and at the end of the day, I know we want the same thing—"

My mouth captured his, cutting off the words I had been so desperate to hear. It soon became clear that the kiss outside the copy room had been only a warning shot of the passion pent up inside of us.

Be careful, Cadie. I heard the still small voice, with its distress signal and urgent plea. It sounded vaguely like my gut, which I had been trusting to guide me, but there was a difference. All night long, my gut had been offering wise, indisputable counsel: don't be too eager, hear him out, understand him, don't wear the overalls. I'd had no problem at all traveling in the direction that all of that wisdom had led me. My gut and my brain, not to mention my heart, had been willing partners.

But as Will kissed me more passionately than he had ever kissed me before, and our hands dared to go where we'd never allowed them to go before; as we sat together on my bed, where we had never sat together before—despite the fact that it was literally placed in the center of my home like an unavoidable temptation—and as we each silently consented to the other, it was abundantly clear.

My gut was attempting to direct me away from the biggest mistake I would ever make, and I was no longer willing to listen.

6

At the End of the Date (But Not of the Day)

"Sadie?" Will called out for probably the fifth
time. "I feel pretty helpless out here."

He was beginning to wonder if she was ever
coming out of the bathroom, and the longer
she stayed in there, the more he wondered if he
should even still be at her place when she did
finally reappear, or if he should ever show his
face again.

He'd been sitting on the edge of the bed ever
since the moment she'd run to the bathroom,
without a word having been uttered between
them. He had gotten mostly dressed, but in the
silence he still felt naked and vulnerable. He
grabbed his dress shirt from its heap on the floor
and buttoned it up over the undershirt he had on.
He slipped on his socks and shoes, fully aware
he wouldn't actually make a run for it, of course,
but having no idea what his next move should
be. Not being able to stand the distance between
them any longer, he approached the bathroom
door and thought he heard her crying.

He took a deep breath as every single thought

passing through his mind began to pass through a different filter. *You're such a jerk,* he lectured himself.

He hadn't been with a woman since giving his life over to God in grad school. He'd had no intention of being with *any* woman again outside of marriage, but no matter how resolute he'd been in his decision to wait, in the moment he'd thought only of her. Unfortunately, even in his thinking of her he'd thought all the wrong things.

"Cadie?" He repeated her name, but this time softly. He leaned his arm against the door and rested his head there, guilt washing over him. "I'm so sorry. I didn't mean to make it just about me." Though he *did* feel helpless. "I just . . . I don't know what to do, or what to say. I wish you'd talk to me." He listened and heard only an occasional sniff. "Are you hurt? If I hurt you, I'm so sorry. You know I never meant to." He didn't know how much more he could take. "Please just talk to me. Please come out. I need to see you."

He backed away from the door in response to the shuffle he heard, and a moment later the doorknob turned. He never could have guessed that seeing her would be more painful than the agony of the door between them, but as she stood before him with a quilt draped around her shoulders and mascara remnants under her eyes, that reality set in.

He hadn't previously known helpless.

"Hi," he whispered. "You okay?" He reached out for her, but she dodged his arms and crossed to the other side of the room.

"I think you should go."

He turned to her, certain he'd heard her incorrectly. Or at least he really hoped he had. "I'm sorry, what?"

"I think you should go," she repeated resolutely.

Will took a deep breath and warned himself not to react emotionally. That wouldn't do anyone any good. He knew it was different for her—he didn't fully understand how or why it was different, but he knew it was.

"Cadie, I'm sorry if . . ." He cautiously took a slow step toward her, and then another. He took another deep breath and exhaled as he begged his mind to come up with the right words to say. "I've always walked away before it was too late, but tonight, I wasn't . . . I mean, like I said, at the end of the day—"

"Oh, that's right." Tears that had been portrayed in the redness of her eyes as a thing of the past once again appeared in the present, and he wasn't sure if his heart would survive it. "At the end of the day, we want the same thing. Isn't that what you said?"

"Yes," he replied with a shrug, daring to take another step in her direction. "Was I wrong?"

She didn't bother to wipe away the tears that were streaming down her cheeks. She only

95

tightened the quilt around herself and, her voice breaking, asked, "What were you going to say next, Will? What's the surprise that was going to make tonight so special?" She turned away from him and looked toward the bed as disdain overtook her face and, he soon discovered, her voice. "Please tell me that whatever it was, you didn't plan for it to turn into *that*."

"No! I didn't plan it, Cadie. You know that." There was no right answer. "That shouldn't have happened, and I'm sorry. You know I'm sorry. But I don't think either of us can deny that the last year has been pretty rough at times, and I think that's, at least in part, because it was becoming more and more difficult to keep from crossing the line. And I haven't always handled that very well."

"Please, Will. Just answer the question." He watched her as she bit her lip and looked down at her feet, toes just peeking out from beneath the quilt. He watched her silent tears flow so heavily that they ran down her neck before absorbing in the cushy bedspread material. "If you didn't plan for *that* to happen, what did you think was going to happen tonight?"

Not feeling like he was allowed to reach out and hold her was nearly unprecedented, and not a sensation he ever wanted to experience again. How had one of the best days of his life turned into this?

The "how" seems pretty obvious, he mentally replied to his own soul-searching. *You were so careful for so long. How could you have let this happen?*

"I wanted to take you away," he muttered, the plan that he'd thought was so romantic just a little while ago suddenly seeming foolish and naïve. "I felt bad about having to cancel on you the other night, so I convinced Kevin to let us borrow his cabin in the Poconos for a few days. But, I wasn't planning for this to happen there, either. You have to believe me. I wasn't planning for this to happen *anywhere.* I just thought we could get away from everything for a little while, maybe reconnect some. Just relax for a bit, you know?"

He watched as she took in all he'd said, and he was as fascinated by her as he'd always been. Her brain moved so quickly, but he'd long ago learned that in most cases, words took their time to follow. Not too much time—just the right amount. She was careful. Cautious. She seemed to understand, as so many young adults of their generation did not, that words are powerful and permanent.

"Pope's nose." Her voice trailed off, along with her eyes.

Admittedly, those weren't the words he was expecting her to land on.

"You know what?" he asked with renewed

vigor. Not that he was *feeling* vigorous, but he knew he had to start digging them out from the despair. "Maybe we should go. To the Poconos, I mean. We can take a few days off work and focus on us, and talk about everything. I realize it's going to take us some time to bounce back from this, but—"

"At the end of the day, I don't know that we've ever wanted the same thing, Will."

"I don't think that's true—"

"I didn't want *this!*" she cried.

Panic and heartbreak rose in his chest. She still wasn't looking at him, and he was glad. He could only imagine what the fear and pain looked like on his own face. "I didn't . . . I mean, you were . . ." Wasn't breathing supposed to be involuntary? Why was he having to put in so much effort? "I blame myself. I do. I take full responsibility. But you didn't give me any indication that—"

"That's not what I mean." She groaned, and more tears fell, then she cleared her throat and went back to staring at her toes. "You didn't do it alone, and you don't have to take full responsibility. I . . . yeah . . . I wanted it in the moment," she whispered. "But at the end of the day?" She slowly raised her head and met his eyes. "At the end of the day, all I've ever wanted is you."

For the first time since desire had completed its transformation into guilt, a smile formed on his face. "And all I've ever wanted is you. See? We're on the same page after all."

"This isn't working. I'm sorry. This just . . . isn't working."

"What isn't working? This isn't working? What is *this?* It's bad. Trust me, I *know* this is bad. But once the dust has settled—"

"Once the dust has settled?" Cadie whimpered, pulling the quilt even more tightly around her. "What does that even mean? What do you think comes next?"

He took a shaky breath. "Hang on. What are you . . . are you saying, *we* aren't working?"

"I think you should go, Will," she said one last time, so softly.

Everything in him was telling him to fight it. To fight *her,* if he had to. She was wrong. He knew it, and he was convinced that once the emotion of the situation cleared away, she would know it too. Ultimately, it was his confidence in that, his confidence in *them,* that caused him to grab his tie, vest, and brand-new suit jacket—all painful reminders of the hope and excitement with which the evening had begun—and walk out of her apartment without saying another word.

7

A Few Days Later (Long Before the Dust Settled)

I know that technically a walk of shame takes place the morning after a sexual encounter— same clothes, messy hair, unbrushed teeth. I'm not sure that walking back into ASN after a sick day and a weekend qualified. I was no longer wearing the black slacks and jade blouse that had failed me so spectacularly, and my dental hygiene was as meticulous as ever. Nevertheless, shame coursed through every inch of my body.

I was sure someone would know. I didn't think that Will would tell anyone, but somehow they would know. And even if they didn't, I knew. I would *always* know. Perhaps every step I ever took, for the rest of my life, was destined to be part of my walk of shame.

"Hey, you," Darby greeted me as I entered The Bench's accounting suite. "Feeling better?"

Such a loaded question.

Better? my brain cried out. *Better than what? Better than the bottomless pit of despair that I've been living in for the past few days? Better than the constant crushing conviction that I'm resigned to be grappling with every time I breathe until the day I die or become a nun, whichever comes first?*

But since I knew she only meant "better than the stomach flu," which I had claimed to have so I could skip work on Friday and blow off Darby all weekend, I replied, "Yes. Thanks."

I knew I would have to tell her. Maybe I wouldn't ever have to tell anyone else, but I would have to tell Darby. For one thing, she would know something was up, and she would keep hounding me until she figured it out. Beyond that, I knew I needed to talk to *someone*. Without Will, Darby would always be my someone.

I walked into my office and set down my bag. It was all so deceptively normal. Set down the bag, like every other day. Hang up the jacket. Check the messages. Sign on the computer. But it was the things that were so unlike any other day that already hurt, even before they happened. It was those things that had caused me to contemplate how long I could call in sick before rumors would begin circulating that I had somehow contracted malaria.

"At least I wouldn't feel guilty about malaria," I grumbled to myself as I pulled out my desk chair and sat down.

"Why would you feel guilty about malaria? Are we supposed to feel guilty about malaria?" Darby asked from the doorway. "I confess I don't know much about it. Is that the mosquitos one?" She paused. "Is there a telethon or something? Should I send a check?"

"I was just . . ." What? What was I *just?* I sighed and crossed my arms on the desk and then lowered my head in defeat. Embarrassingly quick defeat. "I need to talk to you."

"Okay . . ." Her tone was instantly dripping with concern. "Should I shut the door?"

"Yes, please," I muttered, my head still buried in my arms. "And lock it."

I heard the door shut and the lock click in quick succession, and then she rushed over to the other side of the desk. "Do you have malaria? I'm so sorry I was making jokes, Cadie. How do you even *get* malaria in New York?"

I laughed—truly laughed—for the first time in days, and I lifted my head. "I don't have malaria, Darb." She was just a little too easily convinced that I had somehow contracted a tropical disease. Never mind that Coney Island was the farthest south I'd traveled in at least two years.

"So it really was just a stomach flu?" she asked.

And in a flash, the humor was gone and the guilt was back. That had been a nice four seconds.

"Not exactly."

The concern returned to her face as she sat down and leaned in, ready to listen. "Okay, what are you not telling me?"

I took a deep breath and prepared to say the

words aloud for the first time. It sure felt like they didn't want to come out, which I suppose wasn't surprising. But as many times as I had repeated them over and over in my mind, you would think I would be desensitized to them somewhat.

"Will and I had sex."

I had expected shock. Maybe a little bit of shouting. Quite possibly she would track down some ashes and sackcloth for me, just to get the ball rolling. What I hadn't expected was for my best friend to not believe me.

"No, seriously, Cadie. I'm worried. What's going on?"

Well, crap. I was actually going to have to say it again?

"Seriously," I replied in a hushed tone—just loud enough for her to hear but quiet enough that the screaming inside my head might drown it out so I wouldn't have to hear myself say the words a second time. "Thursday. He came over. We had sex."

There it was. Shock was very plainly registered on her face, I was pretty sure shouting was imminent, and I fully expected to get a notification at any moment that an order had been placed in our shared Amazon account for sackcloth and ashes—hopefully with two-day shipping, since we're Prime members.

"But you said . . ."

"I know."

"You said you canceled. Because you were—"

"Sick. I know. I wasn't sick."

"Why did you lie to me, Cadie? Me! You don't lie to *me!*" she, of course, shouted.

"I know. I know!" I lifted my hands in surrender as tears burned my eyes. "I'm sorry. But I knew that if you knew I ended up getting together with him, you would ask if he had proposed. Or, worse yet, you'd assume he had. And then I'd have to talk about it." My lip began to tremble and I reached for a tissue. "And I just couldn't talk about it. I couldn't. I really don't know . . . I don't know how it happened. I feel so stupid."

I collapsed in a heap of tears, and in an instant, she was by my side. In an instant I felt even stupider because I hadn't allowed her to be by my side until then. When would I learn? Darby would never judge me or force me to focus on my failings. She understood I was doing that quite well on my own, without anyone's assistance. She no doubt knew that we'd get around to all of it—the pain caused by betraying my convictions, and my fears about disappointing God so spectacularly, as I knew I had. But there would be time for that later.

She wrapped her arms around me and laid her head on top of mine as I sobbed.

"Okay," she began, the predictably shouty side giving way to the calm and comforting side. "Tell me what you need. Do we talk about this now? Do you want to wait until later?" When I didn't answer, she added, "I'll go tell everyone you have malaria, if that's what you need."

"How would that help?"

She shrugged. "I don't know. Maybe it wouldn't."

"I bet everyone would leave me alone." I sniffed. "That would be good."

"That *would* be good. Although—and bear with me here, I'm just spitballing—if I go out there and tell them, I might not be allowed to come back in. I mean, I don't know much about malaria—"

"Yes, you made that clear earlier . . ."

"But I'm pretty sure if we report a case on Fulton Street, somebody will have to be called in. Like the CDC, or—"

"Will Smith?" I sniffed again as I looked up at her.

She looked down at me, confused. "Um, sure, sure. Maybe they'll call in Will Smith."

"Because of *I Am Legend*, I mean."

She smiled. "Yep. They would definitely call in Will Smith. And then I wouldn't be allowed to come in to see you."

"I don't actually think it's contagious."

"Look, just because *you* apparently know everything about malaria doesn't mean anyone else does, and we can't risk a quarantine where we get separated. So I think what we should do instead is just send a memo from here. 'To: All ASN staff. Please be aware that Cadie McCaffrey in accounting has malaria. She'll be fine. Just let her be for a few days—' "

"And maybe they can drop coffee and bagels through the air vent or something?"

"Okay, so, 'Please be aware that Cadie McCaffrey in accounting has malaria. Send coffee and bagels. And Will Smith.' Will that work?"

I blew my nose and replied, "That works."

Several minutes later, I had finished explaining how Will's really good day at work, his really nice suit, and my mental twisting of every single word he said into confirmation that he was finally ready to commit to spending the rest of his life with me had mingled to result in the biggest mistake of my life.

"So, what are you going to do?" Darby asked me.

"What am I going to do about *what?* I don't suppose there's much to be done. It's not like I can press Command-Z on this one." I sighed as I stared blankly at the trusty iMac on my desk. How much easier life would be if it were like a spreadsheet—no mistake would be permanent, and you could sort and filter until things made sense.

She nodded. "That's true. You can't undo it. But life will carry on in spite of that."

I crossed my arms as I leaned back in my chair. I wasn't entirely convinced she was right about that. At the very least, life as I had known it had come to an end.

"Look, Cadie," she continued. "I know how important it was to you to wait until marriage. I get it. But guess what? You messed up."

"Wow. Thanks, Darb."

She shrugged. "You messed up like we all mess up—in different ways. And yeah, sometimes we even do things we told God—and ourselves—we wouldn't. Now you need to figure out how to move forward. I think after you talk to Will—"

My eyes flew open wide. "Talk to Will? How can I talk to him?"

"You go down the hall, turn right, walk about fifty yards, and then take another right. It's not that difficult."

I was not amused. "I'm serious, Darby."

"I know you are, Cadie. So am I."

She walked over to the window that looked out into the hallway and peeked through the blinds— presumably to try and figure out if Will was in the building. I hadn't bothered to look for myself. He was there. I was sure of it. And it probably wasn't going to be long until he knocked on my door and tried to get me to talk to him.

"I'm not fooling myself that I can avoid him forever." I sighed. "After he tried calling a couple times, I texted him and asked him to give me the weekend. And he did. I told him I'd talk to him soon, and I will. But right now, I don't know what to say. I spent all weekend thinking, and I still really don't know what to say."

Darby walked away from the window and returned to her seat across the desk from me. "What do you *want* to say?"

"What do you mean?"

"I mean, what's on your heart?"

I scoffed. "I don't think I can say what's on my—"

"But if you could," she interjected, tenderly, "what would it be?"

I sighed . . . again . . . as tears sprang to my eyes . . . again.

"That I'm sorry."

"For the other night?"

I shook my head. "No. I mean, *yes*. That too." *Definitely* that too. "But really for everything leading up to the other night. The misunderstandings, I guess, if that's what they were. The year of distance between us—"

"But that wasn't all your fault," she insisted.

I shrugged. "Wasn't it? I really don't know. Is it really his fault if I had us built up in my mind to something more than what we were?" I took a deep breath. "I guess, right now, I would really just want to ask him what the point was."

"The point?"

"Of being together for so long and getting my

heart to where it's convinced that I could never love anyone else like I love him, only to realize we're headed toward . . . nothing. What was the point of any of it?"

It was my turn to walk to the window and look out, but I wasn't looking for Will, or even thinking of him at all, really. Not right then. If anything, I was just searching for a way out.

Once upon a time, my mother had said that when I found the right man, I'd know. She said that there were three characteristics that were nonnegotiable—he had to be a Christian, he had to earn a good living, and he had to be someone she and my father approved of. Of course, at the time I was thirteen and convinced that I was in love with Gabe Thorstun, who was known to his peers as Surge.

I'm sure my mother thought that by laying out those three indisputable qualifications for a boyfriend, she was protecting me from Surge. "Trust me," she said. "If the young man has those three things in his corner, the rest will be easy." *The rest will be easy.*

Will Whitaker had given his life to the Lord, worked hard to make a decent living, and my parents loved him, but for the first time I was realizing that my mom didn't know what she was talking about. Nothing about any of it was turning out to be easy.

"What's been the point?" I repeated as I

continued staring out the window. "I'd almost feel better if I could at least believe it was some sort of long con to get my money."

"You have money?" she asked with a smile.

"No! See? I'm not even worth conning."

She was laughing as she joined me by the window. "If this was a long con, it was the worst long con in history. Let's face it, Will is no Sawyer."

I faced her with a smirk. "Ah. So you're on . . . what? Season two?"

When all the world was obsessed with *Lost*, tuning in every week to see if polar bears or smoke monsters or Others would show up, Darby refused to jump on the bandwagon. It was only a couple of months prior, while recovering from pneumonia and out of things to watch, that she gave in and watched an episode. Now she was just like everyone else—obsessed, confused, and regularly alternating between Team Sawyer and Team Jack.

Okay, so she was just like everyone else *was* . . . in 2005.

"Sawyer just pulled that long con on that Cassidy woman—"

"Oh, the one he had the baby with?" I asked, *fully* aware of what I was doing.

The color drained from her face. "Spoilers!"

"Nope." I chuckled. "Sorry, but the spoiler statute of limitations has expired."

"Anyway . . ." she said, her tone long and drawn out—and annoyed. "Your four years with Will were not a long con." She gave my hand a quick squeeze as she left me at the window and walked to the closed door, where she had apparently left her slipped-off shoes at some point. Sometimes I wondered why Darby even bothered to walk out of her apartment in shoes. They never stayed on.

I faced her and then hoisted myself up onto the little ledge of the window. I crossed my arms and dangled my feet as I said, "I know. But if I could convince myself that he never loved me, at least I could stop trying to figure out why he doesn't love me *enough,*" I muttered, accompanied by my closest companions, sigh and cry. "Why does it feel like that's so much worse? What's wrong with me, Darb?"

"Nothing, apart from the fact that you have the musical tastes of a seventy-two-year-old woman."

I quickly decided that right then was not the moment to share with her that Barry Manilow had been my soundtrack of sorrow throughout the weekend. Not that she would be surprised. Barry had provided the soundtrack for most of the key moments in my life, from the time I was a little girl whose parents only allowed three pop music options in the house: Barry Manilow, Pat Boone, and Debby Boone. Compared to "Love Letters in the Sand" and "You Light Up My Life,"

"Copacabana" seemed positively scandalous.

"For what it's worth, I don't think my musical tastes are what's keeping Will from wanting to spend his life with me. Too bad, really. If it were as simple as that, I could at least figure out how to proceed. What am I supposed to do when the only thing keeping the guy I love from wanting to marry me is, you know . . . the fact that I'm me?"

Darby put her hand on the doorknob. "That's absurd. You are quite the prize, you know. Well, maybe you *don't* know, but I know. And Will definitely knows. I haven't the slightest idea what's keeping him from proposing to you, but whatever it is, it's his problem. Not yours."

That was such a best friend thing to say, and I loved her for it. What's more, I knew she believed it was true. If only I could find a way to make myself believe it.

"I mean, that's weird, Cadie."

"What is?"

"Four years, and you guys never talked about marriage? That's not normal. I don't care if people decide to get married or not, but at *some* point in a relationship that lasts that long, it's going to come up."

"It's not that it never came up."

"So it *has* come up? I don't remember you ever telling me that."

I waved off her interest. "There's no story

there. Seriously. I don't even remember what was said, really. It was about a million-and-a-half years ago." I groaned as I looked at the clock and realized it was *way* past time to get to work. I descended from the window and walked to my desk to finally turn on my computer—thirty minutes after I arrived at the office. "I guess that's not really the point, anyway. Even if he had proposed at the end of the night, we'd have already thrown a lot away. And here I'd thought the worst thing to come from our date would be me breaking up with him. If only."

She opened the door. "You going to be okay today? If you need to take another day off—"

"I'll be okay." I did all I could to present a genuine smile for her. The appreciation I was feeling for her was most assuredly genuine—even if my face didn't want to cooperate. "Thanks, Darb."

I figured I'd be okay, but that didn't stop me from hurriedly moving to the door and closing it behind her as soon as she walked out. My hand hesitated as I tried to make up my mind—to lock or not to lock.

Not to lock. I couldn't stay hidden away forever. If Will showed up, I would just feign malaria.

8

*A Million-and-a-Half Years Ago
(Okay . . . More Like Three)*

H ey, where's that research kid?"
Will knew he should be satisfied—thrilled even—that Kevin Lamont was asking for him at all. He was working his dream job at his dream network, and one of the industry greats knew that he existed. Most days, that was enough. But every once in a while, he wondered if it would be too much to ask to be called by his name. Lorenzo Bateman in legal had finally begun calling him William, and despite the fact that his name was *not* William—even on his birth certificate, it was just Will—he liked to think that progress was being made.

"I'm right here, Mr. Lamont." He set down the cup of coffee he hadn't finished filling and returned the coffeepot to the burner before turning. "What can I do for you, sir?"

"Well, for one thing, you can stop calling me Mr. Lamont. You've been here, what, six months already?"

"A little more than a year, actually."

"And you're dating Cadie McCaffrey from accounting, right?"

Will's eyes flew open, not having expected his love life to come into the conversation. "Yes, I am."

"I like Cadie." He paused before adding, "I like that my sports career means nothing to her."

"I wouldn't say your career means *nothing* to her. No, she's not much of a sports fan, but—"

"That's an understatement!" Kevin laughed boisterously. "But she's unapologetic, she knows who she is, and just as importantly, she knows who she's not. I get so tired of the suck-ups and the yes men. As far as I'm concerned, if someone is good at what they do, they should be confident enough to avoid all of that brownnosing stuff that so many people in this industry fall into."

"My name is Will," he suddenly blurted out. "Not 'research kid' or 'new guy' or even William, or any of the other names I've been called in the past year." His confidence dissipating quickly, he added, "Sir."

Kevin was silent for just a little bit too long, and Will couldn't interpret the mood being communicated through the eyes that were boring holes into him. He quickly decided his safest move was to turn the topic of conversation back to Cadie.

"Cadie does actually try to connect with

the sports stuff, sometimes. She'll use sports analogies to explain accounting to me."

"Hang on." Kevin reached out with one of his legendary-wingspan arms and placed one of his grip-a-basketball-in-his-palm hands on Will's shoulder, the tension seemingly defused. "McCaffrey uses sports analogies?"

"Well, they're awful, of course. Usually they just involve a 'player guy' running a ball down a 'court thing.'" Despite his nerves, and the general uncertainty as to whether or not he had just thrown away his career in a fit of assertiveness, Will couldn't help but smile. "I just like that she tries."

Kevin laughed. "Don't you think for even a minute that she can't keep up with your stuff. She's attempting to dumb down for you. Not the other way around."

"Yes," Will replied. "I am fully aware of that, sir."

"Good. Just so that's clear. I for one am glad I'm married to a woman who's smarter than I am, but the fact that she goes to a great deal of effort to make me feel like I can keep up with her, well . . . let's just say I've got a good one. Sounds like you've got a good one too, Will."

"Thank you, Mr. Lamont," Will said, quite impressed with how well he was hiding the elation he was feeling upon hearing Kevin Lamont finally say his name.

"Seriously, man." He pointed a finger toward Will's face. "If you don't start calling me Kevin, I'm going to go back to calling you 'research boy.'"

Um . . . that's 'research kid,' Will thought and very nearly said before he thought better of it.

"Okay. You got it."

"Good. So, look, we're going to be pulling together an hour special on Jordan. I'm going to have them send you over some questions, and then I want you to meet up with him and prep him before the interview."

"Jordan? *Michael* Jordan?"

"His people are expecting your call. You're probably looking at coffee tomorrow or Friday. Let me know once it's set up, and then you're going to run point on B-roll."

Kevin spun on his heel and began walking away, but Will stopped him.

"I am incredibly flattered. Of course. But I literally just got back from a trip interviewing the Zamboni driver for the Manitoba Junior Hockey League. Are you sure—"

"I'm tired of the suck-ups and the yes men," Kevin repeated. "And you're good at what you do, Will." Will stared at him in silence, afraid to move. "So go do it."

Two minutes later Will was briskly walking—and when no one was around, running—through The Bench's hallways. He'd just been handed the

117

biggest, most important assignment of his life, he was about to make a phone call to arrange a sit-down with one of the greatest, most legendary athletes of all time, and he was no longer "research kid." Only one person could make the day even better.

"Hey," he said as he poked his head into Cadie's office.

"Hey there," she responded in greeting, and the smile on her face—the one he knew was reserved for him—validated his belief that a few minutes with her was worth making Michael Jordan's people wait. "This is a nice surprise."

"How's your day?"

"Not too bad. You?"

"Good, actually." He stepped farther in. "Kevin is putting me in charge of B-roll for a Michael Jordan special, and as if that weren't enough, I get to sit down with Jordan and do some prep." Even as he said it, the reality was still setting in.

"Will!" Cadie squealed, jumped up from her chair, and ran into his waiting arms. "That's huge!"

He continued holding her but pulled back to look at her with a smirk. "Okay, I appreciate the enthusiasm, but do you know who that is?"

"Of course! He's the really good rugby guy!" She winked and then laughed as she removed herself from his arms—despite his resistance— and returned to her desk. "Just kidding. Even *I* know Michael Jordan. I mean, he was in *Space Jam*, so . . . total legend."

He watched her as they continued talking, and he was keenly aware that she wasn't the direction he had imagined his life going. Every woman he had dated before Cadie, on the other hand, had been *exactly* the type of woman he had thought he would spend his life with. The type who had their own season pass at Fenway and gave him a run for his money in Fantasy Football. Cadie McCaffrey was definitely not that type.

"She's unapologetic, she knows who she is, and just as importantly, she knows who she's not."

"What?" she asked when she caught him looking at her so intently. When he said nothing, a slightly self-conscious grin spread across her face and she asked again, "What is it?"

"Nothing," he replied nonchalantly with a shrug. "Just thinking of something Kevin said today. He said he's glad he's married to a woman who's smarter than he is, but he appreciates the fact that she goes to a lot of effort to make him feel like he can keep up with her. And I was just realizing how lucky I am to have *you*. You *definitely* go to that effort for me, and I guess I just wanted to let you know that I see that." He sat on the edge of her desk beside her chair.

She picked up a few papers, carefully placed them in a file folder, and then stood to take the folder to the tall, tan cabinet in the corner.

Then she joined him at the edge of the desk and bumped him gently with her hip. He scooted over in response, and she sat beside him.

"You're a pretty sharp guy, Whitaker. I don't think I have to work all that hard." She leaned over and rested her head on his shoulder. "But that's very sweet. Thank you."

Will kissed the top of her head. "I think we've got a good thing going, McCaffrey."

She turned to face him, and his face was still close. She leaned in just a touch farther and rested her forehead against his.

Will adjusted his angle so that his torso was parallel with hers, and then he draped an arm across her and slid her toward him on the desk, closing the already minimal gap between them.

"I love you," he whispered against her lips.

Cadie smiled and said, "I love you too," as she raised her hands to his face and grazed his jawline with her fingertips. He tilted his head, leaning into one of her hands, as his free hand made its way to the back of her head. He began pulling her toward him, their lips already brushing against each other, but she resisted.

"As much as I'd *really* love to, you know . . . sit here and make out with you, with the door wide open and all . . ."

He sighed as he pulled away from her and stood from the desk, and she followed suit and hopped down. As she pulled the chair out and sat down again, Will said, "So, all in all, Kevin actually seems pretty wise."

"For saying he made the right call by marrying someone who's smarter than he is?" He shrugged and she laughed. "I suppose. I don't know. At the very least, it's more poetic than the marriage advice my parents gave *me*."

"Which was?"

She moved her mouse on the mousepad to awaken the computer that had fallen asleep while they'd flirted. "The guy has to be a Christian, my parents should love him, and he has to have money."

Will laughed. Cadie did not.

"Well, that's a bit passé," he said as he continued laughing.

"Which part?"

He thought for a moment and smiled. "Everything except the Christian part, I guess."

"I don't know," she said—still without laughing. "It's always made pretty good sense to me. I know it's sort of old-fashioned to want my parents' 'blessing,' or whatever you would call it, but I've never really thought that would be a big deal. I guess I've just always known they would love the guy I love."

She looked up at him with big, loving eyes—so tender and guileless—and he knew he would willingly go along with any archaic tradition her heart desired. That was a small price to pay for being the guy Cadie McCaffrey loved. Besides, he was pretty sure her parents already loved him, so he had nothing to worry about there.

He leaned down and kissed the top of her head before crossing to the other side of her desk. "And what about the third piece of advice? How much money are we talking?"

"To satisfy my parents? A diversified stock portfolio and a small yacht should do the trick. They're simple people, really." Finally a smile appeared on her face, but after taking in his expression it quickly faded. "I was a teenager when they said that."

"But it makes sense to you?"

"Well, not the yacht. The insurance premiums on those things are ridiculous." The corner of her mouth turned up again. "All I meant is it makes sense to me to try and marry someone with some source of decent income and maybe some aspirations in life. I mean, they expect that of *me*. *I* expect that of me. Why shouldn't I also expect that of the person I spend my life with?"

He chuckled and nodded his head. "You're right. That makes sense. And you think that's all your parents meant?"

She laughed. "Well, if you pressed them on it, I think they'd say that's what they meant. He should just make a decent living. But in their heart of hearts, I'm pretty sure they meant the yacht."

All the wind was gone from his sails, and he

didn't even know why. He felt as if he had gotten to know Oliver and Nessa McCaffrey pretty well over the course of the thirteen months he'd been dating Cadie, and they were wealthy, ultra-conservative, and literally famous for being Christians. They lived in a huge, beautiful home on two acres in Syosset, and they no doubt wanted the same or better for their only child. Their requirements for their daughter's husband were just what should be expected.

But Cadie had never seemed to care about money. Sure, it's easy not to care about money when you *have* money, but apart from her brown-stone in Greenwich Village, she had worked for everything she had. She never looked down on Will's tiny, modest Morningside Heights apart-ment, which he shared with a revolving cast of roommates.

"Well, I should let you get back to work," he finally said, in a voice he hoped sounded normal.

"And you have to call the Air Jordan shoes guy!" She trilled with excitement for him, and his deflated enthusiasm was bolstered by *her*.

"Actually," he said with a grin, "you can just call him Air Jordan. That was his nickname."

"After the shoes?"

"The shoes were named after him."

She looked up from her computer and shrugged. "Ah. I was close."

"I just like that you try."

• • •

Three years later, Will sat in the same cubicle at ASN he had occupied since the beginning, spinning mindlessly in the same chair.

Sometimes loving your job can be a curse. Sometimes being *satisfied* can be a curse.

But suddenly, he wasn't satisfied. The workspace, where the framed photo of him smiling beside Michael Jordan sat buried on his desk because there was no wall on which to hang it, represented unfulfilled dreams and unacceptable complacency. He'd made a promise to himself to work harder. To speed things along. But here he was, in the exact same spot.

Well, no more.

He bounded from his chair and hurried to The Bench as quickly as he could. Every few feet he was greeted with congratulations and attaboys by co-workers he knew meant well, but he didn't have time to soak in the praise. He rounded the corner and opened the door to the accounting suite.

"Hey, Darb," Will called out as he entered. "Have you seen the overnights? From the Magician special on Friday?"

She turned the rest of her body to face him. "Of course I've seen them. You do know I compile *all* of the ratings, don't you?"

"Were they good?"

"You haven't seen them?"

He shook his head and repeated, "Were they good?"

"Will, they were off the charts. And each replay since has gotten better."

"Can I get a copy?"

"Sure," Darby replied with a shrug, seemingly baffled that he didn't already have one. She walked to her desk computer and began typing.

As she pulled up the reports, Will cleared his throat and asked, "Is she here? Could I see her for a minute?"

"I think she's on a call . . ."

"I can wait."

Darby looked around at the bustling office and then leaned in closer and softly said, "Don't wait. Don't do this here. Okay?"

"At least tell me if she's okay," he whispered as he diverted his eyes.

"I don't know what to say. I really don't. Just give her some time. I could be wrong, but I really think that by this time next week, or the week after, we'll be looking at a different situation."

"Next week?" he asked incredulously. After she texted and asked him to give her the weekend, he'd replied by telling her to take all the time she needed. He'd been hoping she'd be ready to talk by lunchtime.

"Or the week after. You know how she is, Will. She has to—"

"Process," he said with a sigh. "I know."

"So give her some time," she repeated, and then she clicked her mouse a final time. An instant later she was handing Will a paper from the printer behind her.

"Thanks."

"No problem."

She resumed whatever she had been doing, leaving him to stare at the numbers in his hands. She hadn't been exaggerating. In the modern age of social media and online video clips, no one had really expected to ever see those sorts of ratings again.

Will chuckled and muttered to himself, "We may not be talking Syosset money, but I think we're on the right track."

"What's that, Will?" Anna, the new girl in accounting, asked him.

"Nothing. Sorry."

Overnight ratings clasped firmly in his hand, he walked out of the accounting suite, left The Bench, and marched back to The Field, determined to make Darby's prediction come true.

By this time next week, or at least by the week after, they could be looking at a completely different situation.

9

(Roughly) This Time the Week After Next

I think I'm going to get a dog," I said aloud to . . . no one. I was alone in my living room, sitting on my couch. The TV wasn't even on.

That was the moment, I think. The moment when I realized that something had to change.

I groaned as I stood from my couch—not the groan of someone who was frustrated, but the groan of a woman who was suddenly, undeniably old at the age of thirty-four. I brushed the Milano cookie crumbs off my chest and realized that the evidence was indisputable.

I had, apparently, given up.

I wasn't exactly sure when it had happened. Maybe it was just a result of the exhaustion that stemmed from avoiding Will all day every day at a time when it had never been more difficult to go even a few minutes without hearing his name around the ASN offices. It probably didn't help that Darby had been on two dates with the same guy over the course of three days, and that my thoughts had been alternating between the realistically depressing "She's going to fall in love and I'm going to be single for the rest of my life, and she won't have time for me," and the more absurd but equally depressing "I wonder if only one of us can be happy in a relationship at the same time, and if I'm no longer with Will, Darby can finally find love."

The most likely culprit, however, was the phone call from my mother, five days prior. It had been strange, even by Nessa McCaffrey's remarkable standard, and I hadn't been able to shake it.

"Cadie, my love. I have a question." She'd begun the conversation the moment I picked up the phone.

I'd been avoiding her calls since the night I was with Will, certain that she would masterfully combine her motherly intuition with her spiritual gift of discernment and say something to the effect of, "Are you eating enough? Do you need some money? Hang on . . . you're not a virgin anymore, are you?" The upside of getting the topic out of the way so quickly, I suppose, would be that I'd immediately be disowned and could finally stop shuddering in fear each time my phone rang.

I hadn't been counting on the sneak attack call at work. She didn't even call my direct office line where caller ID could have saved the day. Instead, she took full advantage of a new employee answering the general accounting department line, and the call got transferred straight to me.

"Hi, Mom," I said, my voice as normal as I could possibly make it considering the fiery wrath that I knew was only moments away.

"Does Will make you happy?"

It was even worse than I had anticipated. She wasn't going to confront me outright but rather guilt me into submission!

"What do you mean? Why do you ask? That's kind of a weird, random question."

"Honey, I can't explain right now," she whispered. Whispered? Why was she whispering? "I just need to know if he makes you happy. Can you see yourself living a long, happy life with Will by your side?"

How could I possibly answer that? If I said no, I figured she'd come back with, "Well then, I guess you should have thought of that before you engaged in premarital intercourse with him." And if I said yes, I expected, "Then it's really too bad you didn't marry him a while ago, rather than engaging in premarital intercourse." No matter what I said, I just knew she was going to say something about engaging in premarital intercourse, and I didn't know if I would survive it.

It was a hopeless situation either way, so I decided to go with the honest answer.

"No, Mom. I . . ." I took a deep breath and braced myself. "I don't really see myself spending my life with Will. He, um . . . no . . . he doesn't really make me happy anymore."

I heard her sigh on the other end of the line, and then she said, "Okay, baby. We'll talk soon, all right? I love you." And then she was gone, without a single mention of premarital inter-course.

After that call, I'd given in to the misery. The guilt, the regret, the sense of failure, the feeling that I'd spent my entire life believing in something only to throw it all away because *propose* loosely rhymes with *Poconos*, and Will looks good in a suit. Most of all, the misery that came from knowing my heart and Will's hadn't ever been quite in sync—despite my best efforts to convince myself otherwise. I just gave in to it all and let my emotions carry me away. I used a few of my copious accrued vacation days and stayed home the rest of the week, waiting for my mother to call again.

But she didn't call. I never would have imagined that *not* having that awkward, hor-rifying conversation with my mother could be worse than having it, but the longer I sat there, waiting for the phone to ring, the more certain I was that *this* was how she had decided to punish me.

My mother is a wonderful woman. Truly. She loves God, loves her family, and loves America. And an ever-growing but very specific niche of America loves her back. As the host of *Love God, Love YOU!* on the HTT (Holy Trinity Television) network, she is invited by hundreds of thousands of people into their living rooms each weekday morning. To her viewers, she comes across as the mother they probably all wish they had.

Of course it was the one person who'd actually had her as their mother who fully understood how terrifying she could be. I watched her show every day during my vacation, though I hadn't watched a moment of it in years. I was so afraid that she was going to covertly lecture me, with show topics like "When Your Child Brings Shame Upon Your Family" or "Rahab and Mary Magdalene: Finding the Harlot in *You*!"

In one way or another, my parents had been using my mistakes as applicable life lessons for everyone else throughout my entire life. In the books my mom had been writing since before I was born, at the megachurch where my dad had been the senior pastor since I was sixteen, and on the Christian Living program she had been hosting and he had been producing since I was twenty-two.

But that week, she talked about bullying, she spent time in the kitchen with Candace Cameron-Bure, and she began promoting her new women's Bible study book. What she did *not* do was address her daughter's immorality.

So there I sat, making higgledy-piggledy plans to get a dog, wondering if there was possibly a chance that my mother hadn't supernaturally discovered that I'd slept with Will after all, and trying to figure out why in the world she'd asked me if I was happy with him if it hadn't been part of her shame entrapment plan.

Something had to change. I had to snap out of it. I *had* to move on with my life.

I have to break up with Will.

In my mind, we were broken up already. It was as plain as day that we were done. But I wasn't sure our demise as a couple was quite as obvious in Will's mind.

I walked to the kitchen counter, where my phone sat charging in silent mode. Two texts awaited from Darby.

> Is it a bad sign when you cancel your third date with a guy because you're cramping so bad you're willing to trade in Omakase at Sushi Nakazawa for a bottle of Motrin and a heating pad?
>
> Seriously. When is menopause? Do you think there's an early fertility retirement package we can sign up for? Think we can get a 2-for-1 special?

I looked at the date of the texts, certain that my phone company was once again holding my messages hostage in the cloud until they chose to disperse them at the random time of their choosing. Of course the date didn't help at all, since they listed the date received rather than the date sent. I quickly decided it didn't really matter. I could simply look at my own menstrual calendar and know *exactly* when she had messaged me, since we had been on identical schedules as long as we had known each other.

Except Darby hadn't had a third date with a guy in months. Many, *many* months.

I clicked on "Call Back" underneath the most recent text and quickly did some math in my head as I waited for her to pick up. There was no moment of "What does this mean?" or even "No . . . that can't be right." I knew it was right. And I knew exactly what it meant.

"Did you find a 2-for-1? If not, I am definitely willing to pay full price."

"Darby," I whimpered. "I'm late."

"For what?"

"My period."

I heard a slight gasp, but she covered pretty well.

"Well . . . you . . . I mean . . . didn't you *use* anything?"

"You mean like protection?"

"Of course I mean protection, Cadie!" she exclaimed, revealing a crack in the calm we were both trying to pretend existed. "Tell me you used something."

"No, we didn't use anything!" I shouted back,

panic rising in my chest. "What makes you think that either of us would have had anything to use?"

She sighed and muttered, "Good point. But it's only been . . . what? Two weeks? Two-and-a-half? You couldn't be, right? I mean, you wouldn't already be missing your per—"

"I don't know! I'm the girl whose parents held her out of sex ed and said that everything I needed to know about sex was found in the Bible. But I don't remember anything in *Song of Solomon* about ovarian cycles, Darby. I don't know anything!"

"But you took health class, right?"

"So did you, I assume. How sure are *you* that I couldn't possibly be pregnant?"

The pause on the other end of the call assured me that she saw my point.

"Okay . . . here's what we're going to do. I'm going to head over right now. I'll swing by CVS on the way and pick up a test."

"No, I can't wait that long."

"I just live in Chelsea, Cadie. It won't take long."

But I was already slipping on my shoes and grabbing my jacket and door keys. I lived three blocks away from CVS, and I just couldn't imagine sitting there, doing nothing, waiting for Darby to show up.

"Thanks, but I'm just going to go."

"All right. Do you want me to come over anyway? I can probably be there by the time you get back . . ."

I closed my door and locked it behind me and then went down the stairwell and exited onto Bleecker Street. I looked around. My surroundings were so familiar—I'd walked this street nearly every day for almost a decade—but I was still disoriented.

"No. Don't come, Darb. Not yet. I'll call you when I know something."

I stuffed my phone in my pocket and began walking the three blocks. I passed people I saw every day—working, walking, living. I tried to focus on their names, and their dogs' names. Names I would have known if I'd tried to remember them an hour before. Names I couldn't quite put my finger on as I did my best to smile and acknowledge them all.

Instead, all I could think about was how my apartment would be a horrible place to raise a child. Apart from the bathroom and a closet, it was just one big room, really. There was no way to put up baby gates to keep a toddler from the kitchen. And there wasn't a lick of carpeting in the place. I'd have to pull out the oven and make the kid wear a helmet at home.

How would my parents react? They'd be disappointed—and I wouldn't hold that against them. I would be pretty disappointed myself. But would they still love me? *Of course they would,* I answered my own silent question. And they would love the baby. But would they be ashamed of me? Of the baby? Would they hide it all from people as long as they possibly could, so as not to shatter everyone's perception of their life?

How would I tell Will?

That was the one I couldn't allow myself to think about. Not yet. Mercifully I arrived at CVS and was able to focus instead on picking out the best version of something I knew nothing about. The best version among at least a dozen or so brands. How was I supposed to know if I preferred to look for lines or pluses? Words! Yes, I definitely needed the one that plainly stated either "Whew! You got lucky," or "Have fun telling Nessa McCaffrey she's going to be a grandmother!" Would the generic brand work just as well? I am a woman who studies and plans and makes her decisions based on thorough understanding, but there wasn't time for any of that. *Just grab one, Cadie.* Against my bank balance's better judgment, I chose the most expensive one, hoping that it was expensive because it was the best, and then I paid and rushed back home.

My walk of shame continued, as I had suspected it would. As I suspected it would *forever.* I felt as if every person I passed—people who were working, walking, living—knew what I had done. I was pretty sure even their dogs were judging me—probably for briefly believing, earlier in the evening, that I had the emotional fortitude and upright moral character to care for one of their kind.

Without even taking off my coat, I hurried to the bathroom as soon as I walked in. I quickly read the directions, which my clouded brain struggled to understand, even though they really consisted of very little more than "Pee on the end of the stick thing," and then I did it. I peed on the end of the stick thing.

It's not every day that one is acutely aware that they are experiencing the most important pee of their life.

I set the timer on my phone for two minutes, and then I walked away. I couldn't just stand there and stare at the seconds ticking down. I went to the kitchen and looked around for something to do, but of course I was obsessively neat, even on vacation—apart from the Milano crumbs. There were no dishes to put away or spills to sop up, but I still grabbed a Clorox wipe from underneath the sink and began sanitizing every surface.

I told myself it would be fine. I told myself I was worrying about nothing, and that the odds of getting pregnant at thirty-four from my first time were astronomical. Never mind that I had no idea what the odds actually were, and never mind that scenes from movies and TV were rushing through my head—shows like *Degrassi*, which made it pretty clear that *every* woman gets pregnant her first time.

But then, without any warning that it was about to happen, I found myself dropping to my knees in a flood of tears and despair.

"Please don't let me be pregnant!" I cried aloud to the ceiling. "I can't do it. I can't . . . I just can't, Lord. I can't face my parents, or my friends. I wouldn't be able to face Will. Please don't tie me to him forever. Please don't do that to me. I want to move on, and I want to begin putting him behind me, and I don't know how I'm going to do that anyway, but with a baby—"

I was startled out of my heart-to-heart with God—the first one I'd allowed myself to have in far too long—by the sound of the timer on my phone buzzing in the bathroom.

"Not yet!" I shouted, surprising myself.

In that brief moment I had begun to feel God's presence for the first time since before that Thursday when I had chosen to ignore his outstretched arms and had sought comfort in Will's instead. Since then, I hadn't allowed myself to pour my heart out to God or even so much as ask for forgiveness. Instead of running to the Lord with my shame and heartbreak, I had spent the week vegging out in the Garden of Eden, acting like I was simply wearing my fig leaf because it was the latest thing in Madison Avenue foliage wear.

"Not yet," I repeated much more quietly as I rubbed the tears from my eyes and prepared to get real with God. I shifted from the increasingly uncomfortable position of kneeling and sat flat on the tile instead. I pulled my knees up against my chest and rested my forehead on them, and I tuned out the incessant buzzing from the other room.

"I am so, so sorry," I prayed. "You know that if I could go back and make it not happen, I would. It was so *stupid*." I sniffed and banged my head against my knees. "*I* was so stupid."

The tears began to flow even more freely, and I could barely choke out the words that were on my heart. My throat felt thick with shame and despair.

Please forgive me, Lord. I stopped speaking aloud, fully aware that God could hear everything I had to say to him with or without the filter of my voice. *I never meant for this to happen. I'm sorry I'm so weak. I mean, I was pretty strong for thirty-four years, but . . .*

I groaned aloud, frustrated that I was trying to find a way to defend myself even in the midst of my confession and repentance.

I'm sorry I'm so weak. Thank you for loving me anyway. I do really, really hope I'm not pregnant, Lord. "Please," I whispered painfully. *But regardless of what the test says, please help me to deal with it . . . however I'm supposed to deal with it. If I have to be a mom right now, help me to be a good one. If I have to share a child with Will, help me to talk to him, and for us to somehow work that out. If I have to tell my parents about all of this . . .* I shivered at the thought and moved on, unwilling to go to the very scary place where that thought was threatening to take me. *If I have to find a different apartment, help me to accept that—even if I don't get to live this close to the subway again. Even if I have to leave the Village. Even if there isn't a Magnolia Bakery nearby . . .*

On one hand, that felt like the wrong thing to pray. On the other, I was certain that God understood the value of being a few steps away from Magnolia's banana pudding.

Whatever it is, Lord . . . please be with me. Even though I don't deserve for you to be.

I struggled to breathe normally as I stood from my cold, hard, unsafe-for-toddlers tile and replaced the Clorox wipe in my hand with a tissue. The buzzing continued and I began walking slowly toward it, as if pulled in by an invisible force. I tapped my phone to silence it and then picked up the stick.

Not pregnant.

"Thank you," I whispered.

The doorbell rang and I walked to answer—as

if pulled by the same invisible force that had drawn me to my phone's buzzing just a minute or two prior. I wasn't ready for Darby yet, but *of course* she had headed over anyway. Ready or not, I knew that once I saw her I would be glad she was there.

I looked through my door's peephole and jumped at the sight of him. No. No, no, no. If I wasn't ready for Darby, I *definitely* wasn't ready for Will. I backed away from the door, slowly and silently, and made my way back to the bathroom, where my phone remained. Darby would know what I should do. At least, I really hoped so, because I didn't have a clue.

"Well?" she answered before the end of the first ring.

"Will's here," I whispered.

The doorbell rang once again, and then the relatively calm chiming was replaced by an incessant knock and Will's voice calling out my name. "Cadie? I know you're in there. I really need to talk to you. Please open up."

It was very possible that my head was going to explode.

"Will's there?" Darby asked. "Why is Will there?"

"I have no idea. What do I do? He won't stop knocking, and he says he knows I'm in here."

"How would he know?"

"I don't know, but I am! So what do I do?"

"Cadie, did you take a test? Are you pregnant?"

"Yes. It's fine. I mean, yes, I took a test. No! I'm not pregnant. Now tell me whether or not to open the door!" I exclaimed as Will's nonstop knocking continued, every seven beats playing out as an endless remix of "Shave and a haircut—two bits."

"Well," Darby said with a sigh. "You're going to have to talk to him eventually."

Was I? I had very specifically asked God for help with that *if* Will and I had to share a child. Didn't a negative result get me off the hook?

As if my very sanity depended upon a moment of silence—which, let's face it, it probably did—Will stopped knocking, and neither Darby nor I spoke. The pounding in my head continued, but that was to be expected, I suppose.

I sighed as a tear rolled down my cheek. "You're right. I'll call you later, Darb."

"Love you, sweetie."

"Love you too."

I set the phone down on the kitchen counter as I passed from the bathroom to the front door, and I took a deep breath. *If he's still there, I talk to him and end things once and for all,* I prepared myself as I placed my hand on the knob and pulled the door open.

"I was about to give up," he greeted me softly as soon as we saw each other.

"You probably should have."

He held a huge bouquet of roses in one hand and a brown paper bag in the other.

"Is that from Sarge's?" I asked, quite possibly disappointing him by zeroing in first on the familiar packaging of my favorite New York deli.

"Wow, you're good," he responded with a laugh as he used the pastrami-induced distraction as an opportunity to slip past me into my apartment. "Here. For you."

In response to his offer I reached my hands toward the bag. Unfortunately, he tried to hand me the roses instead, and when I looked up at him, he laughed.

"I guess you can have this too."

I snatched the bag out of his hand and caught myself smiling at him. Smiling! No, no, no! This was no time for smiling. In fact, this was no time for pastrami. Sure, one could argue that it was *always* time for pastrami, but one could also argue that it was immoral to accept brined meat from a man you're about to break up with.

"What were you doing way over on Third?" I asked as I opened the bag and plucked out a thin slice of meat. Any less would have just been rude.

He exhaled and ran his hand through his hair. "Walking. Thinking. Look, Cadie, I have some things I need to say. Things like apologies, and

I'm prepared to grovel if necessary. But I feel like, more than anything else, I just need to tell you—"

"It's over, Will!" I exclaimed, startling both of us.

I'm just not sure I could have come up with a worse way to tell him if I'd tried. I was still chewing, for goodness' sake! But I knew he was about to tell me he loved me, and that he was still committed to trying to make it work, and I just couldn't let him say that. I was done. I couldn't keep hanging on, expecting things to change, knowing they never would.

All of the color had drained from his face and the flowers that he had been carefully holding upright began to droop in his hands—matching the general countenance of his face.

"What do you mean?" he asked.

I rolled my eyes. I didn't mean to; I just couldn't help it. What did I mean? What else *could* I have meant?

"I mean it's over. Between us, Will. I'm done. I'm sorry . . . I didn't mean to tell you this way. But then, I didn't expect you to show up at my door unannounced." I reached into the bag and pulled out another lump of mustard-covered pastrami, which promptly got stuffed into my mouth. "But thank you for the pastrami."

"You seem pretty calm," he observed, even as the sweat began beading on his brow and his feet began shuffling, clearly indicating that calmness was not a quality we shared.

And he was right. I did *seem* pretty calm, and in some ways, I suppose I was—although it's difficult to say how much was calm and how much was resignation and defeat intermingled with pregnancy fear, from which I hadn't yet had time to recover.

"I'm sad," I confessed. "Heartbroken, in fact. I never thought we'd end up this way, and I certainly never wanted us to." Tears began pooling in my eyes. I was really breaking up with him. It was actually happening. "I'm really sorry, Will. For so many things. But where can we possibly go from here? We're headed nowhere, and that was true even before we . . ." I took a deep breath, and then another. "There's no moving forward and there's certainly no turning back, so what choice do we have but to—"

"Marry me, Cadie," he suddenly blurted out.

Those words.

"What? I'm sorry, *what?!*"

"Marry me," he repeated as he rushed toward me, removed the paper bag from my hands, and placed it, along with the roses, on the floor beside us. He clasped my hands in his as he said, "I mean it. I know this isn't how we planned for any of this to go, but—"

"No!" I pulled my hands from his as if I'd been burned, and it felt as if I had. "You don't—this

145

isn't—you don't get to—" I released a primal, guttural cry as I backed away from him and the tears overtook my eyes, erasing any projection of calm I had been displaying. "We're done, Will! We're through. And *now* you ask me to marry you? How clueless *are* you? No. No! I won't marry you. You ask me *now,* just because . . ." I groaned in frustration as I picked up the roses from the floor and left the bag right where it was—even in my frenzied state knowing better than to willingly give away a sandwich from Sarge's—and shoved the bouquet against his chest. "I think you should go."

Pain and shock were evident on his face, but I didn't care. He'd had four years. Four years! And for the last of those four years, he'd pulled so far away from me that he'd called nearly every moment of the first three into question. But still, at pretty much any point during those four years, I probably wouldn't have let him get the words out before I'd joyfully accepted his proposal. But *now?* Today?

He finally proposed, and it was nothing more than an act of desperation.

He cleared his throat and swiped at his eyes. "Cadie . . . I love you. I want to marry you."

"Go home, Will," I said—quietly, exhausted.

"I'm sorry, but you don't get to do that. You don't get to kick me out of your life and act like we're not in this together."

"In *what* together?"

"Life, Cadie! Life. I know that having sex changed things. I get that. But—"

"That's the thing!" I shouted. "Having sex wasn't the cause of the change. Having sex was a *symptom* of the change." I choked down the tears that were struggling to break through. "I mean, what are we even doing? Who *are* we? We were hanging on by a thread for the last year, at best, and then we threw away so much of whatever was left, for nothing. Absolutely nothing."

The redness in his eyes made it clear how much that stung him. "I know it was a mistake, but I wouldn't exactly call making love for the first time *nothing,* Cadie."

"Did you ask for forgiveness?"

"You mean, from God?"

"Of course I mean from God."

He sighed. "I guess I haven't really gotten to that yet. All I've been thinking about is *you.* I know it's been rough for you, but it's been pretty rough for me too. No matter how wrong it was, it doesn't change the fact that you and I shared something very intimate, and then you were just gone. *That's* what I've been thinking about, Cadie."

He kept talking, but I didn't hear the words he said. I didn't need to. I knew what he was saying, but I was unable to move on from "I guess I haven't really gotten to that yet." The numbness and the shock and the complete and utter shame that had been controlling every thought for two-and-a-half weeks suddenly gave way to an unspoken fear of mine. A fear that was so much worse than thinking I could be pregnant. Worse than the fear of being a mother, of doing it all alone. Of the judgment I was going to face from everyone in my life. Even worse than having to go out of my way for banana pudding.

My hands began trembling and I clenched them tightly together in front of me. I stared at them, willing them to stay still, as I heard my voice come out as barely a whisper. "What if God won't forgive our sin because you aren't sorry?"

"What?" he asked softly as he took one step toward me. "Is *that* what you're worried about?" He took another step, but my still-trembling hands raised slightly in warning, and he halted his advance. He sighed. "How many times do I have to tell you that I *am* sorry, Cadie? What's it going to take for you to believe me?"

Tears flooded my cheeks. "It was a two-person sin, Will. Maybe it requires two-person repentance. And if you were really sorry, I think you would—"

"You think I would what?" he snapped. "Please, by all means, tell me how *you* think I should handle *my* heart. *My* relationship with God."

My breath caught in my chest. It took him hurling my patronizing, judgmental attack back at me for me to realize how thoughtless my words were.

I shook and lowered my head. "I'm sorry. That wasn't fair."

"Where is this even coming from?" He exhaled and turned and began pacing the room as he chuckled bitterly. "Of course. Your mother."

"My mother?"

"You sound just like her. I can't believe you let her get to you." He stopped walking, and I heard him taking deep breaths and muttering to himself. He was still turned away from me when he said, "At least that explains why you're acting like this. I should have known."

"My mother doesn't have anything to do with this."

He turned, his face carrying with it an expression of forced peace and patience. "This is a lot for both of us, and of course we're having some thoughts and saying some things that aren't doing anyone any good, so I'm going to go." He stepped toward the door without looking at me, and he still didn't look at me as he turned the doorknob and said, "I'm going to ask you again tomorrow. Maybe by then, you can figure out how to think for yourself."

He walked out and slammed the door behind him, leaving me to collapse in a heap on my kitchen floor—with only confusion and pastrami to help get me through until tomorrow.

10

Tomorrow

Tap, tap, tap, tap, tap, tap, tap.

The sound of Will's pencil bouncing repeatedly against his desk was never-ending. He'd been in his new office for two days, and it was a good thing. The cluster of cubicles in which he had worked for four years had been in the middle of an otherwise-open passage-way on The Field, and five minutes would rarely pass without someone cutting through to take a shortcut. If Will had still been sitting at his old desk, tap-tap-tapping away, he probably would have quickly driven every single one of his co-workers insane.

As it was, he was occupying the new office he had demanded. The new office he had *earned.* No one was subject to his neurotic tendencies now except for the one person whose office was directly across the hall from his.

Unfortunately for all involved, that one person was Ellis Haywood.

"Will, man, if you don't stop it with that pencil, I'm going to lose my ever-lovin' mind."

"Sorry," Will called out as he set the pencil down on his desk and raised his hands to show Ellis they were empty—not unlike a blackjack dealer going on break.

"What is your deal today, anyway?" Ellis asked, leaning back in his desk chair.

Will was momentarily distracted by his appreciation for any chair that could fully support a reclining Ellis Haywood. All 335 pounds of him.

"Just trying to get used to the new office," he responded, excusing away his annoying behavior. It wasn't completely untrue, but there was also very little truth in it.

Ellis sighed as he laced his fingers behind his head. "You gotta get your head in the game. You know Swoosh went out on a limb for you—"

"It wasn't *that* much of a limb," Will huffed. "Was it?"

The giant man grumbled as he returned his chair to its natural, unburdened position and stood. He walked around the desk, crossed the hallway, and entered Will's office. Ellis helped himself to the wooden chair across from Will and softly said, "You know his office is next door, right? There's you, there's me, and then this corridor ends with Kevin. The big office. The one with the big window and the view of the Statue of Liberty. Do you get that?"

"I didn't mean to sound ungrateful. If you think he heard me I can go apologize—"

"You're missing the point, man. I'm a pretty big deal around here."

"I know you are . . ."

"*I* have the office next to the boss. I've been here eight years, and I've turned down five different offers to go back to the NFL—to play, to coach—not to mention tons of offers from other networks." He stood from the chair, rested his hands on the desk, and leaned across it, toward Will. "I'm a really big deal."

Despite his imposing stature, and the fact that during his football career he had regularly flattened men twice Will's size, everyone knew that Ellis was the biggest teddy bear at ASN, and maybe in all of sports. His friends—and Will did consider himself one of that group—knew that he would do absolutely anything for them, and his co-workers felt free to go to him for advice, a venting session, or a hug, whenever it was needed.

Yet in that moment, Will felt as if he had a pretty good idea what it must have felt like to be running down the field with a football clamped under your arm—nothing but Astroturf and end zone in sight—only to see Ellis Haywood step in front of you. He had to assume that all of those running backs through the years had seen their lives flash before their eyes.

"I know you're a big deal, Ellis." Will chuckled nervously. "Trust me, I know that. You're the best in the business."

Ellis kept his eyes locked with Will's, and no other part of him moved either, just long enough for Will to begin feeling sweat beading up on his lip. Then the tough façade cracked in one fell swoop as Ellis burst into laughter and settled himself back into the chair.

"Don't butter me up, man," he said through his laughter. His entire face was overtaken by hilarity and his shoulders bounced up and down. "I don't need you to tell me I'm the best. I am fully aware."

Will let out the breath he had been holding. "Okay . . ."

"I'm just saying I'm the best, and Swoosh is the best—like, for real the best. On the other side of us, who've we got? Enzo Bateman, who may be a slime wad but who also happens to be, you guessed it . . . the best. The point is, in about six seconds you went from the cubicle to this office."

"I've actually been here four years, Ellis. And—"

"Hey, you don't have to sell you to me any more than you have to sell *me* to me. You're still missing the point. You're in this office 'cause you're the best. I know it, Swoosh for sure knows it. All of us . . . *The Daily Dribble* team . . . we know it. But the ones upstairs in the suits, sitting in that boardroom? They don't know you, man. The best thing you've got going for you is that Swoosh should technically be in one of those upstairs offices too, running things from a distance, but instead he stays down here and works in the trenches with us so he can personally see to it that this *show* is the best. He sees things, and he saw you. But now you need to get used to this office, real quick. You gotta rise to this. We're talking once in a lifetime. And it won't just look bad for you if it doesn't work out. This isn't just on you. You read me?"

"It's on Kevin. I know," Will muttered quietly.

Ellis stood and began walking back toward his own office. "You know I believe in you. We all do. You've got this. Just put your nose to the grindstone and make the most of this opportunity. Don't let yourself get distracted by life or love, or anything that's happening outside of—"

"Cadie broke up with me."

It was the first time he'd said the words aloud, and he hadn't been prepared for how bitter they'd taste.

Ellis sank back down in the chair, seemingly disregarding his motivational speech about work ethic from two seconds prior. "Why in the world? I thought you guys were solid."

"So did I," Will replied with a shrug.

"Did you fool around on her?"

"Of course not! I really don't know what happened." He caught himself looking away sheepishly but quickly recovered so that Ellis didn't suspect he was keeping something from him. He knew *exactly* what had happened, but it sure wasn't for him to share intimate details of Cadie's life with her male co-workers.

"So how'd you respond? Are you letting it be, or—"

"I asked her to marry me."

Ellis slapped himself on the forehead and then rubbed his big, bald head. "Tell me you didn't."

Well, *that* certainly wasn't the way Will had expected him to respond. "I did. What's wrong with that? I thought you'd tell me it was about time."

With a sigh, Ellis shook his head. "Oh, you know that I think it was well *past* time, but that was not *the* time. Can I safely assume, since you led this conversation with a breakup rather than an engagement, that she said no?"

"I agree that it may not have been the best timing," Will acknowledged as his pride tried to hold its own against the pity in Ellis's voice. "But it will work out."

"My friend," Ellis began as he stood from the chair and crossed to place a compassionate hand on Will's shoulder. "If she doesn't want to marry you . . ."

Will stepped away from the contact and began pacing. No. He wasn't willing to accept that. "She has high standards. She had a pretty strict upbringing and certain values were instilled in her." He was impressed with the restraint he was showing. He hadn't once referred to Cadie's parents as infuriating uptight snobs who had raised their daughter to have unrealistic expectations and impossibly lofty ideals. "It may take a little work, but I don't believe that she doesn't want to marry me."

He felt the anger rise up inside of him, but none of it was directed toward Cadie. No, the anger was reserved for Oliver and Nessa McCaffrey. It had been nearly a week since his last conversation with them, and after seeing how they'd seemingly gotten in Cadie's head, his emotions regarding his interaction with them had gone from frustration and confusion to fury.

"Will?" a voice suddenly called into the room via the phone on the desk, startling them both.

Will quickly scrambled to push the appropriate button and respond. "Yeah? Is she here?"

"Just stepped into her office."

"Thanks, Anna. I owe you one."

He released the button and ran over to close the office door so he could look in the mirror on the back of it. He straightened his shirt, ran his fingers through his hair, and checked that his teeth were free of coffee stains and bagel crumbs.

"What are you doing?" Ellis asked.

"I told Cadie I was going to ask her again today." He opened the door and turned around to face Ellis with a smile. "Wish me luck."

"Oh no." Ellis's words were long and drawn out. "Don't do it, man."

"This is Cadie and me we're talking about, Ellis." Will chuckled, his confidence surging. "We went through a little rough patch, but it's all going to work out."

He whistled his way to The Bench, doing all he could to resist his confidence being overtaken by his nerves. He believed what he'd said to Ellis. It was all going to work out. But he understood that there was a decent chance he was moving too quickly. She would still be processing. Nevertheless, he'd promised her he was going to propose again the next day, and he'd already let her down enough for one lifetime.

"Is she still in there?" he asked Anna as he entered the accounting suite.

Anna nodded. "She is. But if there's anything *I* can help you with, Will, I'm happy to—"

"What are you doing here?" Cadie called out from the doorway to her office, her coldness toward him seemingly unhampered by the presence of her entire staff.

As Will watched her, he couldn't help but realize how his perception of her had changed. No, not changed. *Grown.* Developed. Matured. He had always seen her as sweet and kind, funny and just a little bit dorky. Beautiful, of course, and undeniably sexy, but innocent in so many ways.

Now she was also a woman he had made love to, and the only woman he wanted to make love to for the rest of his life. And despite the fact that it shouldn't have happened, and regardless of how much distance there seemed to be between them, all he knew was that he was more in love with her than he had ever been.

"I work here," he said with a confident smile—confident, because he knew that at the end of the day, there was no scenario in which the two of them didn't spend their lives together. "And I need to talk to you for a minute."

She seemed to suddenly sense that all eyes were on them, and with a sigh she approached him. Quietly she responded, "We have nothing to talk about. I've said everything I have to say. Now I need to get back to work."

She spun on her heel and made her way back toward her office, but his voice cut her off.

"Marry me, Cadie."

She froze, and the entire office gasped. Silence overtook everyone and everything as he began walking slowly toward her. She turned around to face him, but her face didn't convey the joy he'd been hoping to see.

"So what do you say?" he asked, struggling to keep his smile and confidence in place. "Will you?"

Her eyes stayed locked with his until the tears welling up lost the ability to stay put. She looked down at her fingers, tightly intertwined in front of her, and then whispered, "Don't do this, Will." He opened his mouth to speak, not really sure what he was going to say, but she looked up at him again and repeated, "Don't do this. Not here."

She turned back toward her office, and he understood that he was allowed to follow. He also understood that she was imploring him to avoid the public spectacle for *his* sake, not hers. He glanced around the room—friends, co-workers, a few strangers. All of them eyeing him with unmistakable pity. He caught Darby's eyes, and she smiled at him. Sadly. Compassionately.

Cadie really was saying no.

Will hustled into her office behind her and slammed the door. "I don't understand you. How can you act like we're just some casual thing? How can you act like we're over?"

"Because we are, Will." She remained calm as she settled into her chair—presumably to place the desk between them. How was she calm? He just didn't understand.

"No. No! That's . . . that's . . . crazy, Cadie. Since when? Since when are we over? You're going to have to walk me through it, because I don't remember our relationship ending . . ."

She bolted up from the chair, and Will could very nearly hear the wall of calm shatter into a million angry pieces. "Are you kidding me right now, Will? Seriously? Do you have no memory of yesterday? You know . . . yesterday? When I told you it was over?"

"Oh, trust me. I remember that," he growled. "But all that we have between us, all that we are to each other . . . that doesn't just end. Like *that*." He snapped his fingers.

"You're right. It doesn't. It's been happening for a *year!* You have basically been acting like . . . I don't know . . . like my best friend—"

"And what's wrong with that?"

"I already have a best friend! How do you not get it? You've totally friend-zoned me! How's that supposed to make me feel? What am I supposed to think? I used to feel like you couldn't get enough of me. Like I was the best part of your day. But now? Have you seriously not realized how much we've drifted apart? We don't go out nearly as much as we used to, and when we do, you're late." Her comments had begun with as much anger in her voice as he had ever heard and then slowly grown quieter. She spoke in a hoarse whisper by the time she said, "You barely even kiss me anymore, Will. At least you didn't, until . . ." Her cheeks, already burning red as a result of their shouting match, somehow took on an additional shade of bright pink as she diverted her eyes away from his. "I've clearly slipped down the priority list—"

"That's not true!" he shouted, unable to disarm

his frustration and bewilderment enough to match her quieter tone. Will filled his lungs as much as he could, and then he released the air slowly. "That's absolutely not true, Cadie. You have *not* slipped down the priority list. I've just been working a lot—"

"Exactly."

"*For* you! Don't you know that?"

"All I know is that a year ago, on my birthday, I felt like I finally made it clear to you that I wanted more for us. And for about two seconds, that seemed to bring us closer together. But then it was like you—the you I had been with for three years—suddenly vanished. That . . . that *was* instant. Like *that*." She copied his symbolic snap. "If it had happened slowly over time, I mean . . . maybe that happens. Maybe that's just what happens to a couple when they've been together a long time. But it was *instant.* It didn't leave any room for doubt as to what had caused you to step back."

He'd never forget the sight of her, sobbing on the floor of her apartment. Nor the realizations he'd made.

And that had been the night, after he left her apartment, as he walked the streets of Manhattan for hours, that he had decided he needed to speed up his plan to become a man worthy of marrying her—according to her guidelines, her parents', and his own. Not just because it was so difficult to resist her, but because it was so difficult to leave her. He'd wanted to hold her all night long and never have to let her go.

"Of course I stepped back, Cadie," he acknowledged softly. He was still lacking all of the confidence that he had felt early in the conversation, but at least he was pretty sure he was beginning to understand. At least he was pretty sure he could offer up a defense in his favor. "I was trying to make it easier on you."

She laughed. Coldly. Bitterly. "Oh, I see. By making me not want you as much? Were you trying to make it easier on me by making sure I wasn't really so bothered by being stuck in a vast nothingness for the rest of my life, with no reason to believe we would ever become unstuck? Were you trying to make it easier on me by making sure I fell out of love with you?" Tears welled in her eyes and her chin trembled with emotion and determination as she softly added, "Because it worked, Will."

It was as if an invisible hand had slapped him across the face, and the sting raced down his throat, into his heart and lungs, and all the way down to his toes.

"Cadie . . ." he whimpered.

"You're off the hook, Will." She sniffed, but there were no tears in her eyes as they met his. "You're off the hook. This doesn't have to be complicated. I'm not holding you to that guilt-induced proposal, and I'm not blaming you for what happened. I can certainly think of a million things *I* could have done differently. It's just . . . time."

It was as if he'd never seen her before. After four years of loving her every single day, they were strangers.

"What are you even talking about?"

She sighed. "Don't make me go through it again, Will. Please."

The room was spinning around him as the thought registered as reality for the very first time.

"You're saying we're *through?*" For the first time, he realized she actually meant it. He ran his hands through his hair, certain there had to be something he could say that would cause them both to wake up from this ridiculous nightmare they were stuck in. "It wasn't a guilt-induced proposal, Cadie! I was planning to ask you anyway."

She laughed bitterly. "Oh really?"

"Yes, and whether or not you believe that, I need you to believe this: what we've got and who we are is bigger than anything we're going through. We'll sort it out."

"But I'm not in love with you anymore, Will. How are we going to sort *that* out?"

The next few minutes were a blur. He couldn't say for certain if he'd said anything after that, or if she had. The door had opened—he was pretty sure she had done that—and then he was on the other side, watching her vanish behind it. He made his way toward The Field, walking those familiar halls, surrounded by familiar people but experiencing emotions he'd never felt in his entire life.

"How'd it go, man?" Ellis asked from his office as Will walked into his own. When Will said nothing in return, Ellis replied, "Yeah. I was afraid of that."

"Where have you been?" Kevin's deep voice bellowed from the doorway before he made his way into Will's office and threw a file folder on top of the cluttered desk. "I've been looking everywhere for you."

Ellis bounded out of his chair and joined them. "Our man here's had a pretty rough day."

"Well, it's about to get a whole lot better." Kevin knocked his fist on the folder on the desk. "Levinson's office called a press conference for Thursday."

Will pulled his chair out from his desk and collapsed into it, staring blankly at his boss.

"Did you hear me, Whitaker? The commissioner of Major League Baseball is holding a press conference in three days. It's in response to the Magician story. It has to be. And I think our new chief research analyst needs to be the one to cover it, don't you?" There was a smile on his face that made it pretty clear that he not only knew what a huge opportunity he was giving Will but that he was thrilled to be able to give it. "What do you say? Are you up for it?"

"Sure," Will replied softly before turning his chair to face the window behind him. "You can count on me."

Kevin let out a frustrated breath and then turned to Ellis. "Okay, what's going on?"

"Cadie broke up with him," Ellis said.

"Oh." Kevin turned back to Will. "Well, I'm sorry to hear that. I really am. But—"

Ellis wasn't done. "So then he proposed."

That seemed to take Kevin by surprise and, once again, he was talking to Ellis. "And how did that go?"

"Not well."

Kevin sighed. "Sorry, Whitaker. But about the press conference . . ."

"But *then,* he asked her again. Just a few minutes ago."

"You're kidding me. What did she—"

Will couldn't take it anymore. It was painful enough to have just lived the series of events. He wasn't going to stand there any longer and listen to an excruciatingly slow play-by-play retelling.

"She said no again." Will jumped up from his chair and began pacing the room. "She told me she doesn't love me anymore and that we're done. Thankfully *that* part took place in the privacy of her office, unlike the part where I actually proposed and the entire accounting staff understood the answer before I did. Now, unless there are any further questions, do you think we can get back to work?"

He returned to his desk, completely unsure if he was capable of getting his mind back on work—though he talked a good game.

"Okay, um . . . well, the press conference is at the commissioner's office, at noon," Kevin said, doing his best to honor Will's request and also, no doubt, grateful to be finished talking about his employee's personal life. "Take an A/V crew with you and get it filmed, in case it's worth using on *The Daily Dribble*."

"It might be nice to have it on tape anyway," Ellis chimed in, "in case Levinson brutally attacks you right then and there for destroying his game. Might need the evidence for the lawsuit."

Ellis smiled at his joke, but Kevin appeared unamused. Will, meanwhile, was hardly paying attention to any of it. He barely noticed when they both settled into the chairs across the desk, and he didn't so much as blink when they began discussing whether or not to bring Enzo into the mix—in case the legal concerns Ellis had joked about were something they needed to consider. They began making calls—to legal, to programming, even to accounting—but Will was only slightly aware throughout.

His mind was on Cadie, her extremely annoying

cousin Victoria, a McCaffrey family wedding from not all that long ago, and *Dirty Dancing*, of all things.

"I'm going to fight for Cadie," Will blurted out in a near-whisper.

"Why would you fight Cadie?" Ellis asked, pulling his mouth away from his phone, though his ear remained. "We're all sad she ended things, man, but I'm not sure that picking a fight is really the way to go."

Kevin groaned. "He said he's going to fight *for* Cadie, dummy."

Ellis perked up. "Ooh! That's *much* better." He unceremoniously ended his call and returned the phone to his pocket. "Are you for real?"

"I made the commitment to love her forever. That commitment doesn't go away just because she's not in on the plan."

"Well, all right!" Ellis sat forward in his seat. "So what are you going to do?"

The memory of Cadie's cousin and a family wedding had entered his head with a tinge of déjà vu, and it took him some time to even place the context. Once the context was in place, the memory of the conversation came flooding back—as did the memory of what it felt like to have Cadie wrapped in his arms. He could still feel the softness of her skin and smell the lemon and sage scent of her hair as he whispered in her ear.

"No girl, with the possible exception of Victoria, really wants a fantasy world to play out in their life," she'd said. "Oh, sure . . . there are moments when we'd love for our man to turn into Johnny Castle in *Dirty Dancing* and tell our parents that nobody puts us in the corner, but if that were the norm, I think it would just be exhausting."

For whatever reason, that part of the conversation had made its way past his heart and into his brain, where it had remained locked and loaded in the time since.

"In the movies, those things are usually an attempt to save the relationship, aren't they?" he had asked her then.

He jumped to his feet and began frantically pacing across the room. "You okay, man?" Ellis asked, but Will held up his hands to silence him. He squeezed his eyes tightly shut and struggled to remember what had come next.

"In the movies, those things are usually an attempt to save the relationship, aren't they?" He whispered the words to himself, attempting to unlock the rest. He knew there was more. He knew she had said something that he needed to remember.

His eyes flew open as his memory heard the echo of her voice from *then*—when she had spoken to him with a warmth and intimacy that had been missing for longer than he cared to admit.

"So I guess just save all the gestures for some-day," she'd said with a smile. "When the romance is gone. And then you can plan something spectacular . . ."

She'd said those words before they'd had any reason to suspect that *someday* was going to be an issue for them, but Will knew that one thing was true then and it was true now.

If anyone deserved spectacular, it was Cadie McCaffrey.

"I've got to do something big!" he abruptly exclaimed. "Like, like . . ." He snapped his fingers and groaned. *Like what?* "I don't know. I just know she loves those big moments, you know? Like in the movies. They never just talk it out in the movies. Couples don't get back together over a nice quiet dinner in the East Village. Do you know what I mean?"

Kevin sighed heavily and stood from the chair. "I don't have any idea what you mean. Just tell me, Whitaker . . . are you going to be ready to go by Thursday?"

"Oh, I don't know about that," Will replied. "I mean, I'm fired up, but I really need to put some thought into this. I might need the weekend . . ."

Ellis chuckled. "I think he means the press conference."

"We'll find some time real soon to grab a drink and talk, because I really do care," Kevin said. "But I need to know that you understand that the sports world is going to stand still for a few minutes on Thursday, right around noon. I need to know you can handle this."

Okay. Get your head in the game, Will. "Right. Sorry. You bet. I won't let you down."

Kevin patted Will on the shoulder and left the office, and Ellis—still chuckling—stood and prepared to follow him.

"Good for you, man. What you and Cadie have . . . it's worth fighting for. Let me know how I can help."

Will rubbed his temples, so frustrated that his thoughts weren't all coming together the way he wanted them to.

"I wish I knew how to explain what I'm thinking, Ellis. I'm talking gestures. You know? Like, over the top, romantic, no mistaking, make-her-weak-at-the-knees types of gestures."

"You forget who you're talking to. I haven't been married four times without picking up a thing or two about romance. What you're talking about, my friend, is a good, old-fashioned wooing." Ellis laughed and returned to his office, but not before adding, "McCaffrey won't know what hit her."

11

While the Sports World Stood Still

A nna, can you come here a minute?" I asked, pushing a button on the speakerphone on my desk. "And bring the November projections with you, please."

I've always loved bringing interns on staff full-time once their internships were complete. The good ones, anyway. They're so used to working hard and going the extra mile for free that once you add a paycheck to the mix, it's like they can't believe their luck. Anna had made the transition to the land of money and benefits about a month prior, and I had been so pleased that my practice of hiring interns had once again paid off. She was energetic, a go-getter, efficient, happy to be there, and she laughed at all my jokes.

She was also not yet in my office.

"Hey, Anna?" I spoke into the box once again.

"She's down on The Field with everyone else," Darby said as she appeared in the doorway of my office.

"Oh." I looked away and shuffled papers on my

desk with an air of indifference. "That's right."

She sighed. "Are you sure you don't want to watch? Your boy is on fire."

I met her eyes briefly as I said, "He's not my boy," and then I returned my attention to my mindless work.

"Okay." She plopped down in the chair across the desk from me. "All the same, are you sure you don't want to watch? It's not only a big Will moment, it's also a big ASN moment. Commissioner Levinson won't directly answer any of Will's questions, but Will keeps pushing. That room of stuffy, looking-out-for-number-one reporters actually cheered for him a minute ago."

I smiled. I couldn't help it. No, I didn't want to watch, and no, I didn't really even want to talk about it, but I was happy to know he was doing well. How's that for maturity?

It was strange, really. I had expected the official breakup to hit me harder than it had. Of course I was sad. And sure, I had eaten an entire package of Ben & Jerry's "Coffee Coffee BuzzBuzzBuzz" pint slices after getting home from work the day before. And no, I definitely didn't want to watch my ex-boyfriend bring down Major League Baseball on live television. But I really was doing incredibly, surprisingly well. I was sure of it!

Besides, the pint slices didn't even count. Maybe they were breakup therapy, but they just as easily could have been a slightly delayed thank-the-Lord-I'm-not-pregnant celebration. It was impossible to say, really.

Darby threw her ballet flat adorned feet up onto my desk and crossed her ankles. "Want to grab lunch? If we get out now, no one will even know we're gone."

"I'd love to, but I'm meeting my mother."

Darby gasped comically. "What? In the *city?*"

"I know, I know." I stood from my desk and carried the papers I had been mindlessly shuffling to my file cabinet. "You're welcome to join us. It's a rare opportunity to spot the wild Nessa McCaffrey outside of her natural habitat."

"Have you told her about you and Will?"

I sighed, full of dread at the prospect. "No."

"Then I'll pass," Darby said, dropping her feet from the desk and standing.

"She might be fine with it, you know. After that weird phone call, asking me if I was happy with him and all of that? I still think she may have had a hunch something was up. It was just too weird, otherwise." It was pretty weird, regardless.

"She was a big fan, though . . ."

"I know," I replied with a sneer. How many guys had I wanted my parents to like? How many times had I felt so blessed by the fact that they loved Will? But now their fondness for him promised to be a nuisance at best.

"Well, don't worry." Darby smiled and winked. "I think they like you too."

I laughed humorlessly as I grabbed my jacket from the back of my chair, put it on, and pulled my hair out from under the collar. "They used to. When they find out I'm not their innocent little girl anymore—"

"Hang on!" Darby exclaimed and then quickly covered her mouth with her hand. She hurried to the door and made sure no one was around and then shut the door anyway. "You're going to tell them you slept with Will?"

"No! I mean, not intentionally, but come on, Darb. You know my mother. Somehow she always knows. Everything. Which is why I wasn't overly surprised by her call, asking me if he makes me happy." But I was abundantly surprised that she had yet to follow it up with unsolicited advice as to how to best carry on with my life.

That was probably the purpose of lunch.

I crossed past Darby, reopened the door, and was greeted by increasingly eerie silence. I looked at my watch and then poked my head around the corner into the empty accounting office.

"Still?" Darby asked, joining me in the door-way.

"What in the world could be—"

"We could turn it on. Maybe we *should.* Maybe a meteor hit in the middle of the press conference or something."

I smiled at her as I walked backward down the hallway. "Are you kidding? A meteor shutting down the city before lunch with my mother? I'm not that lucky."

"Hey, kiddo," my dad's voice called out as he crossed to our table at Le Bernardin, where I had arrived far too early in order to make sure I had time to breathe.

"Daddy! I didn't know you were coming too." I stood and hugged him and then turned to look for the maître d', to indicate we'd need another chair.

"Not 'too.' Instead." He pulled my chair out for me to sit and then took his seat across the table. "Your mother got pulled into a meeting last minute."

I eyed him warily and smiled. "Really? Or did she chicken out at the thought of the traffic?"

"Chicken out? Never." He chuckled and then softly added, "Think better of it? Possibly."

My dad began intently studying the menu. My mother hates the city, but my dad loves it—and he loves pretty much everything that goes along with it. Especially the food. In Manhattan there are Michelin stars, Zagat recommendations, and James Beard Awards on every corner, and few restaurants had received more of all of them than Le Bernardin. Though I had no doubt that he was glad to have the opportunity to spend a little extra time with me, I also fully understood that my dad was chomping at the bit to satisfy his taste buds with Le Bernardin's three courses of prix fixe.

"I'm thinking of going for the Golden Imperial caviar," he said as he set the menu on the table in front of him. "How about you?"

I glanced at the first course selections, and my eyes flew open wide. "At an upcharge of $155.00 per ounce? I think I'll pass."

"Oh, come on. It's on me."

I took a sip of the iced tea I had ordered and smiled. "I would certainly hope so! Otherwise I'd be drinking water from the tap in the bathroom right now. But still, $155.00 for an ounce of anything feels extreme. Except for perhaps gold . . ."

"Suit yourself." He shrugged as our waiter, Milo, approached the table, and then he proceeded to order in the same charming, elegant, personable way he always had. Within moments, strangers effortlessly became friends to Oliver McCaffrey.

Once orders were placed and out of the way, he launched into small talk—not that it was really all that small at all.

"Will's quite the talk of the town, isn't he?"

"Heard about that, did you?" I bit my lip nervously. I had been hoping for at least a couple of minutes of conversation about my mom's television show or their upcoming vacation to

Sedona before being forced to confront the Will topic.

"Are you kidding? I couldn't *avoid* hearing about it. I was listening to that press conference in the car on the way here. He was really something."

I didn't want to care. Oh, how *desperately* I didn't want to care.

I fidgeted in my chair, twirled my hair, and avoided eye contact as I said, "Oh really? How so?"

Good job not caring, Cadie.

"The baseball commissioner was trying to skirt Will's questions, and Will just wasn't having it. I was pretty impressed. I don't think I've ever seen that assertive side of him before." I still wasn't looking at my dad, but I could feel his eyes on me. "I'm surprised you didn't catch it."

"I was busy, and then I took the subway over here, so . . ."

"Of course," he said with a nod.

Milo returned to the table with our first course—caviar for Dad, mesclun salad for me—and I took the distraction as an opportunity to furiously blink away the threatening tears and take a couple of deep breaths. As Milo left us, my dad grabbed my hand across the table and offered a quick prayer of thanks, but after "Amen" he didn't let go.

"Your mother told me what you told her. On

the phone. About Will not making you happy anymore."

He cleared his throat, and I finally looked up at him. He was as uncomfortable as I was. I knew it because I recognized the same tried and true determination in his eyes that had been present whenever my heart had been broken through the years. He *would* muster all of his strength and find a way through and be exactly who I needed him to be, even if he would rather be just about anywhere else on the planet right then, discussing just about any other subject.

I felt like I was seventeen again, walking into the house after Layton Forrester spent the entire evening dancing with Jacie Anderson—despite the fact that he was my date. And from the look on my dad's face, I think he felt like I was seventeen again too.

"Are you up for this, Daddy?" I asked, pulling my hand away and wiping my eyes on the cloth napkin that had been resting on my lap. "Because if you would rather I talk to Mom about it, we can just sit here and discuss other things, and I won't be offended in the least."

He exhaled slowly. "Honestly, it makes me a little sad that you have to ask me that."

"It's not a bad thing. At all! I just know that it upsets you when I cry."

"Of course it upsets me when you cry, Cadie. Because you're hurting, and I usually don't know how to fix it." He scooted his chair closer, rested his elbows on the table, and placed his chin on his interlaced fingers. "But it is one of my greatest privileges to be the one you cry to."

I smiled at him as tears rolled down my cheeks. So many people had benefited from his genuine concern and attention through the years. My mother had always been a queen in his eyes, the members of the church were all like family to him, despite the fact that there were far too many of them for him to know all their names, and even Milo probably felt as if he'd made an authentic, soul-level connection with him. But I was his little girl. His only one. I knew there was a section of real estate in his heart reserved only for me.

"Will and I broke up," I said softly, and then I picked up my fork and took a bite of mesclun salad. Ignoring all of my good breeding, I continued with my mouth full of greens. "Sunday. At least, that's when it officially ended. In many ways I really think it had been over for a long time. I know how much you like Will, Daddy. I'm sorry."

"Oh, my sweet girl. I hope you don't actually believe that you owe me an apology. All I want is what's best for you. You know that, right? If Will Whitaker isn't what's best for you, then good riddance!"

He took a bite of his caviar and I couldn't

resist laughing at the look of indifference he had plastered on his face.

"Good riddance, huh?"

"Yes. Good riddance."

"Now you don't have anyone to talk about sports with. Or to take to ball games. And didn't you guys actually play doubles tennis together for a while?"

"Yes, but that was a disaster. I just used him for his serve. Once the ball was in the air, he was useless. He was much more likely to trip over his own feet than score a point." He sighed. "And as for talking sports and going to games, I'm really not too worried about it. I have you and your mother, so who else could I possibly need?"

I pulled the crisp linen napkin up to my face again, this time to cover my mouth as I laughed. The thought of Nessa McCaffrey trying to carry on a conversation about athletics was nearly enough to make me spit out my mustard greens. And my father had long ago discovered that there was absolutely no benefit derived from his daughter's cool job. The coolness was wasted on me.

"So, let's have it," he continued, setting down his mother-of-pearl caviar spoon. "Tell me what happened."

I shrugged my shoulders and raised my hands slightly in the air. "I'm not sure I could tell you. I'm not sure I *know*, really. I just know it had been a really, really long time coming."

"How long?"

"A year, maybe."

His eyes grew wider. "A year? You've been unhappy for a year?"

I shook my head. No matter how true the "long time coming" statement was, I knew that going that far wasn't quite fair.

"I don't mean that I've been *continually* unhappy, but it's probably been about a year since I first began worrying it wasn't going to work out."

He studied me for a moment before picking up his spoon again and elegantly spreading caviar on a cracker. "What was the final straw?"

There it was. I knew that I could easily answer his question in a hundred different ways that wouldn't require me to say the words, "I thought he was going to propose and we had sex, but actually he was just planning to invite me to the Poconos."

Nope. I just couldn't imagine saying those words to Oliver McCaffrey, the reverend, and I *certainly* couldn't imagine saying them to Oliver McCaffrey, my dad. However, I had imagined saying them to my mother, and in so many ways that was infinitely more horrifying. Maybe I'd lucked out by my dad being the one to show up at Le Bernardin. Maybe the absolute best thing I could do would be to confess all and let him break the news to my mom. Was it the coward's way out? Sure. Did that bother me? Not so much.

Milo cleared our plates away and, seconds later, placed our second courses in front of us. My dad took a bite of his crab-filled calamari a la plancha and I began fiddling with my red snapper.

Seemingly sensing my hesitation, my dad broke the silence. "I know that whatever happened, it's not like when you fell off your bike and all it took was a bandage and a scoop of ice cream to make you forget it had ever happened," my dad said softly, never taking his eyes off of his plate. "You can tell me if you want, or not tell me if you want. If there's a way I can help, you know I want to." He finally met my eyes and smiled. "Ice cream is always on the table, of course."

"Thanks, Daddy," I replied, returning his smile. "All that really matters, I guess, is that I just couldn't see the point of staying in a relationship that was heading nowhere." I sat up straighter in my chair, increasingly confident in the only version of the truth my dad needed to hear. "The last year was so frustrating. There were so many times I was sure Will was going to propose, and he never did. And each time he didn't, I was left wondering why he wasn't as in love with me as I was with him."

He nodded, and I saw a slight shift in him. I recognized the appearance of the protective defender, who undoubtedly wanted to rake Will over the coals for not loving me enough. As if things were still as simple as when he wrote a note to get me excused from gym class.

"And you wanted to marry him?"

I shrugged—such an indication of indifference and nonchalance, and not at all reflective of my years of absolute certainty that my name would someday be Cadie Whitaker.

"Cadie, whatever happened between the two of you, I am absolutely positive that Will not loving you couldn't have been the problem. Trust me. I saw how he looked at you and heard how he talked about you. How he talked *to* you. I know that he was committed to—"

I placed my hand on his to stop him and then shook my head and lowered my eyes. "Don't do that. Please. I know he loved me. *Loves* me, probably. That's not the point. The point is he didn't—doesn't—love me *enough*."

My dad began studying me again. "You told your mother you couldn't see yourself spending your life with him."

"I can't. Not anymore."

Exquisite, expensive, delicious red snapper with spiced tomatillo nage had never before been subjected to the mistreatment it was receiving from my fork. I poked and prodded and did everything but eat it.

Suddenly I didn't feel as if any part of the story could be told without telling the rest of it. How could I explain that he *had* asked me to marry him but that I had turned him down without also explaining that it took him grasping at straws to try and save our relationship for him to finally take a step toward marriage in the first place?

"It'll be fine," I said, finally diving into my fish. "Work will probably be a little awkward for a while, but we'll move past it."

"You can always come work for us," he countered with a smirk.

I simultaneously laughed and shuddered at the thought. "I'm sure that would go well . . ."

He swallowed another bite of calamari and set down his fork. As he did, he relaxed to the back of his chair and chuckled. "It would go better than you think. We have the studio right there in Syosset now—"

"Which means I would have to commute from Manhattan every day? I don't think so."

"Or you could just move to Syosset."

I had just begun sipping my iced tea, and in response to that fabulous idea, I began sputtering and ever-so-slightly choking on the beverage. And that was nothing compared to how my mind was choking on the thought.

"Okay, okay," my dad said in response. "Maybe not. But there are a lot of great places on Long Island—"

"Daddy! No. I love the city. I have no intention of *ever* leaving Manhattan, and if I do, I'm certainly not ever going back to Long Island.

Nothing personal. I just can't move *backward,* you know?"

"Fair enough. I'm serious about the job, though."

"I know you are, and I'm grateful." I sighed and shook my head at the thought—not only the thought of working for my parents, or even the thought of being back in Oyster Bay. No, I shook my head at the thought of admitting defeat and leaving a job that I loved, all because of a boy. "It really will be fine. Like I said, it will just be awkward for a while. But the truth of the matter is I was there long before Will was, so if for some reason we reach a point where it's too difficult to work together, I don't see any reason why I should be the one to go anywhere."

"Good for you." He nodded with a proud smile. "You're absolutely right. You are established and, frankly, indispensable."

"That's right!" I concurred. Whether I truly believed it or not, my confidence was in desperate need of the boost.

"He's only been there, what? Four years? I doubt they even know Will Whitaker's name." He shrugged in response to my cocked eyebrow. In light of the first part of our conversation, he had obviously overreached. "Well, I guarantee ASN knows how lucky they are to have *you* working there."

Milo reappeared to refill our drinks and remove our second course dishes, but before he could do any or all of that, he froze and gasped. In a very heavy French accent, he asked, "*Mademoiselle, je vous demande pardon*. You work for American Sports Network?"

It was very rare that I got to encounter a sports-obsessed fan, since I was not someone who would ever be recognized. Oh sure, in the old days when Darby and I used to go out to dinner with *The Daily Dribble* crew on Thursdays, we were in the mix of it all. But that was long ago, before we all got too busy and *The Daily Dribble* team grew too large. The timing of Milo's starstruck recognition couldn't have been better—at least for my ego's sake.

My dad seemed to think so too. A smile overtook his face as he gestured at Milo and then sat back in his chair with his arms crossed in a manner that clearly communicated, "See? Told you."

I smiled at my dad and then up at our waiter. "Yes, I do. I've been there about ten years."

The excitement on Milo's face increased. "I am such a big fanatic of the American Sports Network and all of the American sports!" He looked around him to see who was close enough to call over. After all, Le Bernardin is a classy establishment and not the type where you shout across the dining hall, but he did the best he could, considering where he was. He whispered in French to a passing waiter, whose eyes and attention were instantly on me. The conversation continued quietly, in a language I hadn't studied since eighth grade.

My eyes darted back to my dad, who was as amused by it all as I was.

"If I may be so bold as to ask, what do you do at ASN?" the second waiter asked. "Forgive me if I am being too forward."

"No, not at all," I replied. "My job is rather boring, I'm afraid. I oversee the accounting department—"

"For all of the American Sports Network?" Milo asked eagerly.

I know I had just gotten out of a long-term relationship, and I was *so* far away from being interested in dating, but I was keenly aware that each time my dreamy French waiter laboriously referred to ASN as the American Sports Network, he got cuter and cuter.

"Not everything, no, but a lot of it. All of the prime-time programming." I chuckled and shook my head. "See? Pretty boring."

"No, Mademoiselle! Not at all!" Milo argued. "You probably do not work directly with people who we see on the screen, no?"

"I work with quite a few of them, actually." Here we go. Time to name-drop and blow his mind. "Do you know who Ellis Haywood is? I work pretty closely with him sometimes. And Kevin Lamont?"

They both gasped in unison. It was official. I was a superstar.

"He's on TV, of course," I continued, "but he's also the head of prime-time programming—"

"And *you* work in prime-time programming!"

I nodded. "He's my boss."

"*Quelle chance!*" Milo said, nearly tingling with excitement. "*The Daily Dribble* is the best program on the American Sports Network!"

Cuter and cuter and cuter and cuter . . .

"It's a great program, isn't it?" my dad interjected.

The Daily Dribble was just one of the many programs my office worked on, of course, but it was the one that would always have a special place in my heart. I'd been part of the small team dedicated to getting the show up and running in the beginning, and Kevin and I, along with a handful of others, owed our current status with the network at least in part to the show's success. I imagined it would always be gratifying to be reminded of that success.

Milo nodded enthusiastically. "*Le meilleur!* The best! Today we have talked about nothing other than Le Magicien."

Oh, Milo. Why'd you have to go and ruin it?

"Ah yes. That has been a pretty big deal," I said, my smile becoming a little less genuine. I looked at my dad and raised my eyebrows as high as they would go. "So, what are you thinking for dessert?"

"Dessert! *Oui, oui*! My apologies, Mademoiselle. I am afraid I have gotten carried away." He flapped his hand to indicate that his friend should shoo, and I realized I had been somewhat rude.

"Not at all. I'm sorry. I didn't mean it that way. I was more than happy to talk about it."

My dad kicked into gear, reading the situation perfectly, and affably charmed Milo back into certainty that we were the greatest table he had ever waited on in his entire life. I heard the warm tones, I heard the laughter on both sides, but I didn't hear all of the words. I was too distracted by the sight of the second waiter in the back of the room, fervently pantomiming various sports postures to a busboy.

All of a sudden, the two of them were rushing toward our table.

"Pardon," the second waiter said as they approached. "My little brother, Alexandre, is the biggest fan of sports there is. He has just one question to ask you, if it is not too much of an inconvenience, Mademoiselle."

"Of course," I said and smiled, all the while in the back of my mind repeating, *Don't let it be a sports question I can't answer. Don't let it be a sports question I can't answer.*

We all looked intently at Alexandre, but he didn't say a word. His older brother jumped in and said, "I apologize. He has not yet learned English. He knows only . . . eh . . . fourteen words." Then he whispered emphatically to him in French.

I shook it off and smiled kindly at Alexandre, and then the words erupted out of him.

"Le Magicien? Eh . . . how you say . . . Will Whitaker?"

Really? *Really?* So much for my dad's theory that ASN didn't know Will's name. Even busboys who only know fourteen words of English apparently knew his name.

I nodded. "Yes. We work together. I know him."

My dad reached out and grabbed my hand across the table, and I suddenly felt emotionally gobsmacked as I realized my heart was torn in two—half of me was so proud of Will, and the other half hoped the clock was ticking loudly on his fifteen minutes of fame.

"Milo." My dad interrupted the Will Whitaker fanboy moment with a sigh and a sad smile. "I think my girl could use some ice cream."

12

The Bacteria Portion of the Morning

Will was always amazed by how slowly time passed when sleep was elusive. On nights when hours were filled with nothing more than watching shadows on the wall and rethinking every decision you've ever made, it was as if the night would never end—and Will was equally impatient and full of dread, waiting for the moment when it finally would. At 5:40 a.m., when the darkness felt unchanged from how it had been all night long but the sounds outside his apartment indicated the start of a new day, Will finally gave up and climbed out of bed.

He was used to not sleeping very much, but not sleeping at all was new. Usually, when sleep was hard to come by, he could pinpoint why—and more often than not the culprit was his brain, which wouldn't shut off. But that night had been different. He'd practiced all of his tried and true techniques for winding down, but there had been something churning inside of him that hadn't been receptive to any of his normal tricks. By 5:40 a.m. he'd decided to chalk it up to convoluted emotions from the day before, refusing to let go.

It should have been one of the best days of his life. He was so aware of that, all day long—when he walked into the commissioner's press room and saw his name on that chair way in the back corner, while Commissioner Levinson was downplaying ASN's involvement and claiming he had been about to break the story himself, when he tried feeding the reporters that ridiculous story about how he considered The Magician a hero—Will knew through it all. He knew that every single detail was coming together in the best possible way for him.

But all he wanted to do was call Cadie. He wanted to send her a text asking if she saw him on TV, and for her to send some ridiculous text back saying, "Not unless you're on *Downton Abbey*" or something. And he would have laughed, because he would have known that she was watching. He would have known that she was proud of him and that, despite the fact that she would never let him get a big head, she'd be bragging to everyone she knew. All day long he was busy living one of the best days of his life, and he didn't see the point of any of it.

He showered to the soundtrack of his Old School Rock playlist. Songs from Pearl Jam and U2 cut through the steam-filled room—the water as hot as he could stand it and the stereo as loud as it would go in an attempt to drown out his thoughts, which seemed resolved on turning negative.

He was bound and determined to get her back, but a day of not seeing her and a night of not sleeping had left him feeling much less confident that he had any idea how to go about that. His mind kept wanting to slip from thoughts of "This is how I'll get her back" to "But when that doesn't work, I'll have to find a way to survive."

As he shaved he sang along with Bono and tried to comfort himself with the thought that at least he would no longer be forced to listen to the Carpenters and Barbra Streisand or any of Cadie's other horrible music choices in the car when they drove to visit her parents on Long Island.

Come to that, at least he would no longer be forced to visit her parents on Long Island. After his most recent time spent with Oliver and Nessa, he was quite grateful to not have any reason to ever see them again.

Thinking of that wasted, infuriating twenty minutes spent in Syosset, ten days prior, caused a visceral response. Will was glad he was done shaving. It wouldn't have been a good idea to still be holding a razor in his now-shaking hand. He looked in the mirror at the steam coming off his shoulders. He knew it was caused by his body still being warm from the maybe-a-little-too-hot shower and the quickly cooling temperature of the bathroom, but he also couldn't help but wonder if his blood was actually boiling.

He walked to his closet and pulled out a crisp, light blue button-up and a darker blue tie, and began getting dressed. His playlist ended, and silence filled the room, and immediately Cadie's voice was on his heart like a fresh stab wound.

"What if God won't forgive our sin because you aren't sorry?"

He scoffed at the memory of her words. Yep. Without a doubt, those words represented the influence of Nessa McCaffrey, one way or another.

But the words aren't really the point, are they?

He'd been reaching for his wallet and cell phone, to grab them from his dresser and put them in his pockets, but his hand froze in midair. He heard that question in his mind with all the clarity of the one before it, but the voice wasn't Cadie's. And he wasn't completely sure it was his own.

The churning inside of him—his incessant foe, all night long—returned.

He rubbed his face in his hands and attempted to shake it off, attributing the uncomfortable question to a lack of sleep. Dressed and ready to go by 6:25, he finally grabbed his phone and wallet, took one last look in the mirror, put on his coat, and prepared to leave the apartment a full twenty minutes earlier than usual. Typically, he would brew his own coffee and fill a travel tumbler to drink on the commute, but every little bit of penny-pinching he'd been doing suddenly seemed pointless. It was a good day for an overpriced latte.

"Dude. Do you always leave this early?" an unexpected voice greeted him as he grabbed his keys from the hook by the door.

"Hey, Sam," he said as his eyes adjusted to the darkness of the room enough to spot his roommate. Even so, staring straight at him, it took Will a moment to register *what* exactly he was looking at. He flipped the light switch by the door and then immediately wished he hadn't.

Sam was hanging upside down from an inversion bar in his bedroom's doorway, wearing only gravity boots and exercise shorts. Will was exhausted just watching him pull-up and crunch and whatever else he was doing, but Sam was still somehow able to carry on a conversation without getting so much as winded.

"I'm running a little earlier than normal," Will said, finally answering the question. "But this is pretty much my usual time. I don't think I've ever seen *you* up this early. Hope I didn't wake you with the music."

"Nah. I've got an audition at 8:30. Who schedules anything at 8:30? It's ridiculous. But my agent pulled a lot of strings to get me in."

"That's . . . brutal," Will replied as he looked at his watch and realized if he didn't get out the door soon he wouldn't have a chance to grab that latte and still get to the office by his usual arrival time of 7:30. "Well, good luck with the audition."

"Break a leg," Sam grunted as he held on to the bar, unlatched his boots, and hopped to the ground in one fluid motion.

"I'm sorry, what?"

"You don't say good luck, you say break a leg."

"Ah. Sure, sure." Will wished he hadn't turned on the light so that he could roll his eyes without being spotted. Why did he always end up with struggling actors as roommates? "Then break a leg."

He grabbed hold of the doorknob and turned it, but he didn't move quickly enough.

"Hey, so, if it's all right with you, I was thinking of having a few people over tonight, to celebrate this audition—"

"The audition you haven't gone to yet?"

"I don't believe in celebrating the destination. I celebrate the journey." Sam grabbed a clear blender cup full of a nasty-looking green concoction from the floor by the doorway and began guzzling.

"By all means. Celebrate your journey. I'll steer clear—"

"No, I wasn't saying you should stay away.

You should come. I've lived here three months and we haven't hung out once. And bring your girlfriend. Sadie, right?"

"Cadie," Will corrected him and then took a deep breath before correcting him once more. "But we're not together anymore."

"Aw, dude. That sucks. Well, bring another girl—"

"We literally just broke up this week. . ."

"Or some friends, or whatever."

Will opened the door and took one step into the hallway. "That's nice of you, but—"

"I'm serious. Let's hang out. I insist. Bring home some friends from work. You're, like, a science and math guy, right?"

"Research," Will corrected him, but he quickly realized Sam thought he had just confirmed that he was a science and math guy.

"So, you work in a lab or something?"

Sam walked to grab his T-shirt from the back of the couch and mercifully put it on. Will was surrounded by some of the greatest athletes of all time on a regular basis, so he had certainly gotten to a point where he did not intimidate easily. But it was as if his roommate's six-pack had been worried it might get thirsty, so it had brought along an extra six-pack of its own.

"Not really a lab. Look, I need to run . . ." Will was watching his overpriced latte disappear, and that had really been the only thing he was looking forward to—in the morning, in the day, and at that point, in his entire life, really.

"Okay, well, bring home some lab guys. Or lab girls, if that's a thing."

Will was one foot out the door, but he just couldn't let that one hang in the air. "Did you seriously just say 'if that's a thing'? As if you don't know if women work in labs?"

"Oh, dude! No, that sounded bad. I just don't know if *you* work with any women. And that's the point. We don't know anything about each other. I don't know what kind of lab you work in—"

"Not a lab."

"I auditioned for this TV pilot one time where these aliens created this force field thing to keep women from entering normal places they would go. Like, work and their houses. Men were forced to carry on alone, and they could only be with women in this bubble thing that was safe from the force field."

Will felt as if there were a force field keeping him from his latte. "Well, rest assured, my workplace is an alien-free zone."

"I think it was actually a good thing that pilot never got picked up. It was ahead of its time," Sam continued. "It kind of had a *Glee* vibe—"

Will interrupted. "Did you just say *Glee*?"

"Yeah. The aliens were inhabiting the bodies of the people who worked at this singing telegram company."

"As in big teddy bears singing 'Love Me Tender'? Stuff like that?"

Sam laughed. "Wow. *Someone* hasn't gotten a singing telegram since 1954."

Will had known better than to engage. With a shrug he said, "I didn't even know those things still existed."

"Oh yeah, man! There are some pretty good companies, in New York, especially. Lots of Broadway sorts, waiting for the next gig, so you actually get some decent talent sometimes. I'm sure you can even get a big teddy bear, if that's your thing. I'll warn you, though. Your higher quality singing telegram performers aren't going to put costumes and masks like that on their heads. I can't even tell you how gross those things are."

Will had only been half-listening through most of that, but once they entered the bacteria portion of the morning, he decided it was time to check out completely.

"I'm sorry, Sam, I really have to go. Break a leg!" he called out over his shoulder as he hurried into the hallway and closed the door behind him.

The words aren't really the point.

This time, the voice in his head was his own, but it wasn't making any more sense than Cadie's or the unrecognizable voice had.

It did, however, make more sense than any single thing he'd ever heard his roommate say.

"The words aren't really the point," he repeated, this time aloud, as the churning morphed into an ache. "Then what *is* the point?"

And suddenly he knew.

It didn't matter what his thoughts were on Cadie's two-person repentance theory, and it didn't even matter if Nessa had influenced her daughter's thoughts or not. The point was, Will still hadn't asked God for his forgiveness.

"I am sorry," he whispered, looking up toward the desperately-in-need-of-rehab ceiling tiles above him. He looked around the hallway and down the stairwell to make sure no one was around. He wasn't ashamed of his faith, he just really didn't want his prayer interrupted by Ted from next door asking Will if he was a Mets fan, as he did every time he saw him, or by Fabiola from the second floor, doing lunges up and down the stairs as part of her daily workout.

Satisfied he was alone, he leaned against the windowsill, bowed his head, and closed his eyes.

"I *am* sorry, Lord," he said softly. "Please forgive me. I'm sorry about what Cadie and I did, and I'm sorry I hurt her. Please help her to know how much you love her." *Please help her to know how much I love her too.* "And please forgive me for taking so long to bring this to you. I love you, Lord, and I'm so grateful that you love me too. I don't deserve it."

Will definitely hadn't been talking to God enough lately, but he felt secure in his faith. His heart was open, and he was giving it all to God—even if the words were simple and few—and he trusted that he was forgiven. He knew he had a bad habit of putting his desires first, and when he did, God tended to end up on the back burner. That needed to change. And making that change would undoubtedly mean more to a future with Cadie than any mistake of the past.

He stood up straight and glanced at his watch, accepting the reality of having to say goodbye to the promise of espresso, once and for all. Of course he wouldn't trade his couple of minutes with God for all the lattes in the world. His time with Sam, on the other hand . . .

But somewhere in the midst of the most nonsensical conversation he could remember ever having with his roommate, he'd accidentally stumbled upon not only renewed motivation to get Cadie back but an actual place to start.

He'd just have to be sure to avoid the disgusting teddy bears.

"Cadie always said you weren't very observant," Darby said several hours later as she stormed into Will's office and shut the door behind her. She placed her hands on the edge of the desk and leaned over to confront him. "What *was* that?"

"What was *what?*"

"That hip-hop debacle that just took place in the accounting suite, of course!"

He jumped up from his chair. "They've been here already? How did it go? Did she sing along? I just know she sang along. Did she figure out it was from me?"

"Why in the world would she have sung along? We are talking about Cadie McCaffrey, right? The woman whose ringtone is 'Snowbird' by Anne Murray? How in the world would she know a song called 'Sista Big Bones', and why in heaven's name would you *ever* have anyone sing it to her?"

"I don't understand." He sank back down into his chair, confusion giving way to fear that something had gone horribly wrong. "She's obsessed with *Hamilton*. You know that. I was never able to get her tickets. You know . . . since I like to eat and have electricity and all. I wouldn't normally send her anything from NYC Hip Hop Grams, of course, but when they said they were running a special on *Hamilton* tributes, I thought . . ."

Darby stared at him in confusion for several seconds before laughter overtook her. "You lovable dum-dum!" she exclaimed through her laughter. "It wasn't a *Hamilton* tribute. It was an *Anthony* Hamilton tribute."

"Who's Anthony Hamilton?"

"A rapper, I think." She could barely get the words out through her giggle fit. "Or a producer.

I don't know, exactly, but apparently he sang 'Sista Big Bones', which isn't quite the Cadie McCaffrey romance bait you might imagine it to be."

Oh no. "I told them I didn't want a card or anything. Maybe she hasn't figured out it was from me."

"Yeah, maybe she *wouldn't* have . . . if they hadn't ended the song by saying, 'Will loves you, girl, and he wants you back, real bad.' "

"Oh no." Will's arms folded across the desk in front of him, and he slammed his head down onto them.

Her giggles faded away, and Will was grateful that she was too kind and humane to continue finding humor in his moment of complete and utter humiliation.

"So, talk to me, Will," she said as she sat down across from him. "What were you trying to do?"

"I was trying to get her back, of course," he muttered into his arm.

Darby sighed. "I know it's going to take you some time to get over her, but when it eventually happens—"

"It's never going to happen, Darb," he said—softly, with surprising calm.

"You feel that way now, and that's really romantic. It is. But—"

Will shrugged as he raised his head and looked her in the eye—equal parts determination and resignation. "That's not some stupid line I've come up with, like in those ridiculous romance movies you and Cadie love so much."

He ran his fingers through his hair, not sure how to communicate what was in his heart—and not entirely sure why he was putting in the effort.

"I made the commitment to love her forever," he finally said, repeating the line he had spontaneously spewed to Ellis and Kevin. "That commitment doesn't go away just because she's not in on the plan."

She tilted her head and bit her lip, her eyes never leaving his. He maintained eye contact with her as long as he could, until he began to feel uncomfortable.

"What? Why are you looking at me like that?"

"That was a really good line, Will. It was ridiculous romance movie caliber, actually."

"Well then . . . I guess that makes it all okay."

She continued looking at him with that disconcerting intensity that he'd never seen on her face before, and then she abruptly tore her eyes away and swiped a legal pad and pen from his desk.

"What are you doing?"

Without looking up from whatever she was frantically scribbling, she answered, "I'm helping you get her back." The words were accompanied by a sigh heavy enough to convey she'd just agreed to drive the getaway car in Will's heist. "But listen, my relationship with her is my priority. If this goes sour—"

"What are you talking about? 'If this goes sour'? Are we kidnapping her? Are we about to cut out letters from *Sports Illustrated* and send Oliver and Nessa a ransom note?"

"I'm just saying I'm doing this because I love her, and I happen to think you're what's best for her. And clearly you can't handle it on your own."

He stood from his chair. "Hey, today was just a stupid mistake. That certainly doesn't mean I can't handle it. I've been thinking about some things she said a long time ago and figuring out what she'll like. I'm working on some grand, spectacular gestures."

The pen froze mid-word as she looked up at him. "Really? Like what?"

After several seconds of stammering and saying nothing, he finally asked, "So what do I do?"

Darby flipped to another blank page in the legal pad and quickly wrote a few big block letters. She tore it out and handed it to him.

"Research?" he asked as he read it. "What's that supposed to mean?"

"Research! It's what you do!"

"I'm aware, but—"

"Look, Will, you and Cadie have some really big issues to work out. Even if you can get on the same page somewhat, there are still some big things in play."

"Such as?" The look of exasperated disbelief in her eyes made him instantly regret the question.

"I told you you're clueless."

"I know I am." He collapsed back into the chair. With a heavy sigh he said, "Can I ask you something?" She nodded that he could, and Will continued—uncomfortably. "If we hadn't . . ." He paused as awkwardness washed over him, and then he realized he needed to verify that he wouldn't be the one giving away secrets. "Hold on. You do know that Cadie and I . . . you know . . . that we . . ."

Darby's eyes flew wide open. "Yes. I know. But I am *not* talking about that with you!"

"No, no . . . I don't want to talk about it. I just . . ." He sighed again. This was not a conversation he wanted to have, but he knew that no one else apart from Cadie herself would know the answer to his question. And he really needed to know. "Were we okay until we . . . ?" His eyes began to sting, and he could feel them turning red. He was so tired of feeling that way. "It had felt like things were off for a while—"

"I really shouldn't be the one to tell you any of this, Will."

"I know!" he shouted. "But she won't talk to me! She began completely icing me out as soon as we . . ." He groaned. "You know. And if it's all about what happened that night, then I am prepared to continue groveling and do whatever else it takes, but I just can't believe that she would throw everything away over one mistake."

She took a deep breath and leaned closer to him, resting her elbows on the desk. "Can I ask *you* something?" After he nodded, she gently asked, "Where did you think the relationship was heading?"

"What do you mean?"

"Well, it's just that you say you were committed to loving her forever, and I believe that. But usually there is a next step. For some couples that may be sleeping together or living together, but that wasn't part of the plan for you guys—regardless of what actually happened—so what was supposed to be next?"

"Marriage." His tone made it evident that what he was actually saying was, "Marriage. Duh."

"Seriously?" Darby asked.

"Of course."

"She said you never even hinted—"

"Why would I hint?" Will thought back over various conversations he and Cadie had had through the years and began feeling even more confident in the stance he was taking against what Darby was saying. "I asked strategic questions and got the information I needed, in order to make informed decisions."

"So you treated it like—"

"Research." He held up the lined yellow paper she'd given him. "Like you said, it's what I do."

She smiled and shook her head and then handed him the rest of what she'd written. "That should get you started."

"What's this?"

She stood and returned the legal pad and pen to the desk. "In my opinion, it's the key to getting her back."

"It's just a list of movies." He skimmed through all of the titles and felt like adding a bit of additional commentary. It was a list of horrible, cheesy, ludicrously plotted romance movies. "What in the world am I supposed to do with this?"

"Like I said, Will, you two have some major issues to work out. Romance isn't going to just make all of the problems go away. But I think it's a really good place to start."

13

⚛︎

After a Day at the Lab

"Whitaker, when I said we should get a drink sometime, this is not what I had in mind," Kevin said as he looked up and down 109th Street in the dark. "You actually live here?"

Will unlatched the iron gate in front of the stoop of his six-story walk-up. "Oh, come on, Kev. It's not that bad. It's a great old pre-war building—"

"Which war?" Ellis interrupted him. "The Swiss Peasant War of 1653?" He chuckled at his own joke until he realized Kevin and Will were staring at him. "What? Unlike you uneducated jocks, I read and am continually on a quest to pursue the betterment of my mind."

Will laughed while Kevin just changed the subject.

"You really make that commute every day?"

"Every single day. It's not so bad, actually. We'd have made it a lot sooner if you two prima donnas hadn't insisted upon taking a cab. The subway is much faster." Will unlocked the door and held it open for them to walk in behind him.

"When I was in grad school, this place was great. I could walk to campus in three minutes."

"Hang on," Ellis said as they entered the building. "I thought you went to grad school at Columbia."

"I did."

Will almost had the door closed, but Ellis stopped it with his hand and stepped back out onto the front stoop. He looked up and down 109th Street as Kevin had a moment prior, except with slightly more confusion etched on his face.

"Where are we, man?" he asked. "Seriously, where are we? I thought Columbia was on the Upper West Side."

"It is," Will replied with a laugh as he ushered Ellis back in once again and shut the door behind him. "I live on the Upper West Side."

"Nuh-uh," Ellis argued, shaking his head. "*I* live on the Upper West Side. This is, like, Harlem, man."

"Not for another block or two." Will motioned that they should follow him and began bounding up the stairs.

"No elevator?" Kevin asked, and Will could almost hear the exasperated expressions taking place behind him.

"No elevator. But for two big, tough, legendary athletes, I didn't think a few stairs would be a problem."

Kevin pushed him forward, while Ellis just took a deep breath and grumbled as they began their ascent.

"Tell me," Kevin began, alternating the bottle of champagne he carried from one hand to the other. "Why are we coming to a party at your apartment in Morningside Heights—"

"Which is just a fancy way to say, 'Might as well be Harlem,' " Ellis huffed as they rounded the corner to begin climbing the third flight.

"When we literally just left our offices downtown," Kevin continued. "I know you aren't much of a party guy, Whitaker, but for your information, there are a few bars in Lower Manhattan. On top of that, downtown is so close to Tribeca, where I choose to live *because* of its proximity to our aforementioned, recently departed offices . . ."

"Don't dwell on the past, Swoosh," Ellis said from a flight below them. "That was about two thousand blocks ago."

"My roommate is having a thing," Will replied with a shrug.

Both of his friends stopped in their tracks and looked up at him incredulously.

"I'm sorry," Kevin spoke up. "Your roommate is having a thing? What do you mean, your roommate is having a *thing?*"

Will sighed, and after quickly darting his eyes toward the door of his apartment, which they

211

were finally approaching, he ran down a few steps to stand between Kevin and Ellis.

"He's an actor," he explained discreetly. "This morning he was going on about this party he's having tonight, to celebrate an audition he had today."

"He planned a party to celebrate the audition before he knew if he would get the part?" Ellis asked.

"Exactly," Will continued. "I found it really annoying and pretentious, and this guy . . . I mean, he's nice enough, I guess, but between him being out all night, usually, and getting his beauty sleep, I guess, I hardly ever see him. Pretty decent roommate, all in all. But I was just so annoyed by the 'celebrate the journey' crap he was going on about this morning, and I started to feel bad because I think he really was making an attempt to reach out and be nice to me."

"*We* were making an attempt to reach out and be nice to you," Kevin said. "And this is how you thank us?"

"We'll spend five minutes in there and then we'll head up to the roof with that champagne. I get to look like a decent roommate, we get to hang out, I get to tell you about the new plan to get Cadie back, and you guys get to experience a new part of Manhattan. Everyone wins."

Ellis completed the rest of the steps to catch up, and then, still out of breath, stood next to Will and said, "You win, man. Swoosh and I don't win."

Will wasn't looking forward to the noise and the drinking and everyone bumping into each other in the tiny apartment. And he definitely wasn't looking forward to meeting all of Sam's friends, who probably all had abs that made Gerard Butler in *300* look like Steve Guttenberg in *Three Men and a Baby*. But he'd taken Darby's words to heart, though she probably hadn't meant for him to apply them anywhere apart from his relationship with Cadie. He was unobservant and clueless, and he needed to put in more effort with people.

Also, he had to research romance in the movies. Who better to help him with that than a bunch of out-of-work actors?

He glanced back at Kevin and Ellis standing behind him, and he couldn't contain his laughter. The two giant men looked at each other before looking back at Will in confusion.

"What's so funny?" Kevin asked.

"My twentysomething actor roommate invited me to a party with his cool actor friends, and I brought you two! You're both old enough to be his father, and I'm beginning to wonder if this was a mistake, simply because I had an early morning and I'd like to go to bed." His laughter died down to a reflective chuckle. "Sorry, guys. I just feel like I aged twenty years this week."

Ellis placed a comforting hand on his shoulder. "Hey, man, this party might actually be the best thing for you. You were a star on the rise, and at that press conference, you exploded!"

"Don't stars die when they explode?" Kevin interjected.

Ellis ignored him. "And still all you can think about is Cadie. I get that. *We* get that, don't we, Swoosh?"

"Would I be here otherwise?" he answered.

Will smiled at his friends, amazed as always at their depth and compassion—no matter how chill and unaffected they usually appeared to be. Since his confession that he and Cadie had broken up, not one word had been said about it—or about her. But from Ellis going to The Bench on Will's behalf, to Kevin having lunch catered for *The Daily Dribble* team, to Anna, the new girl, sitting in Cadie's chair, representing the accounting department at the daily staff meeting, he knew his friends had been finding ways to care for him.

Although Anna was probably in the meeting because Cadie didn't want to see you.

The thought entered his head, and he knew it was probably the accurate explanation. He preferred his first theory.

"Yep," Ellis continued with a nod, growing more confident in his declaration. "I really think this party might be the best thing for you. You can get your mind off things, flirt with some actresses—"

"Oh, I'm not ready to—"

"Flirting won't hurt you, man. At the very least, you can enjoy them flirting with you, and you can just relax and unwind for a while. You deserve that. You've exploded, my friend. Now your star is going to continue to burn brightly for a very long time."

"You really don't know how astronomy works, do you, Ellis?" Kevin asked.

"I'm not much of a science guy, so sue me."

"Oh yeah, that reminds me," Will spoke up. "My roommate thinks I work in a lab."

"A lab?" Kevin laughed. "Why in the world does he think that?"

"Because I work in research."

Ellis groaned and laughed simultaneously. "Okay, man, let's go. I'm going to enjoy this."

Will smiled and turned his key in the lock, and as they entered, his senses were assaulted by the overwhelming . . . silence.

"That's weird," Will muttered with a quick glance behind him to shrug in confusion. He looked at his watch—9:07. He didn't know much about actors and their wild parties, but surely they didn't start after 9:00, did they? He stepped to the side so Kevin and Ellis could enter fully, and then he shut the door behind them. "Sam? You home?"

"Up here," Sam called down from the second floor.

Ellis took a few more steps inside the narrow entryway and craned his neck to look up the stairs. "There's a second floor?" he asked quietly as he looked around the tiny space. "Is it bigger up there?"

The corner of Will's mouth moved upward. He had never deceived himself. He knew how small his apartment was. But with Ellis Haywood and Kevin Lamont standing in the middle of it, it was almost comical.

"Nope. It's actually smaller. Let me give you the tour." Will stood beside them and showed them around the entire apartment, just by pointing. "That's my bedroom, and there's a little bathroom in there. That's Sam's room, and then there's another bathroom."

"Two bathrooms?" Kevin asked, and he actually managed to sound like he was impressed. "Not a lot of places have two bathrooms."

"What can I say? We live in the lap of luxury here in Morningside Heights."

"Harlem," Ellis muttered. Kevin elbowed him, so he added, "But it's nice, man. Real nice."

Will laughed and continued the tour. "If you want to come upstairs—"

"I'm not sure I *can* come upstairs," Ellis stated, not at all hyperbolically, as he turned sideways to squeeze up the stairway. Meanwhile, Kevin was bent over, practically at the waist, to avoid hitting his head.

Ignoring them, Will continued the tour. It was all simple. Efficient. No frills. It had been a great bachelor pad but a somewhat impractical habitat for an adult man in a serious relationship. For a time, Cadie had made an effort to act as if she found the apartment charming, but before long they were both finding fewer reasons to spend time there.

"In here is the living room," he said, leading them to the final room with somewhat lower spirits, thanks to his Cadie-centric thoughts. "This is my roommate, Sam."

Sam appeared to brush crumbs off of his lap onto the floor as he grabbed the remote to mute the television, then he looked toward the guests and his eyes flew open wide.

"Sam, this is—"

"Kevin Lamont and Ellis Haywood," Sam completed the introduction himself. He jumped up from the couch and wiped his hands on the side of his jeans before putting his hand out for them to shake. "You're Kevin Lamont and Ellis Haywood. In my apartment."

Kevin and Ellis offered pleasantries while only thinly veiling their confusion as they continued to look around the undeniably party-free apartment.

"I thought you were having a party tonight," Will said, ever so slightly worried that he was going to have to snap his fingers in front of his roommate's eyes in order to get him to stop staring at the giant sports heroes in their living room. At least what Will lacked in abdominal muscles he made up for in work friends. But realization hit, and snapping fingers weren't necessary.

"Hang on," Sam said, turning his attention to Will. "You brought Kevin Lamont and Ellis Haywood here for my party?"

"You really don't have to say our full names every time, man," Ellis insisted.

"I did," Will replied after a quick smile in Ellis's direction, to let him know he had heard his aside. "Yet there is no party."

"Nope. No party." Sam sighed and seemingly lost interest in the famous guests in an instant. He collapsed onto the couch and stared intently at the television as if he couldn't bear the thought of missing a moment—despite the fact that it was still muted.

"So, um . . ." Will began hesitantly. "What's up? Decide the journey isn't worth celebrating after all?" Ellis kicked the sole of his shoe. Will looked up at him and silently mouthed "What?"

Ellis shook his head and rolled his eyes at Will before stepping past him and joining Sam on the couch. "Will said you had a big audition today, man. How'd it go?"

Sam finally stopped staring at the silent

television and craned his neck to look up at Ellis. "You're Ellis Haywood," he said declaratively, as if there were nothing else to say.

"I'm aware," Ellis responded.

"You actually care how my audition went?"

Ellis shrugged and said, "It seems that I do."

Sam took a deep breath. "That's very nice of you."

I'm supposed to be the nice one, Will thought to himself as he opened the refrigerator and grabbed a soda, and silently offered one to everyone else in the room. Ellis raised his hand and Will tossed a can, which was easily caught.

"This audition was supposed to be a big deal. My agent told me she pulled a lot of strings to get me in and cashed in a lot of favors, and that it would really make my career if I got the job. So I get there, and the role is 'Guy in Elevator.' Seriously. One line. *That* was supposed to be my big break?"

"Everybody has to start somewhere," Will said.

Sam nodded. "Yeah. But I didn't even get the part. I'm just fed up. When am I ever going to get my chance? I'm not even asking to be a big movie star, I just really want to break into television. I like the security of having work to go to every day for a long time. A solid income. Does that make sense?"

"It does," Kevin deadpanned. "That is, in fact, the reason most people have regular jobs."

Sam shrugged his shoulders and offered up a sad smile. "Ah well. I guess we all have work problems." He gestured toward Will and said, "I'm sure you run into stuff at the lab." All of a sudden he sat up a little straighter and said, "So how do you guys know each other?"

Ellis began to answer. "We work—"

"Um . . . in the same building," Will interjected. He'd confess soon enough that he had a much cooler job than what Sam believed, but for Sam's sake, he knew it wasn't the right moment. "So, Sam, let me ask you a question. As an actor, do you watch a lot of movies?"

"I watch *every* movie," he replied with a laugh.

"Even romantic movies?"

Sam turned his head to first look at Ellis, and then Kevin, before turning back to Will with an expression that said, "You aren't *really* going to make me answer that, are you?"

Will smiled. "Kevin lives in a houseful of women, and Ellis is the most romance-obsessed person I've ever met in my life. You can speak freely."

His roommate cleared his throat and answered, "Yeah. I watch *everything*."

"Good," Will stated as he pulled Darby's list from his back pocket. "I need your help."

14

*Three Weeks, Seven CDs,
and a Billion Tic Tacs Later*

"Morning, Cadie," I was greeted by Helene in Human Resources as I made my way through The Bench's foyer. "About time you show up."

I took a quick glance down at my watch. "Did I forget a meeting?" It was 7:20. *Surely* I hadn't already missed a meeting by 7:20, right?

She smiled, and I detected a hint of fun and joviality in her eyes—which made no sense, considering Helene was the one who had sent out the memo that Casual Friday only applied to those in the office outside of the normal 8:00 to 6:00 work hours.

"Morning, Cadie!" Pam from accounting's sing-song words assaulted me as she passed. "I was starting to think you'd never get here."

"Okay, what is going on?" I asked—of anyone, really.

"Has she been in there yet?" another voice called out from behind me.

"Oh! Good morning, Cadie." This time it was

Anna Alvarez, at the door of the accounting suite.

I took the last few steps toward her. "I know. I'm apparently late." Being late wasn't like me. Having no idea what I was late *for* was as unlike me as you could get. "Did something not get put on my calendar, or—"

"It's not that," she replied, shaking her head. "In fact, if you want to give me a few more minutes I'll get this all cleaned up so you don't have to worry about it."

I glanced over my shoulder at the small crowd that had gathered. I had no idea what was happening, but I was growing increasingly certain that I hadn't missed a meeting and increasingly suspicious that the accounting suite was ground zero of a zombie outbreak.

"I'd like to go to my office, please," I said, forcing a smile for the benefit of all present. My tone, however, was stern enough to get Anna to move out of the way.

What awaited me on the inside of my usually meticulous department sure smelled better than I imagined a zombie outbreak would smell, but apart from that I wasn't able to make a lick of sense of any of it.

Daffodils. Real live daffodils. Hundreds of them. In the accounting department. In November, for goodness sake! Not in pots or vases, but somehow laid out as if there were a field of them.

"What in the—" Darby's voice came up behind

me, but I couldn't tear my eyes away from the sight in order to look at her. She groaned and softly muttered, "Will."

Of course it was Will. Over the course of the past week or so, I'd received gifts from him every single day. Silly, insignificant, easy-to-ignore gifts like candy and CDs of music he'd picked out and burned for me. But a field of daffodils? That was a little more difficult to ignore.

I have to admit, the sight was pretty spectacular. My mind began to play wonderful tricks on me, as boring gray desks transformed into sunny hillsides, and various filing cabinets became multilevel rock gardens. Against all reason and better judgment, I found myself wanting nothing more than to invite Will into the accounting department for a picnic.

"Gordon? Are you okay?" I heard Helene ask.

I didn't pay much attention until Gordon's emphatic assurances that he was fine were interrupted first by a sneeze that I'm fairly certain deposited Gordon's lung onto Pam's shoes, and then a horrible wheezing sound that made me wonder if I'd been right about that zombie outbreak after all. He hadn't walked through the door. He hadn't even fully passed by. But apparently something about cramming half the Flower District into the accounting suite had been enough to set him off.

"Are you allergic to flowers, Gordon?" Helene

asked in a loud, clearly enunciating tone—I suppose in case his face had just swelled past his ears.

"No," Darby whispered to me. "He probably just had some bad shellfish for breakfast."

I shot her an expression of warning, which of course was laced with a smirk that clearly stated, "I'm in management. Don't you dare make me laugh right now," and shooed her away so I could focus on Gordon.

Right about then, Gordon began pointing to the fanny pack around his waist. Helene unzipped it and pulled out an EpiPen, which Gordon quickly administered with skill and ease. Soon after, the injection began working its magic and Gordon began apologizing to me.

"Sorry, Cadie. My allergies are so bad, you can't take me anywhere during the blooming season. This has happened a lot."

I grabbed his hand as the EMTs some quick-thinking individual had thought to call stepped off the elevator and approached with a stretcher. I only jumped a little upon discovering that if I'd had to differentiate between Gordon's hands and Mickey Mouse's right then, I'd have been at a complete loss.

"Hey, don't *you* apologize. I'm the sorry one. You just take care and let us know if you need anything. Okay?"

Minutes later the crowd had dissipated, Gordon

had been moved to someplace less allergenic, like Mount Sinai hospital, most likely, and the custodial staff had seen to transforming ASN back to our usual workspace—and a little less like Eliza Doolittle's.

"You have to admit," Darby mused as we watched the final clusters get carted out, "that was pretty romantic."

"Romantic?" I scoffed. "I'm not sure Gordon sees it that way. Which reminds me . . . will you have Anna send him some—"

"Balloons?" she asked, a sheepish grin on her face. "Surely you weren't about to say flowers."

I giggled . . . and instantly felt bad about it. "I've never seen anyone's face take on that Gumby quality before." Poor Gordon. "What in the world was Will thinking, bringing so many daffodils in here like that?"

She bent over and picked up scattered petals from the carpet. "In Will's defense, I don't think he *was* thinking." She clutched the remnants to her chest like a bouquet. "He was only *feeling.*"

"Well, I'll be sure to put that on the worker's comp incident report." I groaned and shook my head at the thought of how bad it was, and how bad it could have been.

"You heard Gordon. He said you can't take him anywhere in the blooming season. It could have happened anywhere."

"But the poor guy should have been safe

indoors in November. Where did Will even *find* that many daffodils this time of year?" I asked rhetorically as we walked into my office, which was, mercifully, flower free. "And why daffodils? Daisies are my favorite. He knows that." I caught myself focusing on the wrong thing. Although, really, what was the *right* thing? The fact that after all these years, he didn't know my favorite flower, or the fact that we'd been broken up for weeks and he shouldn't be sending me flowers at all?

None of the above, Cadie. What matters is the way Gordon's lips resembled the giant koi fish at the Brooklyn Botanic Garden.

Darby shrugged. "There are greenhouses and such, right? And as for the why . . . I don't know, but it's kind of like in that one movie you love. Which one is that, where Ewan McGregor plays the younger version of the guy who played Daddy Warbucks? And his son is trying to sort out how many of his dad's stories are actually true?"

Recognition dawned. "*Big Fish*?"

"That's the one!"

Ah yes. *That* was why I'd experienced a short moment of déjà vu while observing the seemingly endless array of yellow flowers. But there had been no time to place the memory once Gordon's anaphylactic shock set in.

"Nah." I shook my head. "Not a chance. Will's never seen *Big Fish*. Not exactly his type."

She shrugged again. "Be that as it may . . ."

"Don't you start!" I laughed. "It's not romantic, Darb. I mean, was there a moment when I found myself getting caught up in the grandeur of it all? Sure."

"It sure smelled good."

I shut my office door and then turned around quickly to face her. "It was like he found a way to give me the gift of spring."

"And *that* isn't romantic?"

I sighed. Begrudgingly. "Okay, sure . . . it was romantic. But it was also kind of sad, actually." I leaned back against the door. "He can't heal all the scars of the past year by making the office smell good and copying *Big Fish*—"

My mouth abruptly stopped working as I saw the image of the daffodils in my mind again. I walked over to my desk and picked up the CD Will had burned for me and slid under my office door the day before, to add to the collection of the six he had given me already, one for each of the six work days prior.

"Is he doing some movie homage thing?"

"What do you mean?" she asked.

"Think about it. We've got the potentially fatal *Big Fish* attempt, and the CDs, and the lifetime supply of orange Tic Tacs? There is no possible explanation for the Tic Tacs unless he's trying to channel *Juno*."

"So he bought you candy and made you some

227

mixtapes. That's not unique to the movies. I mean, aren't mixtapes pretty much the soundtrack of our generation's lives?"

"Sure, sure," I agreed, "but the cover art? I mean, it's a little *Nick and Norah's Infinite Playlist*, don't you think?"

"Did he put any Manilow on the CD?"

I raised my eyebrows. "I don't think so. Why?"

"Just making sure he hasn't gone completely off the deep end." She winked, delighting as always in giving me a hard time about my musical tastes.

I was used to it. "But what's next? Is he going to storm the castle to keep me from marrying Prince Humperdinck? I've already been kissed. Otherwise would he be waiting for me on the pitcher's mound?"

"That wouldn't make sense. Drew Barrymore was the one who had never been kissed, and *she* was the one waiting on the pitcher's mound." When I didn't laugh, she smiled and added, "I love you, but you're overreacting. He sent you flowers and candy and made you a mixtape. Eh, so he went a little overboard, but he basically just did what every guy trying to win back a girl has *ever* done."

I sighed. "You're right. I'm sure you're right. But I wish he'd stop. How am I supposed to move past him if he won't get out of the way?"

• • •

"McCaffrey, I need you in this meeting," Kevin barked from the entryway to The Field.

I'd known better than to go down that hallway. For about a month and a half I had carefully avoided that entire section of ASN headquarters. For the extra effort I'd received not only the satisfaction of limited interaction with Will but also the daily commendation of my Fitbit.

"I've got some reports that need my attention, Kevin, but I can send Anna—"

He crossed his arms and his brow furrowed. "Who's Anna?"

"Anna Alvarez. You know Anna."

"The intern?"

Kevin Lamont was a brilliant man, but after working with him as long as I had, I was aware that he remembered the details that mattered to him. Those details received his complete focus while many others slid through the cracks. Those who understood such things said that his focus was part of what had made him one of the greatest basketball players of all time. I suppose that same focus had resulted in his rise to the top of sports broadcasting, but I couldn't help but wonder if any of his teammates had ever found it as frustrating as I did.

"She's not an intern anymore, remember? I hired her to take over after Debbie left."

I could tell by the distracted look in his eyes

that he wasn't going to remember those details this time either.

"Fine, bring her. It will be a good opportunity for her to learn some things. But she doesn't have the experience to take this one and run—"

"I'll send Darby too," I replied a little too eagerly.

We'd been having the entire conversation about ten feet away from each other, with various ASN employees passing between us, but he quickly took a few steps to bridge the gap before quietly repeating, "McCaffrey, I need you in this meeting."

I bit the inside of my cheek and nodded. "I'll be there."

He spun on the heel of his designer Italian loafers and returned to The Field. I, meanwhile, lamented the fact that I had not only let down my daily step goal—I had let myself down too.

I'd done a pretty good job of avoiding all of the major Will Whitaker moments at ASN—no small feat considering *every* moment at ASN had seemingly been a Will Whitaker moment. He needed to sign off on the policies and procedures for his new expense account, I sent Anna. We needed to look at the budget for that week's "Will Whitaker is the greatest thing to happen to baseball since catchers decided to wear facemasks" special, I sent Darby. The staff got together for drinks or dinner or celebratory cupcakes in the shape of magicians' hats, I just went home. It had been working for me.

Except it really hadn't been working at all.

I was exhausted. I was miserable. I was continually walking on eggshells. *And* I had missed out on far too many opportunities for free food.

Ten minutes later, *The Daily Dribble* conference table was completely full, minus one empty chair that was reserved for a noticeably absent Will Whitaker.

Hey, why should he be on time? It's not like it was his meeting or anything.

Oh, wait. It was *totally* his meeting. Completely, 100 percent all about him and how we could best thrust his goofy ears and shaggy head of hair on the world just a little bit more. Because it obviously wasn't enough that ASN had begun sending him everywhere to cover everything. There were plans for him to be on the fifty-yard line at the Super Bowl and drive the pace car at next year's Indy 500. That, of course, was all in addition to his new seat beside Kevin and Ellis on *The Daily Dribble* and reruns of his Magician special, which seemed to run every hour on the hour.

Yes, clearly the world was suffering from a Will Whitaker shortage and we simply had to do something about that.

"Do you have a problem with that idea, Cadie?"

Kevin asked, interrupting my mental snark session.

Had Kevin Lamont taken to reading minds?

"A problem?" I asked.

"Yes, a problem. I just laid out the plan, and every other person at this table oohed and aahed and said they were on board, while you rolled your eyes and let out the biggest groan I think I've heard in my life. You've always been an independent thinker and I respect that about you. So, I would love to hear what it is about this particular idea that you object to."

Well, crap.

A big part of me wanted to be completely honest and say, "Sorry, Kev. Wasn't listening to a word you said. Not exactly sure what I rolled my eyes and groaned about, but you can be assured that all eye rolls and groans in the foreseeable future will have *something* to do with Will."

With a roomful of eyes on me, I was too proud for that, of course. Instead, I would answer in a generic, insightful way that would once again set me apart as an independent thinker, and not just a yes man to Kevin, unlike the rest of them.

"I'm not sure, exactly," I improvised. "I'm looking at it from all angles and trying to find the upside, but—"

"But you're having a difficult time overlooking the cost and how tight it could make the margin for the next quarter, until the dividends begin to roll in?" he asked, making my concerns sound much more legitimate than they would have if I'd been allowed to continue speaking.

I nodded. "Yes."

"There you go again, kid," he said, his smile conveying his approval. "Thinking the thoughts no one else thinks. Or at least that no one else dares to say." He looked around the room, the smile of approval becoming a glare of discontent. "Cadie's going to take lead on this."

Um . . . what's that now?

"So sorry I'm late, you guys," Will called out as he rushed into the conference room and took his seat.

"I hope the tardiness is for a worthwhile reason?" Kevin asked Will.

"Yes," he responded. "That is, if you call getting the commissioner's office to confirm that the 'Make Good, Do Good' game is actually happening a worthwhile reason."

The entire room seemed to be holding its collective breath as Kevin prodded, "And?"

"And . . . ASN has exclusive first run coverage rights."

Hoots and hollers erupted around the table, and Will just sat there soaking it all in, enjoying the praise. Kevin patted him on the back and then shook his hand in that same way Dr. Houseman shook Johnny Castle's hand at the end of *Dirty Dancing*—after he'd been informed that Johnny had not, in fact, been the one to get Penny in trouble, and after Johnny and Baby had demonstrated that they could pull off the lift.

The problem with the whole situation wasn't everyone's excitement. It wasn't Kevin's approval, or even the fact that Will was reveling in (admittedly extended) fifteen minutes of fame. The problem was that I didn't think about *Dirty Dancing* all that often. Okay, maybe *that* wasn't the problem. If anything, it just proved I had ultimately grown out of my teenage dreams of spending summers at Kellerman's, learning to dance the pachanga. But because I didn't think about *Dirty Dancing* all that often, my mind immediately flashed, without my permission, to a time when Will and I had talked a little bit about *Dirty Dancing* and a lot about romance.

We had been at the wedding of my cousin Justine, and our senses had just been assaulted by my cousin Victoria. I had warned Will, as Victoria approached, that her life was fabulous, mine was a joke, and every other word out of her mouth had always been a lie. She wasn't even a very good liar, but no one ever called her on it, so she just kept on lying.

Will had called her on it. He'd caught her in her lies and stayed one step ahead of her the entire time. And when she told us she was about to marry Aimè Meunière, whose family supposedly owns most of the vineyards in France (mostly in Provence and Bordeaux, but they have the *cutest* little 20,000-acre estate in Côtes du Rhône, according to Victoria), he'd asked to see her engagement ring. An engagement ring she didn't have—because of course the whole story was made up as an attempt to prove that I was pathetic and she was to be envied.

It didn't take much effort at all to transport my mind out of the boardroom and back to that church. To remember how warm and secure I'd felt as Will wrapped his arms around my waist and rested his chin on my shoulder from behind, as we faced the aisle and waited for the bridal party to oh-so-slowly make their way to the pulpit.

"Do you know how many romance movies you've made me watch?" he asked. "I'll tell you how many. All of them. And I've paid attention. There is rarely ever a ring when a man proposes in those movies. Do you realize that?"

"I guess I've never really thought about it." I shrugged and leaned my head against his. "Also, you really think you've seen all of them? You've watched ten. Fifteen, max."

"There are more?" he asked and I giggled. "Well, anyway, the man just never seems to see it coming. That's absurd. Don't you think that's absurd? Maybe the woman doesn't see it coming, but how does the man not see it coming? I don't think that's how it happens in real life."

"You don't think so?" I asked with a smile. I wasn't sure if it was being at a wedding or if it was being surrounded by my family and realizing how comparatively normal I was, but we were skating dangerously close to an actual marriage conversation. I was determined to say as little as I possibly could so I didn't mess it up.

"I don't," he continued to whisper. "I mean, you wouldn't really want any of that movie stuff to happen in real life, would you? Do women really dream of John Cusack with a boom box or Patrick Swayze carrying a watermelon?"

"Jennifer Grey carried the watermelon," I corrected him. "But . . . yeah. Maybe sometimes. I mean, not all the time, certainly. No girl, with the possible exception of Victoria, really wants a fantasy world to play out in their life."

Even as I said those words—through tight lips meant to disguise the fact that we were chatting our way through the bridesmaids' processional—I realized I had no idea if they were true or not. I wasn't sure what other girls wanted. But I had watched all the movies, and though I knew I couldn't live my life like Baby Houseman on vacation in the Catskills, I couldn't deny that once in a great while I wanted a guy to tell my dad that no one puts me in the corner, and then we'd dance and I'd finally do the lift. Metaphorically, of course.

"In the movies, those things are usually an

attempt to save the relationship, aren't they? You never see the happy couples making grand gestures."

"True," I whispered. I smiled and sighed before adding, "So I guess just save all the gestures for someday. When the romance is gone. And then you can plan something spectacular and give Aimè Meunière a run for his money."

The warmth and security of the past dissipated in a cloud of very present sadness as I watched him across the conference table. Yes, I had been slowly getting over him for a year, but it was equally undeniable that not that long ago neither he nor I could have imagined a future apart. And Darby was right, no matter how much I hated to admit it—even to myself. The flowers, the Tic Tacs, the mixtapes . . . even "Sista Big Bones," in its own catastrophic way. It was all romantic.

Why had I told him to wait until *someday?*

I felt the tears that were defying gravity but threatening to give in at any moment, and a small amount of panic set in. No. Crying was not an option. There is no crying in baseball meetings. I grabbed a tissue from the box on the conference table in front of me and gently dabbed at my lower lashes.

"Sorry," I spoke up, choosing to be proactive. "What's the 'Make Good, Do Good' game?"

Silence filled the room as all eyes were

instantly on me. There were only two sets that I paid attention to—my boss's, which were looking at me as if I had grown a second head, and my ex-boyfriend's, which, if I'm not mistaken, hadn't noticed I was in the room until right then.

Something flashed across his face, but it all moved too quickly for me to try and interpret it. There was a moment of slack-jawed calm that quickly morphed into tightly pressed lips squeezing against each other until they became slightly discolored. His eyes and mine were locked, and then it was as if his eyes could only focus inward.

Slow down, I thought. I could read him so well. I had *always* been able to read him well. The fact that I couldn't now made me feel as if I were caught in a tailspin—or at least I was witnessing one. *Just make your face stay put for half a second, Will!* I hated that I couldn't figure out what he was feeling, but not nearly as much as I hated that I cared.

"Where's Anna?" he abruptly asked—so instantaneously calm that the only logical conclusion I could reach was that I had completely imagined the tailspin.

"Um, she . . . I thought . . . I mean . . ." *Snap out of it!* I lectured myself before opening my mouth to try again. Thankfully Kevin beat me to the punch.

"I wanted Cadie here. So much of this is going

to require her approval that it just makes sense to cut out the middle man."

Will nodded. "Of course. Makes total sense. I was just expecting Anna, since she'd already been briefed on the event."

"And you must have just misheard the name a moment ago, Cadie." Kevin's eyes bore into me, and I understood that he was simultaneously frustrated with me and bailing me out. " 'Make Good, Do Good.' The project you were just given lead on."

Will looked at Kevin and then quickly back to me. "Great. I mean . . . that's . . . sure thing, boss. If you think . . . great." I saw his Adam's apple bounce up and down as he swallowed repeatedly.

Have you gone bonkers on me, Whitaker?

"Yep. Great," I stated calmly. Sure, I didn't know a single thing about the project I'd just been given lead on, but I wasn't too worried about it. When someone from The Bench was given lead on a project, it usually just meant someone from The Field needed a project manager. Or, more accurately, a babysitter with administrative skills. I'd have Anna fill me in as soon as I got back to my office. I just had to remain vague and noncommittal until then—and try not to get too caught up in trying to figure out why Will was acting as if he were struggling to chew a particularly tough cut of meat.

Kevin groaned softly. A groan that I interpreted

to mean, "This is why no one should ever date anyone they work with." My imagination's version of his thoughts made a good point.

"Okay, well, I think that's all," he finally said, standing from his chair. "You two call me from Staten Island."

"Sure thing," Will replied, and when I looked at him in response to his affirmation, I saw his Adam's apple going crazy again.

"*Who* two?" I asked in sudden panic. "*Us* two?"

"Dinner meeting with MLB's legal reps and some representatives from each division," Will answered quietly.

Oh no. No, no, no. "On Staten Island? Why would any meeting of people who *all* have their offices in Manhattan . . ." A low growl began making its way up through my torso. "Kevin, so sorry . . . can I speak to you for a moment?"

Just as before, those two sets of eyes were the only ones that mattered. My boss's eyes looked at me as if yet another head had been added to the cluster atop my neck, and my ex-boyfriend's . . . well, my ex-boyfriend's began busily looking around the room at absolutely anyone else.

"Now?" Kevin asked, more than a little annoyed with me, I was certain.

I nodded. "It's important."

He began walking out of the conference room, gesturing that I should follow. I picked up my things and walked out after him, down the hall-

240

way. When we reached his office, he entered in a huff. As soon as I had cleared the threshold, he slammed the door behind me.

"What is your problem today, McCaffrey?" he shouted.

I took a deep breath before softly saying, "I'm sorry. I really am. I don't have any excuse, but—"

"I'm not looking for an excuse, I'm looking for an explanation. I've known you for ten years and you've never once been as unprofessional and unprepared as you've been today."

"I know."

"You'd better know," he barked. "And if you know, you need to do something about it. I've tried to be understanding. I know it's been a tough few weeks for you and Will—"

"Oh, sure," I scoffed. "It's been a real tough time for the golden boy."

He put up his index finger in warning. "No. Sorry. I care about you, Cadie. You know that. I think the world of you, but you are not going to put me in the middle of the two of you at work."

I sighed. "That's not what I'm trying to do, Kevin. Really."

"I have all *sorts* of thoughts and feelings about you guys—together, apart, all of it. If you want to come over to the house sometime, we'll put some steaks on the grill and Larinda and I will gladly tell you everything we think about the two of you breaking up. Spoiler alert: you're both to blame.

But today? Today all I want to do is finalize plans for the biggest opportunity in the history of this network. I realize how uncomfortable it must be for you that Will is the guy at the center of it all, but that doesn't mean you can keep sending in Tennyson and Alvarez. It's time to get back to work, McCaffrey," he concluded definitively, obviously referring to so much more than the current meeting.

I quickly weighed my options. I did *not* want to go to Staten Island with Will, but there was no chance I was going to allow myself to be known as the one out of the two of us who couldn't handle it.

I sighed. "Of course. Sorry, Kev."

He held the door open for me and I made my way back into the hallway. I didn't get very far before he called after me, "And Cadie? On the ferry, be sure to ask Will to tell you what 'Make Good, Do Good' actually is. It's plain as day you didn't hear a word I said, but you're still the best one for the job—even when you're making it up as you go."

15

A Few Hours of Moving Forward
(or Moving Back)

Will sure hadn't expected his day to end this way—on the Staten Island Ferry, staring up at Lady Liberty, looking back at the lights of Manhattan, with Cadie by his side.

Well, Cadie on the same ferry, anyway. He'd lost track of her shortly after they left the dock at Whitehall in Manhattan. She was probably inside where it was warm, not to be seen again until they docked at St. George Terminal. November weather in Manhattan can be pretty unpredictable, sometimes swinging fifty degrees from noonday to shortly after sundown, but this day was just plain cold, all day long.

If he thought she was inside *just* to stay out of the cold, he'd probably be feeling a lot better about things.

"This isn't working," he muttered to himself over the railing, with only New York Harbor and the steam from his breath around to overhear.

He felt bad about Gordon. Really, he did. But

even if Gordon's face hadn't blown up like a balloon animal, he wasn't sure it would have made any difference. He sent her music every day, and she never said a word. And, unfortunately, he hadn't had a chance to be close enough to her to find out if her breath carried the scent of orange Tic Tacs. He was trying to convince Kevin to take part in some *13 Going on 30*–esque "Thriller" flash mob, but so far he wasn't having any luck—despite the fact that Ellis had tried to get it started in the lobby every single day since they watched that one.

I can only watch so many, he silently fumed. *I do have a job.*

Sweet Home Alabama and *The Proposal* hadn't given him much to work with. What was he supposed to do? Try and get them struck by lightning? Pretend he was Canadian and beg her to marry him so he didn't get deported? She'd probably buy him a Mountie hat and a one-way ticket to Niagara Falls.

"Or *over* Niagara Falls," he grumbled.

"Are you planning to jump?" Cadie's suddenly present voice behind him *did* make him jump a little, actually.

He chuckled and turned to face her. "No current plans."

"So, we've got about four minutes until we dock. Tell me what I need to know."

He couldn't imagine that anything would

ever hurt as much as her treating him like a coworker—and not even one she liked.

"Sure. 'Make Good, Do Good' is essentially going to be an All-Star game. American League versus National League. Basically the best of the best who *weren't* caught up in the scandal. It's a 'make good' for the fans and they'll 'do good' at the same time, by donating all of the proceeds to the newly formed MLB Anti-Doping Foundation."

She nodded in acknowledgment. "How much of all of this was your doing?"

He shrugged, wondering if there was any way to state the truth without sounding full of himself. "All of it, I guess." Probably not.

He swallowed down the onslaught of emotions—complicated, conflicting emotions—and worked very hard to maintain eye contact for as long as he possibly could. He tilted his head and studied her, trying to interpret every expression on her face. If he wasn't mistaken, she was attempting to do the same with him.

If only they were reaching the same conclusions.

She pulled her eyes away from his and cleared her throat. "It sounds like a great idea, Will. Really."

"Thank you," he replied softly.

In a hundred years, he would never get used to not being allowed to touch her.

She took a few steps forward and stood beside him—beside him, but distant—at the rail, staring out at Brooklyn across the bay. He turned to face the same view.

"What's tonight about?" she asked. "Working out logistics?"

"On paper maybe. Yeah, they'll send you back with some figures for the network, and I'll explain to them what *The Daily Dribble* has in mind for some of the exclusive lead-up coverage. But it's really more about convincing a few key people that I'm not out to ruin Major League Baseball—or any of their players, in particular. Kevin got this idea in his head that my career as an on-air sports personality will have more potential for long-term success if the major representatives for America's favorite pastime don't hate me right out of the gate. They're all a little gun-shy about working with me at the moment, it seems."

"I can't imagine why. I mean, you're only the guy solely responsible for there being no World Series for the first time since the strike in 1994."

He laughed. "Actually, I like to think that the guys injecting steroids into their bodies had a little something to do with it."

"Whatever it takes to ease your conscience."

He glanced over at her and was surprised to see a warm smile on her lips. It had been far too long since he'd had the pleasure. The frigid Atlantic wind blew strands of her russet hair across her face, momentarily masking her eyes and lips, alternately, and he desperately wanted to reach out and remove the interference. But he knew that once he touched her hair, her skin, the only thing stopping him from pulling her close and capturing her mouth would be *her,* and he just couldn't bear it.

"I'm proud of you, Will," she said softly. Emphatically. As she did, she took care of brushing her hair out of her face, removing one distraction. But her words had provided a new one. "So many people get ahead in this business by being underhanded and shady, and by ruining careers—ruining *lives*—without a second thought about how those people will survive. But you . . ."

Their New Yorker instincts simultaneously kicked in, and they grabbed the rail as their weight shifted from one foot to the other, and back again, as the ferry pulled in to the dock. The outside deck, which had been theirs alone, suddenly filled with passengers making their way to the exit, the tourists all commenting on the cold, as if they just hadn't seen it coming.

"Shall we?" she asked.

He wanted her to finish her thought. She was about to say something nice about him, and he wanted—*needed*—to hear it. But he quickly

247

realized he was okay settling for once again, even for a moment, being a part of *we* with her.

Three-and-a-half hours later, they were reboarding the Staten Island Ferry, the massive Andrew J. Barberi vessel having been traded out for the comparatively quaint Alice Austen, which ran during the less busy hours.

"That was the most fun I've ever had at a three-hour meeting," Cadie said with a laugh as they took their places along the rail.

"And that's saying something," Will joked. "You've been in three-hour meetings consisting of nothing but Enzo reading the whistleblower policy."

"Well, I mean apart from that, obviously."

"Obviously."

They stared at each other, and Will couldn't help but wonder if the past few hours had moved them forward in time or moved them back.

"You were fantastic, Cadie. I'm pretty sure Kevin's got his work cut out for him in the coming days. If MLB and the players' trade union haven't already begun making plans to steal you away from ASN, I'd be shocked."

And they wouldn't be the first to try. Cadie had gotten a *million* job offers. Every network, not to mention every other corporation inhabiting office space in a five-block radius, had attempted to steal her away through the years. She'd received countless offers she shouldn't have been able to refuse, and yet she always had. Everyone thought Ellis was the hotly sought-after commodity around ASN, but it was Cadie.

"Me?" She laughed again. Joyous. Free. "Are you kidding? I was just the designated pencil-pusher."

Will shook his head. "No, you were much more than that. You were in control of that room, Cadie. I bet Kevin gave you lead because he intends for you to be producer on this thing."

Laughter erupted out of her. "I don't think so. You know I've been telling him for years I have no interest in producing. I actually *like* being the pencil-pusher."

He knew that was true, and he knew how adamant she had always been about not wanting to have any part in the production side of things. But after seeing her at work on Staten Island, he could say with absolute certainty she was the right person for the job. He didn't think much of Kevin's chances when it came to convincing *her* of that, however.

"Besides, *you* were the one in control of the room, Will. As far as they're concerned, you're some new kid stepping on their toes, but within about five minutes, they all trusted you. You had them eating out of your hand. That was impressive stuff, Whitaker."

Should he say it? If there were ever a moment, this was it. Would it backfire? Would she step away? Would the joy and freedom—the warmth—fade away and be replaced by the freeze they'd been consumed by for weeks?

"I guess we actually make a pretty good team," she said, and he had to do a double take. The words had been in his thoughts, but they came out of her mouth. And in her soft, lilting voice, they held so much more power.

He smiled. "I guess we do." He was so torn between keeping it light and making sure he didn't miss the opportunity to take things deeper. "Good thing too. If we'd messed this up, Kev would've killed me."

"I think he would've killed *us*."

Will chuckled. "No, I don't think so. I'm pretty sure you can do no wrong in his eyes."

"He just knows he can trust me, and that suits him just fine—because that means he doesn't have to spend too much time thinking about the numbers. But *you?*" She whistled through her teeth. "You're the favorite."

Will's humility rose to the surface, along with his disbelief that his career had taken such a rapid acceleration toward success. He opened his mouth to respond in the same way he'd responded to *Sports Illustrated*: I'm just a guy doing what he loves who happened to be in the right subway car at the right time. But then he remembered who he was talking to. The one person who actually knew him.

"It's crazy, isn't it?" He laughed and turned to face her, his elbow on the railing. "I feel, for about twelve hours every day, like I'm just going to somehow screw it all up."

She smiled at him and mirrored his position. "And what about the other twelve hours?"

"Well, I'm asleep for eight of them . . ."

"I don't believe that for a second."

How well she knew him. "Okay," he relented. "I'm asleep for about five of them. For probably six of them I'm too busy to think about it. And then for one glorious hour each day, I think I've got this. I think I'm the right guy for the job."

She reached out and put her hand on his forearm. "Listen to that one, Will. That's the hour that's not lying to you."

He wondered if there was any way to use that moment to propel them past all the pain between them. He wanted to take her in his arms and make sure she understood how in love with her he was—how in love with her he would always be. He knew that if she understood that, they'd be able to work through the rest. The only thing stopping him from trying to propel them into the future was the overwhelming desire to not let the moment end. He hadn't realized until right then that if he could only be her friend, he'd take it. He'd never be satisfied, of course, but he'd take it.

She pulled her hand away gently. "Want to go inside? It doesn't look too crowded, and I'm pretty sure my face is about to freeze off."

A few hours earlier he'd have gone anywhere she asked, without question. A few hours earlier, he never would have expected to be invited.

"Thanks, but you go ahead," he replied. He watched the Statue of Liberty getting larger by the minute. "I can't ever quite pull myself away. At least not until my face freezes off."

She nodded and smiled, but she didn't walk away. She simply turned back toward the harbor and took in the view alongside him.

Please don't let me ruin this, Lord, Will silently prayed before clearing his throat. "Cadie, I'm sorry I got so focused on the job and lost sight of what was happening between us."

"Will—"

"No, please." He tilted his head to look at her and found she was doing the same toward him. "Please just let me say this."

She sighed and turned her attention back to the water, nodding as she did.

He took a deep breath. "I think I got it in my head that I wasn't good enough for you." Her head snapped around to look at him again, but she didn't say a word. "Actually, I *know* that's what happened. And I think I thought that if I could make some progress in my career, get ahead, get a better title, make more money—"

"I never cared about that stuff," Cadie inter-jected.

He nodded. "I know. I know that *now*, I guess. I think I got it in my head that only a certain type of guy could ever be worthy of you. The type of guy your parents would approve of. The type of guy you deserve. Because, that's the thing, Cadie. I think for a long time I thought I was trying to become the guy everyone else thought was good enough for you, but I was actually just trying to become the guy *I* thought was good enough for you. But that guy doesn't exist, as far as I'm concerned." He exhaled and watched his breath as it dissipated into the night. "I'd give anything if I could go back and focus on becoming the guy you needed me to be."

She chuckled—not the response he was expecting—and he turned to see what she found so funny.

"I think a tear literally just became a piece of ice on my face. I know that's not supposed to happen, because it's saltwater and all, but I *know* it's happening." Her laughter increased. "Maybe I've just become so coldhearted that I cry out ice."

"Maybe your tears are so pure that they're actually freshwater," he contributed.

"Yes! I like that explanation. Let's go with that."

The laughter died away but the smiles remained

253

on their faces as they faced each other, neither saying a word. Cadie sniffed and swiped away her icy tears as her smile became more subdued and a little sadder. She reached out to touch his arm again, as she had earlier, but Will caught her hand and pulled it against his chest, and then he brought his other hand up to join the cluster. Grasping her hand with both of his, he lifted it to his lips and planted a tender kiss on her knuckles.

Neither of them reacted to the feedback noise that began over the loudspeaker a moment later, though it was startlingly loud against the backdrop of the waves rushing beneath them, and the silence of Lady Liberty towering beside them.

"The Staten Island Ferry and the New York City Department of Transportation wish to extend a very special welcome to Murray and Sylvia Fliegelman of Brooklyn, New York, who met as children on the Staten Island Ferry, eighty-seven years ago, and tonight are celebrating their seventy-fifth wedding anniversary—along with their four children, thirteen grandchildren, and forty-two great-grandchildren."

"And seven great-great-grandchildren!" a voice called from inside.

Will and Cadie turned toward the voice and saw, through the glass, the entire Fliegelman family, hugging, laughing, and celebrating—Murray and Sylvia at the center of it all.

Cadie squeezed Will's hand and whispered, "Would you take a look at that."

"Murray and Sylvia," the announcer concluded, "this is for you."

The opening piano notes of Tony Bennett's "The Way You Look Tonight" squeaked their way out over the speakers, and as the frequency issues resolved themselves, Murray stood from his seat, put his hand out for his bride, and took her in his arms for a dance.

"Wow," Will exhaled.

He looked down at Cadie, her face still turned toward the Fliegelmans, her hand still in his, and he knew. Any little bit of lingering doubt was gone. Maybe they hadn't figured it out as young as Murray and Sylvia, so maybe they'd never celebrate seventy-five years and seven great-great-grandchildren, but they were just as real. Just as forever.

"Dance with me, Cadie," he said, not waiting for an answer before placing one hand on the small of her back and gently pulling her closer.

She pulled her attention away from the romance playing out twenty-five feet away and silently consented to being in Will's arms. Her eyes met his as she leaned into him and wrapped her free arm around his shoulders. Through a few bars of the music, they were strangers, holding each other for the first time with all of the awkwardness of two eighth graders at a school dance.

Then Cadie chuckled softly and a smile appeared on her face.

"What is it?" Will asked.

"I was just trying to remember the last time we danced together."

"Ellis's wedding."

She nodded and her smile grew wider. "Yes. Do you remember the time before that?"

He thought for a moment and then burst into laughter. "I'm pretty sure that was also an Ellis wedding."

"Maybe that's why we fell apart, Will. Ellis stopped getting married, and we forgot to dance."

They laughed together, and he spun her dramatically—and when he pulled her back, their bodies were close enough that even the cold winter air couldn't come between them, and the awkwardness was gone. She rested her head on his chest and pulled her hand from his, so she could throw her other arm around his shoulders, and he circled both of his arms around her waist, the familiar scent of lemon and sage overpowering his senses as her hair fluttered in the wind.

All thoughts of Murray and Sylvia were gone. The song was for them. The entire night was just for them.

He felt her pull away in his arms—just slightly—and he wanted to hold her tighter. *No. Not yet. This can't be over already.* But he allowed her the space he instinctively knew she was desiring, and he looked down at her, ready to beg her not to go. But the intensity in her eyes was so different from anything he'd expected, anything he'd feared. She didn't want less of him. She wanted more, and he was more than happy to oblige.

Will brushed his thumb across her chin, and it landed on her jaw as the rest of his hand wrapped around the back of her neck. One corner of his mouth rose in a smile as her lips separated and her breathing grew heavy and a little ragged.

As he prepared to kiss her, silently vowing to never go that long without kissing her again, a tiny snowflake fell on her nose. And then another. And another. Will's half-smile took over his entire face in response to the girlish giggle making its way out of her parted lips. He tore his eyes away from hers and looked up at the diminutive white specks against the dark gray sky, eerily lit up by the approaching lights of lower Manhattan.

He looked back down at Cadie, and everything had changed. The anticipation in her eyes had been replaced by accusation, and the soft expectation of her lips was a distant memory. Her mouth formed a tightly clenched line, broken only slightly by the tremble of her chin.

"Cadie, what's wrong?"

At first there were no words, only a dramatic release of air as she abruptly pulled out of his arms.

"What's wrong?" he repeated. "Are you okay?" He reached out for her, but she recoiled at the nearness of him.

"How stupid do you think I am?" She shook her head. "How stupid *am* I?"

"What are you talking about? What in the world happened?"

She rubbed her eyes and continued shaking her head as a groan escaped. "I know them all!" she shouted. "I can't believe I fell for this."

He threw his hands up in the air. "Fell for *what?*"

"What comes next? You're a bird, I'm a bird? This is real life, Will. All our problems don't go away because you buy me a snow globe of Florence or a new diary so I can make a fresh start!" She was shaking from head to toe, but her voice was strong. "You didn't have me at hello, and you don't complete me. I am perfectly complete without you. How *dare* you interfere in my life and act as if I'm not? You had no right to do that. So tell me. Tell me what comes next."

The ferry docked at Whitehall and they each instinctively secured their footing. Will knew his posture was the only thing about him that was stabilized. He reached out one more time, hoping to grab her arm and pull her aside from departing passengers, but as the snow fell more rapidly and the wind grew fiercer, he lost her in a swarm of Fliegelmans.

16

From Friday Night to 3:15

H e's going to try to talk you out of it, you
know," Darby said with a sigh, early the
following Monday morning.

"I know."

I nodded but remained otherwise unaffected
by the thought. I was completely aware that
Kevin would be shocked to receive my resignation, and yes, he would no doubt try to talk me
out of leaving ASN. But I wouldn't be moved.
Things had gotten out of hand, and I'd had
enough.

"Can you hand me that vase over on the book-
shelf?" I asked her as I continued cramming my
things into a banker's box.

She handed me the vase. "I think you're making
a mistake. I think you need to take some time to
think about it."

"I took all weekend to think about it! How can
I possibly stay here? This crossed a line, and I
think you agree with me on that, whether you
care to admit it or not."

"If what you think happened actually happened,

260

of course it crossed a line. But I don't know. It doesn't really make sense to me."

I placed the newspaper-wrapped vase in the box and threw my hands in the air. "Whose side are you on, anyway?"

She smiled and replied with our oft-used phrase as she handed me a figurine that needed to be wrapped and packed. "Yours. Always yours."

"It was all such a setup, and I felt like an idiot for not recognizing it sooner. I mean, the Staten Island Ferry? Of course. We're Kate Hudson and Matthew McConaughey in *How to Lose a Guy in 10 Days*. And then dancing on a boat to *The Way You Look Tonight*? Now we're Julia Roberts and Dylan McDermott—"

"Dermot Mulroney."

"Whatever. It's *My Best Friend's Wedding*. I haven't figured out the sweet little Jewish couple yet, but I'm sure it's something. I'm just wondering how much they had to pay all those people. And the snow? I mean, come on!"

"Oh, now you're just being ridiculous. Will and Kevin planned the snow, did they?"

"For the golden boy? I'm sure the network would see what they could do."

She chuckled. "Okay, let's say for a moment that all of that is true—"

"It is."

"And that Will planned all of that in a huge, last-ditch attempt to win you back."

261

"He did," I stated and then yielded—just a bit. "Maybe not the snow."

"Well then, Cadie McCaffrey, I think that's just about the most romantic thing I've ever heard in my entire life."

I scoffed. "If your ex and your boss getting together to sabotage your career is what you find romantic—"

"If giving you a great opportunity to excel on a major project that everyone else in this office would kill to be a part of is what you call sabotage . . ."

"That's not the point!" I didn't know how to explain my feelings further. I only knew that it was a huge violation of trust, and I wasn't sure how to recover from that.

She exhaled and sat on the edge of the desk. "Look, I hear you. I do. But it *was* romantic."

I joined her on the desk as tears began pooling in my eyes. I was so angry. So hurt. And so upset with myself that I couldn't stop thinking about how good it felt to be held by him again. Will and his ferry, and the intensity in his eyes, his explanation of where his mind had been for a year—of where *he* had been for a year—and his blasted Fliegelmans.

You weak, sappy pushover.

I nodded. "In the moment? You bet it was. But," I repeated, "it crossed a line."

"So tell him that. Tell Kevin that. Make it clear

you won't stand for it. But the fact of the matter is Kevin would have wanted you on the project anyway. You *know* that."

"I can't be sure of *what* I know anymore, Darby, and that's the point."

I hopped down from the desk and grabbed more newspaper from the pile to continue wrapping up ten years of history at a job I loved.

"I quit, Kevin." As I said the words, I felt the weight of the world lifting off my shoulders. "I can't do this anymore. I'm really sorry. Do what you want, of course, but I strongly recommend Darby as my replacement. She's competent, loyal, and I've already taught her everything I know. If you want to require I give notice, I will, but I have a ton of leave stored up, and I think we both know that the sooner I'm out of here, the sooner everyone can—"

"What are you talking about?" he asked as he shut his office door.

"This is what I need to do. I think you know that just as well as I do."

"No. No, I don't," he replied, his voice forceful but his face bewildered. He grabbed the resignation letter from my hands and dropped it to the floor beside us before reaching out, taking my hand, and pulling me with him to the leather couch in the center of his enormous office. As we sat he said, "Talk to me, Cadie. It hasn't really come to this, has it? I'm sure we can work something out so that you don't actually have to interact with him."

"This isn't about Will," I insisted, hanging on to my adamant assertions that I wouldn't give up a job I loved because of a boy.

Of course it *was* about Will, but it was also about Kevin. And integrity. And professionalism. And I was prepared to tell him all of that, but he started talking again before I had the chance.

"Maybe you *were* onto something by sending in Tennyson and Alvarez. Actually . . ." He jumped from his seat and began pacing near the south-facing window that covered an entire wall. Suddenly he turned back to face me. "You're due for a promotion. You're overdue, actually. Maybe it's time to move you up to the 92nd floor."

It's funny how you can be completely confident about a decision one second and the next wonder what you could have possibly been thinking.

"Kevin, I . . . wow . . . I appreciate that. Really."
Really.

He hunkered down next to me on the couch again. "It really is overdue, and if it means we don't lose you, well . . . now's the time."

The 92nd floor. The corporate office. More money, a better title, more authority, and seven floors between Will and me. It was very tempting.

But then my mind was flooded with the memory of one of the best nights of my career—

not to mention one of the most romantic moments of my life—and I felt like a fool once again.

I shook my head and forced a smile. "I can't do it, and it's really not because my ex-boyfriend works here. It's just time for me to move on. I'm very grateful for all of the opportunities and for all the support you've given me through the years."

"You're really doing this? This is for real?" I nodded that it was, and he placed his hand on mine. "And there's nothing I can say to change your mind?"

I held on to his hand and was filled with affection for him. Oh, I was still furious that he had gone along with Will's harebrained ferry scheme, of course, but as my emotions tempered, I was increasingly aware that it had been just that. *Will's* harebrained ferry scheme. Kevin was just an ill-advised accomplice.

Unfortunately, that awareness didn't take away any of the reasons I had to leave.

I sniffed. "I'll never be able to thank you enough, for everything. You've created something special here, with *The Daily Dribble* and all you're doing for the network. I'm proud that I got to be a part of it. But it's time."

Kevin rubbed his face with his hands and grumbled as he stood from the couch. "Go clean out your desk and get out of here. I'm heading into the staff meeting, and I'm going to talk very slowly to give you some time to leave the building. I'll call HR to meet you on The Bench." He looked at his watch. "I figure you've got about an hour, so don't dawdle. Once those people in there find out you've quit—and especially once a certain someone finds out—I can't be held responsible for the aftermath, so—"

"Thank you." I stood up and threw my arms around his waist. He towered over me as he wrapped his arms around my shoulders and held me tight for a moment.

"Keep in touch, okay? I mean it. Maybe if we're not working together every day we can actually find time to talk once in a while."

I pulled back and wiped away my running mascara before it got on his suit jacket. "I will." I grabbed my resignation letter from the floor and handed it to him.

"Tennyson?" he asked.

"Absolutely. Anna is great, and her day will come, but Darby's ready. Anna will be louder and more determined to get ahead, while Darby will happily keep doing whatever you ask of her. But she really is ready. And you know what? She'll make an amazing producer someday. And *she* actually wants it."

Kevin chuckled. "Got it. Anything else?"

I shook my head. "No. I think that's it." I spun on my heel and reached for the doorknob, but I stopped before grabbing it. "Actually, yes.

Despite everything . . ." I sighed and faced him one more time. "You're right to throw everything into supporting Will. Right now he's going on adrenaline and a fear of missing his opportunity, but at some point he's going to get lost in his head. He's going to doubt . . . everything. Don't let him take himself too seriously, okay? You need to build him up while still keeping his head from getting too big. That's the key. Stay with him through it. Don't give up on him."

"Forgive me, but I kind of feel like telling you the same thing."

I nodded, completely understanding everything he was saying and everything he *wasn't* saying. But I also understood that nothing about my decision to leave ASN—or my decision to leave Will—had anything to do with giving up.

"The important thing, Kevin, is that I've finally made the decision to not give up on myself."

I extended as high as I could on my tiptoes and kissed him on the cheek, and then I hurried out of his office before he could tell me how pretentious I sounded.

Sometimes the truth is pretentious.

"Hey," Anna greeted me as I walked back into the accounting suite. "I got the liability waiver back from Ellis for him to parachute into Wembley for that stadium special, but he's wondering if Will should do it instead."

I had gotten pretty good at appearing unaffected by the constant stream of Will news through the office, but that one took me by surprise. I stopped in my tracks and did a double take.

"Will? Why would Will do it?"

I knew it wasn't my responsibility any longer, and I knew I had to let Anna know that, but first I needed to know what the heck she was talking about.

"Ellis said he thinks it would be good to take advantage of Will's popularity right now. A spectacle like that could go a long way toward letting audiences know that he's not just the smart guy making headlines for asking the tough questions. He's also fun and entertaining." A smile spread across her face as she handed me Ellis's signed waiver. "Although, if I know Will, he probably begged Ellis to let him go."

I felt as if I had no choice but to discredit that theory. It was my moral obligation. "Not likely. He's not a fan of heights, so I really don't think—"

She interrupted me with her laughter. "Are you kidding me? Not a fan of heights? Ever since we went indoor rock climbing a couple weeks ago, he's been trying to get a group together to go climb Mount Marcy in the Adirondacks. I don't think heights are a problem for him, Cadie." She smiled and began heading back to her desk. As she walked she glanced at her watch and asked, "The network meeting's at 3:15, right?"

"Um, yeah, but I think Darby's got it," I replied, unintentionally forgetting to tell her I no longer worked there and would not be in said network meeting. The world had abruptly stopped making sense.

"Are you sure?" she asked. "I've been developing a pretty strong rapport with the guys, so if you want me to—"

"I said Darby's got it!" I cut her off sharply and then caught myself. I didn't even know if that was true, and it certainly wasn't my call to make. I took a deep breath. "Sorry. I didn't mean to snap. I appreciate it. Really. But the truth is—"

"I can tag along."

I saw Darby stand from her desk, behind Anna's. Her eyes were wide, and she was looking at me as if I were a lion, and she were my tamer— and she just wasn't sure if she could get between me and my prey in time.

"I really need you here," Darby said, and Anna turned to face her. "I'm pretty sure the ratings composites are going to hit my desk in the next fifteen minutes or so, and we're going to have to dive in. That will be the priority for the rest of the day."

Anna turned back to me. "Is that okay?"

Hopefully "the guys" can live without you. "Sure. Thanks." That was all I could manage.

I began walking toward my soon-to-be-cleaned-out office, eyes straight ahead. As I passed Darby I simply said, "Now," to which she replied, "Yep," and followed me into my office and shut the door behind her.

"What was that?" I asked breathlessly as soon as we were alone. "What in the world was that?"

"I was going to ask you the same thing. What happened? I didn't hear much, I just saw the expression on your face."

"She went indoor climbing. With *Will!*"

Leaning against the wall, I forced myself to take a deep breath and let it out slowly. That didn't make me feel any better so I repeated the pattern. Still nothing.

Darby's eyes filled with compassion—no-nonsense compassion. "Okay."

"Now she 'knows' him?" I asked rhetorically, snide air quotes running amok. "She has a 'rapport' with 'the guys'? When did that happen?"

"It's been more than a month, Cadie."

"Yes, but for weeks he's been ridiculously attempting to win me back. Friday night he was dancing with *me*. Almost kissing *me!*"

My best friend shrugged. "You know I love you, but I think you really need to push pause for a second and remember all that's involved in that *almost*. He's been attempting, but you haven't been letting him get very far."

"Whose side are you on, anyway?"

"Yours. Always yours."

Tears pooled in my eyes. She was right. Of course she was right.

I groaned and shook my head. "I'm just emotional. After everything."

She nodded. "Totally understandable."

"It's really not that I even care," I explained. "It's just . . . you know . . . I didn't see it coming. More accurately, I hadn't given it any thought at all."

"You hadn't given *what* any thought? The idea of Will with someone else?"

Will. With someone else. Someone who wasn't me.

How could I explain it without sounding crazy? How could I explain that while being absolutely resolute in my decision that Will and I should not be together, there had also not been one moment in which I imagined either of us ending up with anyone else?

Come to that, how could I explain it to myself?

"Yeah. I just hadn't really thought of it," I said as casually as I could. I offered her a dogged smile and then grabbed a tissue and dug a mirror out of my purse to begin pulling myself together. "It's a relief, really, now that I think about it. I'm free. If he's dating Anna, I'm completely off the hook."

"Off the hook from what?"

"I don't know," I said with a sigh, throwing the mirror back into my bag and grabbing my iPad and setting it in the box of my belongings. "The feeling that we would always be connected, I guess. The feeling that if I bumped into him at some restaurant in SoHo it would be awkward."

She laughed. "Oh, suddenly that feeling is gone, is it?"

Who was I kidding? Certainly not Darby, and probably not myself. It would always be awkward, regardless of whether or not he was dating Anna Alvarez, or anyone else.

Note to self: learn how to cook so you never have to eat out again.

17

*About an Hour Later
(the Aftermath)*

"Okay, everybody," Will concluded as he closed his binder and looked around the table. "Good work. If you have any questions, you know where to find me."

Everyone stood to go, but the deep, commanding voice of their boss at the head of the table caused them to freeze.

"Before you go, there's one more thing," Kevin said, pretty softly by his standard. But with Kevin it wasn't about the volume—it was about the authority and respect he carried amongst his staff. Everyone was immediately seated once again.

Will, for one, hadn't even bothered to get out of his chair at what he thought was the end of the meeting. His work was only beginning, and he was scheduled to be in attendance at two more meetings in that very conference room before the end of the day. He knew better than to hold out hope that Kevin's "one more thing" announcement included news that either of those meetings were cancelled. In fact, he was fairly certain that whatever Kevin was about to say would somehow result in more work. It seemed like lately no one could open their mouth without it resulting in more work for him.

It's what you've always wanted, he reminded himself—grateful to be kept busy on this day in a way he rarely had been before.

Once the room had quieted back down, Kevin calmly stated, "Effective immediately, Cadie McCaffrey is no longer an employee of ASN. Succession determinations will be made in the coming days. For now, if you run into something that can't wait, talk to me. My plan is to have a memo out to everyone by tomorrow with some info on who will be running point on various projects—at least temporarily. If you're in touch with Cadie, just know that we parted on the best of terms, and everyone here is so grateful for the contributions she made as a longtime valuable member of this team. Questions?"

"That's impossible!" Will exclaimed with a laugh. He wasn't sure *why* he was laughing, but then he really didn't seem to have any control over anything anymore. "What—what—what are you even saying? What is that even supposed to mean?"

A stunned silence had overtaken the room in response to Kevin's announcement, but the silence deepened and grew nervous in light of Will's slightly unhinged outburst.

"Okay, thanks, everyone," Kevin said gently. "That's all."

As everyone apart from Kevin and Will stood to go, soft murmurs replaced the silence. The momentum and energy that had been coursing through the room moments earlier had been sapped by the news of Cadie's departure. After all, no one around that table had been at ASN longer—not even Kevin. The announcement likely came as a sad surprise to the entire staff.

But there was nothing like a well-timed torrent of unprofessional emotion to pick things up again.

Will remained in his seat, still staring at Kevin, though he was fully aware that as his coworkers left they all watched *him*—no doubt hoping he would shout again or maybe punch the wall or something before they lost line of sight. He didn't have time to be bothered by the busybodies and the inevitable churning of the gossip mill. He was just waiting for the unexpected twist or the punch line, or whatever *had* to be coming.

Kevin stood and reached out to press the intercom button on the phone in the center of the table. "Miranda, will you please let Ellis know we're ready for him?" While still holding down the button, he glanced at the clock on the wall. "We may need to order some takeout. I'll check with Ellis and Will and get back to you. Thanks."

Cadie McCaffrey is no longer an employee of ASN.

Will played the words over and over in his mind, attempting to make sense of them. He'd fully expected Kevin to announce that she'd been taken off the "Make Good, Do Good" project. That wouldn't have surprised him in the least after everything that had occurred between them on Friday—*whatever* that was. But this?

The door to the conference room opened and Ellis appeared. "About time you guys finished up." He shut the door behind him and then joined Kevin and Will at the table. "I'm starving. If you want me to be at all productive, I'm going to need some food here in the next twenty minutes." Ellis looked at his two friends at the table—from one to the other and then back again. Neither said a word. "What? What's going on?"

The tension built for a few seconds more and then Will jumped up from his seat. "When were you going to tell me?" he shouted at Kevin.

"It literally *just* happened—"

"You expect me to believe that?" Will scoffed. "The woman doesn't take an early lunch without sending a memo."

Kevin raised his hands helplessly. "Be that as it may, it's the truth. I came straight in here after meeting with her. She quit about an hour ago."

"Who quit?" Ellis asked. "What did I miss?"

Will had his hands on the headrest of the rolling

chair he'd been sitting in, and his fingers were digging into the leather more forcefully by the second. He felt his anger and regret bubbling to the surface, and all he could think of was every single thing he should have done differently.

"Why didn't you *stop* her?" He pushed down on the chair, sending it careening into the dry-erase board on the wall before tipping over and landing on its side.

Kevin kicked his own chair out from under him as he stood and issued a warning. "Son, you need to calm down."

"Cadie quit?" Ellis asked. "Oh, man. I didn't even get to say goodbye. Is she still here?"

Will's eyes flew open. One more regret for the list. Had he wasted too much time? He hurried to the door, not willing to let one more second pass.

"She's not here, Will!" Kevin called out after him as he ran down the hall.

Will heard him, but there was no way he wasn't going to check it out himself. There was no way he wasn't going to do all he could to catch her before it was too late. Until she turned in her keys, until she did her exit interview, until Human Resources submitted the termination paperwork. Until all of those things happened, he still had a chance to convince her she'd made a horrible mistake. He was sure Kevin and ASN would take her back in a heartbeat.

In less than a minute he was crossing the common area between The Field and The Bench, and two hallways later he was running into the accounting suite.

"Hey, Will!" Anna greeted him from her desk. "Is everything okay?"

"Where is she?" he huffed.

"Who?"

"Cadie. Is she still here?"

She couldn't have left without saying good-bye. Without saying *something*. She wouldn't do that.

Anna bit her lip as she stood and walked over to him. "You didn't hear? Wow, I'm really sorry to have to be the one to tell you—"

"No, I know!" he said with an involuntary groan. *Stop it,* he lectured himself. *Anna's not the one you're angry with.* "Sorry. I didn't mean to . . . sorry, Anna. I'm just—"

"Will?"

He heard the voice coming from Cadie's office, and for the most fleeting of moments he was optimistic. When he looked up and saw Darby standing in the doorway, he knew for sure he was too late.

"Can I get you something?" Anna asked, her voice rich with concern. "You don't look so great."

He wasn't trying to be rude, but he didn't have time for Anna. He really didn't. "Darby?

What . . . I mean, why did she . . . why didn't . . ."

"Come on back, Will," Darby kindly commanded.

He walked past the other desks that he'd passed so many times through the years. He'd never really taken note of any of them. Sure, he'd always said hello to whoever was present, and he and Darby had shared all sorts of ridiculous secret handshakes that had been exchanged through the years, but he was always focused on that moment when he would round the corner, step into Cadie's office, and see her.

This time, his attention was drawn to each desk, and the containers full of orange Tic Tacs that sat on all of them. Pain erupted into rage when he spotted Anna's desk and a stack of CDs he'd spent hours creating. With the back of his hand he sent the stack crashing to the ground, and countless little orange candies went flying through the air.

He owed Anna another apology, but right then he knew he couldn't trust any words that might come out of his mouth.

"Will, come on," Darby commanded again, a bit more sternly.

He walked into Cadie's office, and rage gave way to sadness. "How is it already empty?"

Empty was an exaggeration, of course. Everything work-related was still present. Filing cabinets, a computer and papers on the desk, chairs and a coatrack. All that was missing were any signs that Cadie had ever been there.

Empty.

"Let's sit," Darby said as she shut the door behind them and grabbed his hand to pull him to the two chairs on the near side of the desk. "Can I get you some water or something? Anna's right. You're really pale."

He shook his head. "What happened? Friday night went so well . . . until it didn't. And I have no idea what changed. Whatever it was, it couldn't have been worthy of *this*. Did she get another job? Where's she going to be? I totally understand if she got a better offer or something, but it's not like her to not even give notice."

Darby sat back in her chair and tilted her head as she studied him. The silent contemplation continued a long time, and enough curious expressions passed across her face that Will began to worry. What had he said? What had he done? Why in the world was she looking at him that way?

Finally, a sad smile began to form on her lips, and he had to ask. "What?"

"You're such a good guy, and I'm sorry things didn't work out. I really am. But you know I can't tell you anything. That's not my place—"

"You're her best friend!"

She nodded. "Exactly. And I never should have interfered in the first place."

"You mean the list?" he asked. "That's . . . yeah, I need to go back to the movies, I guess. Maybe you can help me figure out which ones in particular—"

"No, Will." Darby grabbed his hands to cut him off. "No. That was a bad idea. I'm sorry. I thought it would be good, but . . ." She took a deep breath and squeezed his hands firmly. "It's over. She's out there today, starting her new life. It's time to let her go."

18

Three Weeks Later
(When Cadie _Actually_ Started Her New Life)

"Nope. No, Darby, you can't let Enzo get into that habit with you."

"But he said—"

"Oh, let me guess what he said. Depending on the mood he was in, I'm pretty sure it was either, 'Swoosh and I see eye-to-eye on this,' or 'I know you don't understand the precedents at play, but I don't have time to explain the law to you. This isn't _Boston Legal._'"

She laughed. _"How to Get Away with Murder,_ but yeah."

I touched the button on the screen to put the call on speaker and then set my phone down on the couch beside me so I could pull on my pantyhose. _Pantyhose!_ Ugh. Though I had undoubtedly dressed for success every single day of my career at ASN, I had long ago begun wearing slacks most days. In addition to plain practicality, wearing slacks had also carried with it the joy of only requiring the appropriate-for-grandmas but non-chafing-and-less-restrictive knee-high stockings. Reinforced toe and all. Alas, not today.

"At least he stays up on his legal shows. Before me it was probably *Ally McBeal*, and *LA Law* before that."

"So he's playing me?" she asked with a sigh.

"He's totally playing you, Darb, but don't sweat it. It's not personal. That's just Enzo. He's going to test the waters and see what he can get away with." I stood and pulled my pantyhose up over my hips and then lowered my dress back into place and smoothed the creases. "Everything else going okay?"

Her side of the call was so quiet that I wondered for a moment if I had lost her.

"When you ask that," she finally said, "what are you asking?"

I chuckled as I grabbed the phone from the couch and carried it with me into my walk-in closet to slip on my shoes. "I'm asking if everything else is going okay."

"But do you mean work, or—"

"Since when do you and I have to clarify which aspect of our lives we're talking about? We just talk, right?" She was silent again, and the line suddenly felt tense. "I don't have time to explain friendship to you. This isn't *Friends*."

She giggled, and the tension disappeared as quickly as it had arrived. "You're right. Although . . ." She cleared her throat. "It is a little bit like after Ross and Rachel broke up. You know?"

"It's fine." I stepped into my best black pumps and took one last look in the mirror on the back of the door before grabbing my purse and returning to the main room. I took her off speaker and put the phone to my ear. "I don't want you to feel weird about it. I mean, I don't know that I need updates on his personal life or anything, and *please* don't tell me if he and Anna climb Kilimanjaro, but I'm good with the work stuff. Really."

"For the record, I still don't think anything is going on between him and Anna."

"La la la la la!" If I'd been talking to her in person I would have plugged my ears with my fingers to further demonstrate my point. "I just said I don't need updates on his personal life."

"I know!" She laughed and talked louder—probably in case I did actually have my fingers jammed in. "But this isn't an update—it's a retraction."

"Even if that's true, it doesn't change a thing, Darb. I refuse to be that girl who doesn't want a guy but doesn't want anyone else to have him, either."

"I get that," she replied. "I just think that if you guys had actually tried to talk things through—"

"He *did* try, remember? And I would have none of it."

My three weeks of unemployed solitude had allowed me to do a lot of thinking, and the one thought I kept coming back to time and time again was that none of it was simple. Yes, I probably should have been more open to talking with him—after we slept together, after we broke up, before I quit ASN. But looking at all of that through the lens of hindsight, with the luxury of distance and a few weeks of healing, could make it all appear so much simpler than it actually was.

If only we'd talked. If only we hadn't had sex. If only I'd focused, in the moment, on the great lengths he was going to, attempting to win me back. If only I'd kissed him on the Staten Island Ferry.

Those were all very good *if onlys,* and it was an appealing notion—the thought of letting the *if onlys,* in all their simplicity, overtake the more complicated truths. Because romance is one thing, and God's grace is bigger than our sin, but I still had no idea if Will truly loved me quite enough to want to spend the rest of his life with me, or if his attempts to win me back stemmed from guilt and regret and a desire to turn back time.

Again, simplicity was very appealing. Maybe we *could* turn back time. Put God back into our relationship where we'd set him aside. Maybe we could both forgive—each other, ourselves—and find a way to pick up where we left off. Only now we'd be a little wiser. A little more cautious. A little more appreciative of what we'd always loved about each other, and what had made us so good together. Maybe we'd even be engaged, if that's what he thought it would take. But if I still couldn't be sure that he loved me enough for a shared vision of *forever,* how long would it be until *more* turned into *still not enough?*

I shook my head. For my own benefit, I guess. "Darb, can I ask you a question?"

"Of course."

I took a deep breath and prepared to unleash a few of my solitary thoughts. "Do you think God has specific people he wants us to be with?"

"Yes," she replied without hesitation. "Mine is Prince Harry."

I blinked. "Um, not sure if you heard, but he's kind of married now. Don't feel bad about not knowing. It was just a small, quiet wedding that didn't really get a lot of press coverage . . ."

"Well, you didn't ask if I thought God was going to *get* us together, just if he *wanted* us together."

I laughed as I grabbed my keys and walked outside, locking my front door behind me. I turned right and began walking down Bleecker Street.

"But seriously?"

I heard her sigh. "Seriously . . . I don't know. I mean, I don't think God plays matchmaker or anything. But I guess since he can see the whole plan and the whole big picture, it makes sense to think he knows which relationships will lead to the best outcomes."

"That's where I keep landing too. And I keep thinking maybe Will just isn't my best outcome." I rounded the corner onto Christopher Street. "I'm going to have to run. I'm about to go underground."

"Okay. Good luck! Remember, you don't owe anyone anything. You've already got two other offers—"

"One of them is on the other side of Queens. That doesn't even count."

"And about twenty-nine other interviews lined up."

"Seven."

"So if they don't offer you what you deserve, you need to walk away."

"If they don't offer me what I deserve, they'll probably just remind me that they paid for my apartment, and college, and my braces . . ."

She sighed. "Be that as it may, you're just going to hear what they have to say. You really don't have to take the job if it isn't something you want."

"I know. But the pay for my unused leave is going to run out pretty soon. I need to figure something out."

"You took a week to relax, you took a week to

submit resumes, and you took a week to field calls from every single company you sent a resume to. You're not exactly desperate yet, Cadie. You *do not* have to take this job." She sighed again. "I'm worried you're going to somehow get stuck with this job. Are you sure you don't want me to go with you?"

"I'm fine!" I laughed. "But thank you. I'll see you tonight?"

"Yep. Thoroughly looking forward to getting all Maniloony with you."

I took one step back from the stairs descending to the Christopher Street Station to move out of the way of a string quartet attempting to maneuver their instruments through the crowd.

"I appreciate it, Darb. Really."

"Not a big deal. I like Barry Manilow as much as the next girl," she professed.

"No, you don't."

"Not if *you're* the next girl, no. But as much as most girls I would be next to, probably . . ."

"See? I don't even need a boyfriend. I've got you! Will would never in a million years be caught at a Barry Manilow concert. And that was *before* he became someone who people recognize. Now? Not a chance."

"But he did give you the tickets," she countered.

"Gift-giving was never Will's problem." Even as I said the words the image of a conspicuously empty antique ring box floated through my mind as Defense Exhibit A, but that well-intentioned misfire was an exception to the rule. "But how many sports bars did I go to? How many ball games? How many times did I watch *Field of Dreams*?"

"You like *Field of Dreams*."

"Of course I like *Field of Dreams*. But I don't necessarily believe that all of life's lessons can be found in *Field of Dreams*. I don't get choked up every time Ray Kinsella and his dad play catch."

"Then something is wrong with you." She was quiet for a moment before adding, "Do you think that's why Will cares about baseball so much?"

"What do you mean?"

"I guess I would just assume that he loves *Field of Dreams* because it's a baseball movie, but maybe with his dad dying, and that movie meaning so much to him with the father/son stuff . . . maybe that's where his love of baseball comes from."

"Whose side are you on, anyway?" I asked with a chuckle, even if the chuckle was more than a little forced, as I realized there was a very good chance there was at least a little something to Darby's theory.

"Yours," she replied. "Always yours."

"That's better. See you tonight."

She stopped me before I could hang up. "Why don't you meet me at the office? It's practically on the way—"

"From Syosset?"

"Well, *nothing* is on the way from Syosset, but at least we can ride over together."

No matter how desperately I did not want to drop by ASN three weeks after my grand declaration of independence, the siren call of shared cab fare to Brooklyn was irresistible.

"Okay. I'll call you from the lobby."

It had been at least a year since I had visited my parents at work. The last time I had walked into their network's studios they hadn't even been located in Syosset but rather in that exotic Long Island hamlet known as Cold Spring Harbor.

Truthfully, there is nothing exotic at all about Cold Spring Harbor, but I'd always had a fascination with the name—probably because it was the name of a Billy Joel album. I suppose that wasn't enough to entice my mother. After years of suffering the garish thirteen-minute commute through meticulously cared-for tree-lined roads, she'd convinced the network to build a satellite location in Syosset. It had been well worth their investment, of course, to keep their biggest star happy.

"Cadie, is that you?" Eileen Hardwick greeted me the moment I walked through the door. "I didn't know you were stopping by."

Eileen had been my mom's personal assistant for three decades or so, though my mom didn't

290

refer to her that way. She thought it was pretentious to have a personal assistant. She seemed to see nothing pretentious, however, in asking her "prayer partner" to fetch her coffee and pick up her dry cleaning.

"Hi, Eileen." I opened my arms to receive her hug. "I can't say with absolute certainty that Mom knew I was coming. I actually have an appointment with my dad."

"Look at you." She was smiling from ear to ear. "You look gorgeous. Absolutely beautiful." I opened my mouth to thank her for the generous compliment, but before I could get a word out she added, "I imagine the eligible bachelors are just lined up at your door now."

Instead of the intended expression of appreciation, a groan escaped. "She told you?"

"That's really cute that you thought there was a chance she wouldn't." She winked and squeezed my hand before gesturing that I should follow her. "Can I safely assume that you're here to interview for a job?"

I sighed, as I had every single time I'd thought about it since two days earlier when my dad had convinced me to at least discuss it with him. "You can. But I'm thinking it's not a great idea."

"I'm thinking it's a *horrible* idea!" She entered her code into the key pad on the door and pushed it open once the whirring of the gears ceased.

"So tell me, how do we feel about the guy?"

"What do you mean?"

"I mean, is he a dirty rotten scoundrel and I should boo and hiss whenever his name is mentioned, or is he the one who got away and I should bow my head in reverence and say a little prayer that it's not too late?"

I laughed in spite of myself. "Probably somewhere in between. Maybe he is the one who got away, but I don't think the prayers are necessary. It's definitely too late."

She stopped walking, and I followed her lead. She turned to face me and said, "Are you sure? If you want me to pray for a miracle—"

"No!"

I didn't mean for my no to burst out with as much vehemence as it did, but I had to shut that down before Eileen got to work. "Prayer partner" may have been a deceptive title for Eileen's paid position on my parents' staff, but that didn't change the fact that she was a fierce prayer warrior whose unceasing faith I had always admired.

I shook my head, embarrassed, and began to apologize and explain my outburst, but Eileen began laughing.

"Jill Golding had the same look on her face when I offered to pray for her to get pregnant."

"Didn't Jill Golding have her tubes tied a couple of years ago?" I asked.

She shrugged. "All things are possible with God."

The smile on her face, followed by another wink, allowed me to feel comfortable enough to giggle freely without insulting her. But I stopped giggling as I thought to myself, *Not all things, of course.*

As soon as the thought entered my mind, guilt washed over me. My eyes flashed to Eileen, so afraid that her spiritual spidey senses had somehow detected my thought, which I was pretty sure was blasphemous. Thankfully she didn't seem to notice that anything had changed.

"You can go on back," she said, pointing to my dad's office at the end of the hallway. "I'll let him know you're here."

"Thanks, Eileen," I muttered the best I could through my lips, which were clenched to within an inch of their life.

I hurried down the hall and entered my dad's office in a flurry of unleashed tears. I immediately shut the door behind me and pulled the mini-blind down over the window in the door.

"What was that?" I cried aloud. Throughout the course of my life I had said stupid things and thought stupid things—and I had certainly *done* stupid things—but I couldn't remember a single sentence ever before making me so overwhelmingly uncertain of who I was.

Five little words had shaken me on a soul level,

and not just because they were words I hadn't meant to think.

They were words I hadn't known I believed.

"There's my girl." My dad's voice greeted me warmly as the door opened.

I turned to face him, fully aware there was no way to conceal my anguish. I couldn't even come up with a way to try.

"Daddy," I sobbed as I ran to him and threw my arms around his neck.

"Sweetie, what's wrong?" he asked with concern and love as he embraced me.

It had been more than two months since I'd thrown away so much of what I believed in exchange for one night of *him*. One night of passion. One night of being all that mattered in the world to Will Whitaker. What did I have to show for it?

I was broken, and the worst part was I suddenly didn't know if my brokenness was the cause or the effect.

"I have to tell you something," I whispered as I buried my head in his shoulder as I had throughout my entire life. I couldn't look at him, but I needed his help. And I couldn't think of any way to ask him for his help without telling him everything. "I'm worried you're going to hate me—"

"Cadie . . ."

"At the very least you're going to be very

disappointed. But I don't know what to do, Daddy."

He sighed and pulled out of the hug, grasping the sides of my face in his hands. "I can't promise I won't be disappointed, but I can promise that no disappointment in the world could be bigger than my love for you. You know that, right?"

I nodded, and he took my hand and led me to the couch along the wall. As we sat I heard the unmistakable cadence of Nessa McCaffrey's high heels approaching on the wood floor. My eyes flew open, and I began making furious attempts to remove the evidence of tears from my face—a hopeless task.

My dad squeezed my hand and said, "That goes for her too."

I knew that was true. I *knew* how much my mom loved me. But I also knew that there was a very good chance her disappointment would manifest itself in more mortifying ways than my dad's.

"Oliver, are you in here?" she asked as she knocked on the door and pushed it open at the same time. She peered around the door and saw us on the couch. "Do my eyes deceive me or is that Cadie McCaffrey I see? Is the big city girl actually gracing Oyster Bay with her presence?" She seemed to suddenly take in the woebegone climate of the room. "What's wrong? What's happened? Cadie, are you hurt?"

"Cadie was just saying that she's afraid we're going to be disappointed in her," he said to my mom. "But she knows how much we love her. She knows that comes first."

I watched them look at each other as he spoke, and I knew that, somehow, he was communicating more to her with his eyes than he was with his words. I grew increasingly sad as I realized that at the rate I was going, it was highly unlikely that I would ever be able to experience that sort of connection with someone. What was happening between my parents could only have been honed over the course of their nearly forty years of marriage.

"Of course that comes first," my mom said, turning her eyes from my dad to me, her tone so much softer and warmer than usual. "You can tell us anything, baby."

What had my dad's eyes said to her?

I took in all of the air my lungs could hold and then released it slowly. "It's . . . I mean, I don't know how you're going to react. It's kind of . . . intimate. And I—"

My mom crossed to the couch and placed her hand gently on my head. She ran her fingers through my hair like she used to when I was a little girl and she was trying to get me to relax at bedtime.

"Oliver, sweetheart, would you give us a minute?"

My dad leaned in and kissed my cheek, and then without a word left the office, shutting the door behind him. My first thoughts were not of how considerate my mom was being, or how uncomfortable the reality of telling my dad would have actually been. At first, all I could think about was how I'd never felt the need to be perfect for my dad, but for my mom I'd never really believed anything less was acceptable.

And if less than perfect wasn't acceptable, *I* had certainly never been acceptable. And that was *before* the confession I was preparing to make.

She took my dad's seat on the couch next to me, crossed her legs daintily at the ankles, and then waited. I felt her watching me, but there was no pressure. No impatience. She was just *there,* and I knew she would be ready when I was. I took one more deep breath and then blurted out, "I slept with Will." My cheeks were burning, and my hands had gone ice cold. Not even the constant motion of trembling could warm them up. "A couple months ago, before we broke up. I was planning to break up with him, actually, but then I thought he was going to propose, and . . . I don't know. I don't know why that changed things, but it did. It didn't *really* change anything, but it made me *feel* like things had changed. I regretted it. Like, instantly." I stared at my fidgeting hands, unable to bring myself to look at her. A tissue appeared in my hands, and

I blew my nose as the tears fell more quickly. "I knew it was wrong. I *know* it was wrong. We'd waited. For four years, Mom. And then we just threw it all away."

"Sweetheart," my mom interjected, a tremble in her voice. I forced myself to look at her, and it hurt more than I could have imagined. "I know who you are, Cadie. You don't have to try and convince me of anything."

Oh, how the sobbing grew. "You say that, but look at you. You're crying. I made you cry. I don't know that I've *ever* seen you cry."

She exhaled and reached her arms out to pull me close. "Cadie, I'm not crying because I'm disappointed. Life is full of disappointments, and they rarely make me cry, but seeing you in pain breaks my heart."

I threw my arms around her and held on to her in a way I hadn't since I was little—if I ever had. My dad had always been my comforter and my protector, while my mom had been my teacher and moral compass. But in that moment, in the arms of my mother, I found more comfort than I had ever known.

I began again, softly. "A few minutes ago, Eileen and I were talking and she said 'All things are possible with God.' I've heard that all my life. I've believed that all my life. But the thought that passed through my head was, 'Not *all* things.' The worst part is, I meant it. I don't think I believe it—not really—but right then I meant it." I sat up straight again. "I never would have thought something like that before. I used to talk to God all the time. Constantly. But now . . . I don't know. It's different. I pray, of course, but I feel like I ruined it."

I had fully exhausted that first tissue's usage so she handed me the entire box from my dad's desk. I destroyed three in quick succession.

"Ruined what?" she asked.

I shrugged. "I don't know exactly. My relationship with God, I guess. And I know that's not how it works. I asked for forgiveness and I know I got it, but—"

"No, Cadie. There is no 'but' there. You asked for forgiveness and you got it. That's the end of the sentence. It's just not the end of the story, and I think that's where you're struggling. God's erased it. It's gone. Can you say the same?"

I scoffed through my tears. "Of course not! It's messed up my entire life. I was a mess as it was, but then he proposed—"

"Will proposed?" she asked—every bit as surprised as she should have been.

"Yes. And that was probably the most painful moment of my entire life . . ."

"Why? Because you knew you were going to say no?"

"No, because he only asked because I was breaking up with him. After being together for so long, and loving him so much," I cried, "he only asked out of desperation."

"But you just said yourself, you were breaking up with him. Clearly you'd decided—"

"Mom, I was only breaking up with him because I'd finally realized he didn't love me as much as I loved him." I rested my head on her shoulder, and she didn't even say a word about the way my tears and mascara were destroying her silk blouse. "I couldn't just keep waiting forever, could I? I convinced myself he was never going to want to marry me, so what choice did I have but to end it?"

"Oh, baby girl," she whispered against the top of my head. "And then he asked."

"So I said no. I broke up with him, and that was supposed to be the end. But he kept trying all these stupid things from movies to try and get me back. And mostly, I didn't even care. I mean, I always thought I wanted that sort of romance, but when I had it, all I could think about was how it meant he hadn't been able to come up with anything on his own. But then . . . a few weeks ago . . ."

My voice faded away and I wasn't sure I could talk about it. It had been easy to talk about it to Darby right after it happened, because then all I'd really been feeling was anger.

"What happened a few weeks ago?"

I sighed and braced myself for the further onslaught of emotions. "We had to go to Staten

Island for a meeting. Just Will and me. And at first there was nothing romantic about it. At all. But I watched him work, and I was so proud of him. I don't know how to explain it. It was like he'd become the best version of himself and he was living up to all of the potential he's always had, and the best part was he was loving it. I was just . . . so proud. And we talked, and he apologized for being kind of distracted the last year of our relationship. And I saw it, Mom."

"Saw what, sweetie?"

I just didn't know if my heart could take anymore. "For a few minutes, I actually started believing he loved me as much as I loved him. And it was like everything was coming together. But . . ." I blew my nose and grabbed another tissue. "But it was just more stuff, stolen from movies. We hadn't had a breakthrough and nothing had changed. It was just more of the same. And it got in the way of work. I felt like he tricked me. How could I really trust that work was work and life was life, and how could I ever move on with either if that were the case? So I left ASN. And now I'm thirty-four years old and actually considering applying for a job working for my parents—no offense. My entire life has changed because I made one stupid decision. How can I erase it? How can it just be *gone?*"

She cleared her throat, and I raised my head to look at her. There seemed to be questioning in her eyes. If she was, without words, deciding not to hire her only child, I would know that I had hit a new low.

"I'm grateful for the job opportunity, though. Really."

She smiled at me. "You know it goes without saying that you have a job here if you want it—because you're good at what you do, not because you're our daughter. And if I'm being honest, we would love to see you every day. You could do a lot of good around here. I was even thinking, just now, that you could be on the show and talk to all of the young female viewers about the importance of maintaining their purity—"

I groaned. "Mom."

"Sorry. The point is we would be thrilled to hire you, but I really don't think you should run away. You felt it was the right thing to leave your job, and I understand that, but working here is the easy answer, Cadie. Major corporations have been after you for years. Talk to some of them. And talk to Will—"

"Mom!"

"Hear me out. I'm not lecturing you or trying to tell you how to run your life, but right now it's difficult for you to believe all things are possible with God because you don't see a way out."

"Of course I don't see a way out. Going back to him is kind of unthinkable—nothing has changed and we'd be right back where we were a few months ago, except what was lying dormant has now been all stirred up." I sniffed and peeked upwards, certain that at any moment this heart-warming mother/daughter moment would reach its conclusion, and she'd send me to my room to pray and read Lamentations. But so far she was hanging in there with me. "I think I'd be questioning every moment. Wondering what was real, worrying about the future, wanting him to want me . . . being afraid of wanting him."

She shrugged her shoulders. "So you don't go back to him. Seems like an easy choice, when you lay it all out."

Tears flooded my cheeks. She was right. That definitely seemed like the easy choice, and it was the choice I had made. Undoubtedly.

That didn't make it any less unthinkable than the other option.

"I think a big part of the reason you feel so out of sync with God," she continued, "is that you haven't forgiven yourself, and you most certainly haven't forgiven Will. There's some work to do there."

Apart from her belief that *Love God, Love YOU!* on Holy Trinity Television actually had young female viewers, there was so much wisdom in everything she said. She was right. I hadn't forgiven Will. Probably not for the one night, and certainly not for the year leading up to the night. I didn't need to actually speak with him in order to do that, but I realized that in order for us both to get the closure we probably needed, that was going to have to happen. And while I didn't relish the thought of talking about any of it with him, or even seeing him again, if that's what it took to make things right again, between God and me, I had to bite that bullet.

But what needed to happen in order for me to be able to forgive myself? In order for me to actually believe it was all in the past?

I took a deep breath and released it slowly.

"I don't even know that Will's asked for forgiveness yet, Mom. From God, I mean. He apologized to me, but—"

"Cadie," she interrupted me softly. "That sounds like something that's between Will and God." She cradled my face in her hands and wiped away the fresh tears. "So what does that have to do with you, my love?"

A new round of sobs was unleashed and I was welcomed into her loving arms once again. Eventually, once my tears had ceased and my breathing had returned to normal, she squeezed my hands and kissed the top of my head as she said, "Forgiveness is the way out, Cadie."

"I'll see what I can do," I conceded with a sigh.

She gently pulled away from me and stood to reopen the door. "Can you stick around for dinner?"

I guess she thought we had said all there was to

say, but I had avoided Lamentations, so I couldn't complain.

"I can't. I need to be heading back to the city so that I have time to change clothes, then I'm heading to Brooklyn with Darby."

"Brooklyn?" she asked in a condescending tone that had nothing to do with Brooklyn specifically. It was the same tone with which she had discussed the dreaded commute to Cold Spring Harbor for years. "Why in the world are you going to Brooklyn?"

"Barry Manilow, baby!" The second those three little words were out of my mouth I knew what a dork I was, though I didn't care. Not one little smidge. "Will bought me a couple of tickets months ago when they first went on sale."

"I've always wondered about the proper etiquette," Dad said as he reappeared in the doorway and opened his arms to me. "In the event of a breakup, does one get to keep the Manilow tickets? Apparently so."

I groaned, but the groan quickly transformed into a laugh. "I'll see you later." I hugged each of them and then began walking toward the door. I stopped with my hand on the door handle and added, "Thank you." I looked directly at my mom and said, "You don't know how much I needed you today."

"Talk to Will!" she called out after me.

Yeah . . . I'd have to build up to that one.

19

When All Is Said and Done

Will stepped off the elevator onto the 85th floor and saw Darby standing there. He wasn't quite sure what gave it away—her impatiently crossed arms and tapping toes, the death glare she was giving him, or the twenty texts and missed calls from her on his phone—but he was fairly certain she'd been waiting for him.

"Hey, Darb."

"Where on earth have you been?"

He quirked his eyebrow as he walked past her. "*Specifically* where on earth? 245 Park Avenue. Today was the exclusive with the commissioner, remember? Why? What's up?"

"Are you and Anna dating?"

Will stopped in his tracks, fairly sure he had never heard more ridiculous words strung together in his entire life. In fact, he wasn't even completely certain he could make sense of them. He did a double take and looked around to make sure no one was privy to Darby's less-than-subtle questioning—particularly Anna.

He resumed his brisk pace to The Field, and she followed after him.

"Anna Alvarez?" he whispered. She nodded and he answered, "Of course not. Why would you even think that?"

"I didn't. But Cadie does."

He stopped so suddenly, mid-gait, that she came only about a nose-length away from running into him.

"What in the world are you talking about?"

Various employees walked past and nodded their greeting, and suddenly Darby was the one trying to be discreet. She motioned that he should follow her, and she took the lead as they resumed the commute to The Field.

They rounded the corner to the executive hallway and walked down to Will's office. As they entered, Will took off his coat, shaking the snow off of it, and hung it on the coatrack.

As Darby shut the door behind them he asked, "So now are you going to tell me what you're talking about?"

"Somehow Cadie got it in her head that you and Anna are dating. That's all there is to it, really."

"I have a really difficult time imagining she would care."

He leaned over and ran his hands through his hair to shake the remaining snow out of it. He sat down at his desk and used his dark computer monitor as a mirror as he tamed his wild mane.

And then he asked. He just couldn't help himself.

"Does she care?"

She shrugged. "She's using it as additional evidence that it's too late for the two of you."

As Darby took a seat in the chair across the desk from him, he powered on his computer and grabbed a spare T-shirt from the cabinet behind him to sop up the drops of melted snow that had fallen from his hair to his desk.

"It *is* too late." It hurt to admit it, but he knew it was true. "I tried, Darb. I really did give it my all."

"And you got so close!" She threw up her hands in exasperation. "I gave you that list of movies for research, you know."

"I researched. Believe me. You haven't known a wild Friday night until you've been at Kevin Lamont's house watching *27 Dresses*, and Odell Beckham and Alex Rodriguez show up, because Kev forgot to let them know a cocktail party had been rescheduled."

She gasped, but it quickly turned into a laugh. "That didn't happen!"

"Oh, I assure you, it did. But it worked out okay. With Alex there, we breezed through *Maid in Manhattan* and *The Wedding Planner* too. So I did research, Darby. Enough research to last a lifetime." He added under his breath, "A lot of good it did me."

She jumped up from her chair and threw her

arms in the air again. "But you just *copied* stuff. I didn't mean for it to be a Civil War battlefield reenactment, except for romance movies. I thought you would just get some inspiration."

Hmm. That might have been nice to know.

"Ah, well. What's done is done." He sighed sadly. Hopelessly, but with great resolve.

Surprise appeared on her face. "Seriously? You're giving up? Just like that?"

"Just like that? Really?" He laughed bitterly and looked up at her. "How many times—you know, according to proper romance movie etiquette—should a guy put his heart on the line and allow it to be smashed to smithereens before he finally gives up? I was thinking three. Four, maybe. But maybe I should do some more research. Maybe I should try to piece it back together one more time, so she can smash it, one more time. You think?"

Darby's lip began trembling and Will felt bad. He knew she only wanted what she thought was best for both of them—or at least what she thought was best for Cadie. He regretted playing the martyr card with such fervor. Even if it *was* an accurate representation of how he was feeling.

"You're right," she acknowledged as tears pooled. She shook her head and dismissed the tears with a swipe of her hand across her eyes. "Sorry. I have no right to put this on you. I know how hard you tried."

"Look, Darb—"

"But the thing is, no matter how unfair I know it is, there's a part of me that wants to say *yes*." She stepped closer to the desk, put her hand on the edge of it, and leaned over him before emphatically repeating, "Yes."

"Yes, what?" he asked, just the tiniest bit intimidated by her all of a sudden.

"Yes, you should keep trying. Yes, you should put your heart out there again. Yes, you should allow it to be smashed to smithereens again, if that's what it takes. And she should too. We *all* should, if given the opportunity. It's *love,* Will! That's what you do. That's what people *should* do."

"Life is not a romance movie!" He stood, and the motion caused his chair to roll back and hit against the wall. "Don't you understand? I have nothing left! You know I love her, Darb. You *know* I do. But for whatever reason, I can't convince her of that. Or maybe she knows and it's not enough. Whatever. All I know is that on that ferry, I thought I had her back, and it was probably the best moment of my entire life. And then she was gone. She was just . . . gone. I can't go through that again. I can't keep trying to figure out what I did wrong, when—"

"You just shouldn't have interfered with work, Will." Darby exhaled and softened her posture and tone. "She'd been so convinced she could keep everything compartmentalized, but your little battlefield reenactment on the ferry called all of that into question."

He tilted his head and stared at her in confusion. "What are you talking about?"

She settled back down into the chair, their own battlefield moment having passed. "I thought it was romantic, but she thought it crossed a line. And I do see her point. How was she supposed to keep doing her job to the best of her ability if she always had to wonder if she was being assigned projects on her own merit or as part of a setup?"

Suddenly lightheaded, he pulled his chair back over and collapsed into it. "What setup?"

"Oh, come on, Will. At first I wasn't sure, but that whole thing was like Rom-Com 101. You even got lucky with the snow."

He shook his head. "I didn't plan that night. I didn't plan *any* of it. I promise you."

"You guys ready?" Kevin asked from just outside the office as he used his massive wingspan to simultaneously open the doors to both Will's office and Ellis's across the hall.

Will slapped himself on the forehead. "That's right. I totally forgot." He rushed back over to the rack, grabbed his still-damp coat, and put it back on. "Sorry, Darb. I have to run."

Ellis walked in and responded to the confusion in Darby's eyes. "Enzo's awful annual poker night. I don't know why he doesn't just start

311

officially calling it that and list it that way on the invitations. That's the only way I've ever heard anyone refer to it."

"Then why go?" she asked of the room in general.

"Because *everyone* goes," Will answered.

Kevin nodded. "It's true. Last year LeBron James, Peyton Manning, and Danica Patrick were all so distracted by a game of Texas Hold 'Em that they agreed to occupy the ASN booth at the Stanley Cup Finals for the next three years."

On his way out the door, Will grabbed Darby and pulled her in for a quick hug. "You know how bad I want her back," he whispered in her ear, "but I'm not quite sure my heart can survive more rejection." He pulled away from her and smiled at her sadly, and she returned the emotion and the gesture.

"You could come with us, Tennyson," Kevin offered.

She chuckled. "Oh, that is a tempting offer, but I'm sorry—*very* sorry—to say I have a Barry Manilow concert to go to."

"That's tonight . . ." Will muttered to himself.

"Larinda's going to that concert with some friends, but that's not surprising. I love my wife, but she has horrible taste in music. Why are *you* going?"

"I love my best friend, but she also has horrible taste in music."

They all walked down the hall together, and Will, Ellis, and Kevin stepped into the elevator, and there was conversation the entire time. But Will didn't hear a word of it. He was remembering the day he gave Cadie those tickets. She'd squealed and hugged him and made a comment about loving the fact that he knew her so well.

If only that were still the case.

"Did you know she was coming here?" Kevin asked eighty-five floors later as the elevator doors opened into the lobby.

Will looked up questioningly, and then everything stopped when they saw Cadie stepping out of the revolving door and onto the white marble floor. He struggled to catch his breath. It had been more than three weeks since he'd seen her, and the sight of her was enough to replenish his soul and make it feel as if it were being sapped dry, simultaneously.

Ellis placed his hand on Will's shoulder. "She looks—"

"Breathtaking," Will muttered, fully aware that he had never before seen an actual personification of the word.

She stepped aside to the corner of the lobby, out of the way, and looked down at her phone, her thumbs tapping rapidly. Will was grateful she was distracted. He would need a moment. He hadn't seen her dressed like that in a long time—he wasn't sure when the last time had been. Her long overcoat opened up as she shook away the snow, and he was able to see the black and white dress that couldn't have been more flattering to her figure if it had taken to speaking in sonnets. It stopped just above her knees, revealing long legs he hadn't had an opportunity to stare at since a summer day at Coney Island. Had that been last summer? The summer before?

Her hair was shorter than it had been on her last day at ASN. She'd worn it short not long after they met, and he'd forgotten how much he'd liked it that way. Not that he hadn't thought she was beautiful with it long, of course, but when it was short his fingertips had always found their way to the back of her neck. He loved touching her there. He loved that when his fingers brushed across her skin she got ticklish but didn't want him to pull his hand away.

"Shall we go say hello?" Kevin asked, yanking him kicking and screaming out of his memories. "Are you up for it?"

In response Will began walking toward her. Whether or not he was up for it was irrelevant. There was no way he was going to miss the opportunity to hear her voice. Maybe even smell her perfume.

She looked up as they approached and seemed to spot Kevin and Ellis first. It was nearly impossible *not* to spot them first. She reacted with a warm smile, but as her eyes met Will's the smile morphed into something different—no less warm but certainly more complicated.

"You are a sight for sore eyes," Ellis greeted her with his usual charisma, the words accompanied by a hug and a kiss on the cheek.

She wrapped her arms around him—at least as much as she could—and then said hello to Kevin in the same manner. There was no hug for Will, of course. Only a friendly, "Hey, Whitaker. Nice to see you."

He tried to make himself respond in a similar tone. He knew what he was supposed to say. He knew what was acceptable—a simple "You too, McCaffrey," or maybe even a more lighthearted, "Can't stay away from this place, huh?" Either response would have been adequate, but right then, with her looking the way she looked and him feeling the way he felt, neither was good enough.

"You look beautiful, Cadie."

The three who heard the words all looked somewhat uncomfortable, as if he had broken an unspoken rule and they were suddenly unsure what was supposed to happen next. Will didn't feel that way at all. If given the opportunity, he was prepared to say a million more things he shouldn't say.

"Thanks," Cadie finally replied, her eyes darting to the floor. "I was going to go home and change but the train was running late. Mechanical something or other. Anyway—"

"You're always gorgeous in anything, but *this?* Wow."

He watched the heat rise to her cheeks and he felt ashamed of himself. How many opportunities had he missed? How many times had he neglected to tell her that she was the most beautiful woman on the planet?

"Um, so . . . what have you been up to? Where are you working?" Kevin asked, no doubt in an attempt to defuse the awkwardness.

Cadie laughed and replied, "All those years of never taking vacation are finally paying off. I'm happy to say ASN is still supporting me. But I've gotten a couple offers, and I have a few more interviews lined up."

"I hope it goes without saying, but if you need a letter of recommendation, just say the word."

"Same goes for me," Ellis chimed in.

She smiled. "Thanks. I really appreciate that."

The three of them stood there uncomfortably for a few seconds more and then Kevin said, "Well, it really is good to see you, but we need to be taking off."

Cadie's cell phone lit up in her hands and she took a quick peek at the notification before stuffing it into her coat pocket. "Oh, that's right. Enzo's awful poker thing is tonight. Have fun losing all your money to whichever Williams sister it is you always lose your money to."

Ellis rolled his eyes. "Venus. It's always

Venus." He kissed Cadie on the cheek again and reiterated how good it was to see her.

Will wasn't ready to say goodbye, but there was also no natural way to do anything else.

"Well," he began, but Cadie quickly interrupted him.

"Hey, before you go, could I talk to you for just a quick second?"

Please talk to me forever. "Of course." He turned to Kevin and Ellis, who had taken their first steps toward the exit, and called out, "I'll meet you guys out there."

Once they were alone, though surrounded by dozens of bustling Manhattanites coming and going, she said, "You were invited to Enzo's, huh? That's a pretty big deal. I hope you don't lose all your money to Venus too."

He chuckled. "I left my wallet at home for this express purpose, so I will be prey for no Williams sister this fair night."

"Smart," she replied with a smile. She looked around the lobby and then back at her feet before finally locking her eyes with his. "So, um . . . look, Will, I know now isn't the right time—you've got to go and Darby will be down in a minute—but I've been thinking a lot. Today, especially. I don't know if you would be open to it, but it might be a good idea if we could sit down and talk. Only if you're okay with that. If you think it would be too weird, um—"

317

"No!" he interjected, not even worrying about how much his evident enthusiasm removed any façade of coolness, and certainly disregarding all of his recent resolve to protect his heart. "That would be great. Honestly, I've been doing a lot of thinking too, and then seeing you tonight . . . I think if we—"

"Hey, Cadie! I didn't expect to see you here!"

Will couldn't help but groan aloud as Anna walked up behind him. It was nothing personal against her. If Ken Griffey and the rest of the 1975 Cincinnati Reds lineup had been the ones to interrupt him, he would have greeted them with the same groan.

"Anna. Hi there." Cadie greeted her with a smile. "I'm just meeting Darby. You doing okay?"

"Doing great," she replied, and then she looped her arm through Will's. She rested her other hand on his bicep and looked up at him to say, "I think I'll just ride over to Enzo's with you, if you don't mind."

Apart from the fact that his moment alone with Cadie had been interrupted, Will was unaffected by it all. "Sure," he replied dismissively, determined not to break eye contact with Cadie. As long as she hung in there with him, they could get back to their conversation, which had been so full of promise.

But suddenly her eyes tore away from his and

landed on Anna's hand resting on Will's arm. He looked down, and then back at Cadie, and it was as if he was suddenly able to see the entire situation through her eyes. Was Darby right? Did Cadie actually believe that something was going on between him and Anna? Between him and *anyone?*

"You were invited to Enzo's poker night, huh?" Cadie asked Anna. Her focus was on Anna's face, but her eyes still occasionally darted to hands and arms. "That's . . . wow . . ."

"What? Does that surprise you?"

"No, not at all. Well, okay . . . maybe a little. I've just never known them to invite anyone who's not on-air, or at least in management." Cadie plastered a smile on her face. A smile Will didn't recognize. "But that's great. I'm sure you'll have a great time."

Anna laughed. "I may not be in management . . . yet." She winked. Very annoyingly. "But I've become close to so many of the guys."

She squeezed Will's arm and he couldn't help but flinch. He pulled away from her, not wanting to be rude but understanding more by the second that everything Anna was doing and saying could potentially give Cadie the wrong impression.

"Cadie, can we finish what we were saying?"

He leaned in and grabbed her hand, and nearly lost the ability to breathe when she flinched as he had just done in response to Anna's unwanted touch. She pulled her fingers out of his grasp but not before he could feel how she was trembling.

"There's Darby, so I need to go, actually." She looked at Anna and said, "You guys have a great night. Good to see you." Then she walked past them to meet Darby in the middle of the lobby.

Will saw Cadie speak briefly to Darby and then they began heading toward the door together.

"Darby!" Will called out. She stopped, but Cadie kept walking as Will ran over.

"What did you do?" Darby seethed as Will approached. "She texted me two minutes ago and she was in a great mood. And now—"

"I know. Listen, please tell her—"

"I've got to go, Will. We'll talk later."

She hurried out after Cadie, and Will was left feeling more alone than he could remember ever feeling. That feeling didn't change when Anna joined him in the center of the lobby.

"You ready to go?" she asked.

Dear God, he silently prayed—finally straying from his terrible habit of trying to figure his own way out of a predicament rather than calling on God. *I'm falling apart here. It's all falling apart. Help me, Lord. I thought I was done. But I don't think I will ever be done. Please don't let me lose her. Please don't let me screw it up any more than I already have.* He cleared his throat in a hopeless attempt to clear away the accompanying emotions. *I know I messed it all up. That's on me.*

But don't let me lose her. Help me become who she needs me to be. Help me become who you need me to be. Help me know what to say. Help me know what to do.

"Will?" Anna placed her hand on his arm again, and he immediately turned to face her.

"I think I owe you an apology. If I somehow gave you the impression that there was something going on between us apart from friendship . . ."

"No, not at all."

She smiled, and he felt relief course through his veins—not that the relief lasted very long.

"I know you're not ready to start dating yet," she continued. "I understand that. I want you to know that I'm in no hurry. When you're ready, *I'll* be ready."

He closed his eyes and sighed. How clueless *was* he? What else had he completely missed?

"Anna, I'll never be ready."

She giggled. "You say that now, and that's totally understandable, but I mean when all is said and done. You know . . . at the end of the day."

"I am madly in love with you, Cadie McCaffrey, and at the end of the day, I know we want the same thing—"

He shook his head. "You are a really great person, so please don't think this is anything against you. It's just that there will never be

321

anyone else, and I will never move on. There will never come a time when I'm not madly in love with her, and at the end of the day, it will always be her. I will *always* choose her."

He looked at his watch and then ran to the door, turning right onto Fulton Street to head toward where the car was supposed to be parked. He heard Ellis calling his name and he ran back the other way, where he saw Ellis's head peeking out of the window of the black town car.

"I'm not going," Will said as soon as he reached them. "Sorry to keep you waiting, but—"

Ellis laughed. "Yeah, we figured. Get in. We'll take you to Manilow."

"I appreciate that, but the concert's in Brooklyn. You guys don't want to—"

The front passenger side door opened and Kevin's massive build appeared beside the car. "Get in, Whitaker. Now."

"Yes, sir." He opened the door and climbed in beside Ellis, who had scooted to the other side.

"So where exactly in Brooklyn are we heading, gentlemen?" the driver asked.

All eyes were on Will, either via turned heads or the rearview mirror, but he had no idea.

"That's a really good question." Suddenly his mind was jammed with other really good questions. How would he find her when he got there? What was he going to say? "How am I going to pay?" he asked aloud with a guttural groan. "I have my phone, my ID, my Metro Card, and my keys. That's it! I left everything else at home so I wouldn't lose any money tonight."

"No problem, man," Ellis said calmly as he pulled out his phone. "I'll get online and get the tickets."

"Okay, thanks. I'll pay you back." Will pulled out his own phone and performed a quick search. "Barclays Center," he called out to the driver, who nodded and turned onto Vessey Street.

Will experienced ten short seconds of hope, combined with the thrilling adrenaline of action, before Ellis burst his bubble.

"Sold out," he declared.

The three of them looked at each other skeptically.

"That can't be right. Can it?" Kevin asked.

"Are you sure you're looking at the Barry Manilow concert?" Will asked, leaning over to peek at the phone.

Ellis turned his phone toward Will and shrugged. "That's what it says."

"What would you like me to do?" the driver asked as they merged onto the Brooklyn Bridge ramp.

Will stared out the window and replied, "We've come too far to turn back now." They hadn't even traveled a half mile from the office, but he knew that didn't make the words any less true.

• • •

"So what's the plan?" Kevin asked thirty minutes later as they shivered in the cold outside the Barclays Center.

"We'll wait," Will said as he blew warm air into his hands and then rubbed them together.

"Sure. Good plan, Whitaker. Can I make one little suggestion though?" Kevin pointed to the other side of Flatbush Avenue. "Why don't we wait in that warm-looking pizza place right there?"

"What if we miss her?" He was already running through scenarios, trying to determine how the three of them needed to split up to best cover all the exits. It was then that he realized one-third of any scenario he could come up with was missing. "Hey, where's Ellis?"

"Who's the man?" their absentee friend suddenly boomed from behind them. "I'm the man!" He fanned three tickets out in his enormous hand.

"You got tickets?" Will exclaimed. "How in the world did you get tickets? Never mind. I don't care. Let's go!"

"*You* may not care, but I certainly do." Kevin fumed as he snatched the tickets away from Ellis and got in his face. "I'm all for helping Will get McCaffrey back, but your face is literally on anti-ticket-scalping billboards all over the city. I saw you on the side of a bus yesterday! If anyone saw you . . ."

Ellis shook his head and brushed off Kevin's concern. "No one saw me." He laughed and patted Will on the back. "Besides, it's all in the name of love. Let's do this."

Will and Ellis took off toward the entrance, but Kevin lagged behind. "Um, guys . . ."

"Oh, good grief, Swoosh! I'll film a new PSA to salve your conscience, just come on!"

"It's not that." Kevin groaned as he handed the tickets back to Ellis and faced Will. "We are the proud bearers of three tickets to a concert by a Barry Manilow tribute band known as The Merry Granilows, happening now at a venue called Pete's Candy Store."

Ellis grimaced as he turned to Will. "I'm so sorry about that. But hey, I don't know why I didn't think of it sooner, but between the three of us I bet we can sweet-talk someone into letting us in. Take some selfies, sign some autographs . . ."

"Or, here's a novel idea," Kevin said. "Maybe we can maintain our dignity for the rest of the evening. I think it's time to call it, Will."

Ellis elbowed Kevin in the ribs. "Don't listen to him. We're with you, whatever you need."

Will had no doubt that Ellis was interpreting his silence and hanging head as resignation and defeat, but nothing could have been further from the truth. Yes, he regretted the wasted time, but he was more determined than ever to win Cadie back in a grand and spectacular way.

"Who lives closest?" he asked.

"To here?" Ellis asked. When Will nodded, he answered, "Kev."

"Then we're going to Tribeca."

"Why are we going to my house?" Kevin asked.

"You're closest, and you said Larinda went to the concert, so she's out tonight." He pulled out his phone and quickly found his roommate in his contacts.

"Yes, but—"

The call picked up on the third ring. "Sam? Hey, it's Will. Are you home?"

"Dude." Sam laughed. "I can't tell you the last time someone actually called me, like the old-fashioned way. The sound kind of freaked me out when it rang."

"Are you home?" Will repeated emphatically as he began walking back toward where their ride was parked.

"Yeah, I'm home. What's up?"

"I'm going to give you an address." He snapped his fingers over his head and pointed toward Kevin. In response Ellis asked Kevin for his address, which Will promptly repeated to Sam. "Meet us there as soon as you can. We'll be there in about a half hour. I need you to bring a few things with you. Do you have something to write this down?" He paused to give Sam a moment to find a pen and paper and then he said, "You ready? Okay, bring as many of the movies from

326

the list as you can get your hands on, bring some white poster board, a marker, and bring a boom box."

He was supremely proud of the entire conversation. It felt like the type of definitive conversation that would occur at the end of a scene in one of the movies, right before a montage of Will and his friends putting the plan into action—a montage that would probably be accompanied by some great eighties pop ballad.

But he forgot his roommate was a child.

"What's a boom box?"

"You know, like a big stereo."

"Okay. So do I need to bring speakers too? Do you need, like, subwoofers and all, or—"

Unbelievable. "No, Sam, the speakers are built in."

"So why don't you just use your phone or an iPod or something?"

"Because it won't be loud enough."

"Oh, so you just need me to bring a Bluetooth speaker to connect to your phone. Got it."

Will let out a frustrated groan, and Ellis took the phone from him and smiled as he whispered, "Allow me." He put the phone up to his ear and said, "Sammy! It's Ellis. I believe our man is planning to attempt a *Say Anything* moment. Yes, exactly. Okay, thanks. See you soon."

Ellis ended the call and tossed the phone back to Will.

From several feet behind them, Kevin sighed. "I should have known that it was too much to ask that we maintain our dignity for the rest of the evening."

20

The Rest of the Evening

"I am so glad I bumped into you girls!" Larinda said as she hugged Darby and me outside of the Barclays Center.

The three of us had been chatting since we ran into each other in the merch line immediately following the concert. I'd always loved Larinda. Through the years I'd spent a lot of time visiting with her at various social functions and the occasional dinner party at their house, but in all that time we had never connected the dots regarding our shared Manilove. Thanks to Barry Manilow, we were now bonded for life.

The only surprising part of any of it was that Darby was right there with us.

Now clothed in a red "Very Barry Christmas" sweater over her regular clothes, with a "#1 Fanilow" beanie on her head and various other goodies bursting out of her "Barry Manilow: Live!" tote bag, it was safe to say that Darby no longer looked down on my Manilow fandom.

Larinda prepared to step into the cab that had pulled over to the curb in response to her signal, but then she took a look back at us—most notably, my pantyhose-clad legs.

"It's freezing. Why don't you two take this one, and I'll get the next?"

"That's very sweet." I shivered, in spite of my best intentions to the contrary. "But if it takes too long I'll just borrow Darby's fleece Barry blanket."

Darby scoffed. "I didn't end up buying the blanket, remember? It was too expensive, and I needed to be able to buy the coffee mug."

I smiled at Larinda. "We'll be fine. Thanks."

She got in, shut the door, and waved as the taxi pulled away, but after driving about ten feet, the car suddenly stopped with a screech. Larinda's window rolled down and her arm motioned us over.

"Why don't you come over to the house for a while? Kevin's at Enzo's poker night, so he won't be home until tomorrow morning sometime. I'm not quite ready for the fun to end yet."

It had been a very long day and I was beyond exhausted—physically, mentally, emotionally. I had long ago broken my own personal record of time spent with nylon constricting my legs like sausage casings, and though I was used to wearing heels, I wasn't used to wearing them across multiple New York City boroughs and Long Island.

But I, like Larinda, was having a lot of fun,

and all that awaited me at home were quiet and loneliness and reminders of decisions that had to be made—all of which were the very opposite of fun.

"I'm in if you are," I said, turning to Darby.

She nodded enthusiastically, and Larinda rolled up her window. Darby and I stepped off the curb to approach the other side of the car and then climbed in—Darby in the front, me in the back by Larinda.

As I fastened my seat belt and got settled in, Larinda said, "I've actually been meaning to have you over for a while. Truthfully, ever since Kevin mentioned that you and Will split up. You know . . . to get the scoop. But I thought I should wait the appropriate amount of time, so it didn't look like I was just seeking out gossip."

I laughed. "Though clearly . . ."

"Yes, I *really* want to know what happened. Have I waited the appropriate amount of time?"

In the front seat, Darby was apparently in her own little Barry bubble. "What's *your* favorite Barry Manilow song?" she asked the driver.

I shrugged and told Larinda, "There's not much to it, really. We were heading nowhere. It just took me a long time to figure that out."

She tsked sadly. "Well, I was really sorry to hear things didn't work out. Are you doing okay?"

"I am. A lot better since I decided to leave ASN, actually."

"That would be difficult, I imagine." She shifted in her seat and elegantly crossed her legs. I couldn't picture a day when I would ever have the capacity to elegantly cross my legs in a cab. "Seeing him every day, especially when his career is really taking off, would be awkward, I would think. It would be pretty near impossible not to feel some resentment toward him doing so well."

I considered that for a moment and then shook my head. "No, I don't think I felt any resentment toward his success. Toward his name and face being everywhere? Yes. But his success?" I shook my head more fervently. "I'm happy for him. He deserves it."

The pattern beneath our feet changed as we drove onto the Brooklyn Bridge and began our trek back across the East River. As I reflected on the different sounds that accompanied the shift in roadway, I also began reflecting on the truth of my statement. I *was* happy for him. No matter how much I wished he had done things differently in our relationship, and no matter how much I still felt confused and bewildered that something that had once been so good had resulted in so much nothingness, I didn't have it in me to hate him, or even dislike him. I wanted him to be happy and successful and, someday, in love.

Slow down, Cadie, I thought in response to the

tightness in my throat and the sinking feeling that had invaded my stomach. *One step at a time.*

"He's a good guy," Larinda said. "And I'm sure that in his own time he'll find a way to move on."

"From me?" I chuckled because it felt like the appropriate response—not because the thought of Will moving on in any way filled me with humor. The thought that he would have to "find a way" was, I admit, somewhat amusing. "I really don't think he'll have much trouble."

"What makes you say that?" Larinda asked, and I noticed that Darby had begun paying attention. I could always count on her to be standing by with a rebuttal for whatever self-deprecating comment I uttered.

But I wasn't feeling self-deprecating at all. Just factual.

"He's a catch, for one thing," I began. Both ladies looked at me with wide eyes, and I laughed. "What? I don't have any problem admitting that. When I met him, I was completely smitten within minutes. He's charming and smart and hilarious, and really kind."

"He's also a stud," Larinda muttered.

I laughed once again, but Darby laughed harder.

"You don't really have a type, do you?" Darby asked. I understood her point. Physically, it was difficult to piece together a single similarity between Kevin Lamont and Will Whitaker.

Larinda joined us in our giggling. "I *do* have a

type, and I assure you, I'm married to it. But that doesn't keep me from appreciating what Will has going for him."

Darby twisted more in her seat in order to face us. "I've never really seen it. I love Will, but he's kind of a dork."

"Oh, he's totally a dork," I agreed, and Larinda laughed and nodded. "I think that's what I found so attractive about him. I always loved that he wasn't caught up in his looks like a lot of guys, or even *aware* of his looks. He's certainly never had any clue how women look at him." I sighed. "I don't know . . . I think he's kind of a Picasso. Most of the individual aspects don't really make sense together. The pieces don't fit. But when it all connects and you see the whole canvas, it's rather artistic and beautiful."

We pulled up to the Lamonts' gorgeous Federal-style townhouse in Tribeca and all reached into our purses to gather money for the cab fare. Larinda shooed our money away and took care of it herself, and then we all stepped out.

I'd always loved their home. I'd always loved Tribeca, actually. It was my favorite residential area in New York, and though I had no intention of ever leaving Greenwich Village, if I did, it would be for Tribeca. To live in Kevin and Larinda's townhouse, I'd have left the Village in a heart-beat, before you could say "banana pudding."

We walked across the private cobblestone

mews to their four-story home, and I marveled as I always did. They lived only a couple of blocks, in various directions, from the Hudson River, Holland Tunnel, various subway stations . . . and yet you couldn't hear a sound.

Darby had never been there, and I watched her take it all in as we walked up the front stoop and into the rustically decorated living room. It had the quaint and comfortable feel of a family farmhouse and yet the extravagance of the multimillion-dollar property that it was.

"Take your coats off, ladies," Larinda insisted. "Cadie, kick off those shoes. Hot tea, coffee, a glass of wine?"

"Coffee," Darby and I answered emphatically in unison.

Our hostess smiled. "You've got it."

She headed off toward the kitchen and we made ourselves at home as we'd been instructed— though Darby's Manilow hat didn't leave her head.

"So why didn't you ever tell me?" Darby whispered when we were alone.

"Tell you what?"

"How gorgeous this house is. I have such house envy right now it's not even funny."

"Oh, I know!" I laughed softly as I looked at her. "I kind of thought you were going to ask me why I never told you Barry Manilow would change your life."

335

She looped her arm through mine as we began walking toward the kitchen. With a sigh she said, "You did tell me that. And I was a fool for not believing you."

"So, Cadie," Larinda began as soon as we appeared in the doorway. "You were telling us the reasons you don't think Will will have difficulty moving on."

Our journey indoors hadn't been enough to distract from that lovely conversation. Goody.

"I think I was done."

She shook her head. "No, you said, 'he's a catch, for one thing,' which must mean there is more than one thing."

I looked to Darby as she and I climbed onto barstools at the island in the center of the kitchen, but my best friend was no help whatsoever. She just shrugged and said, "You did say that."

Unable to come up with any way out of the conversation, I said, "In a lot of ways, I think he was over me a long time before we broke up, so I don't think that moving on will really be a problem. That's all I meant. Besides, I'm pretty sure he's already in a relationship with Anna Alvarez."

Darby groaned and faced Larinda. "This is what I deal with." Her attention was back on me as she said, "How many times do I have to tell you there is nothing going on there?"

With a shrug meant to convey all of the indifference I knew I was supposed to be feeling, I said, "Maybe there wasn't before, but you should have seen the way she just walked over to him earlier and grabbed on to him." I felt the heat rising in my cheeks and I was suddenly aware of the scornful way I was feeling. I could have no doubt that the scorn had overtaken my face, as well. "And I don't care, of course," I quickly qualified, "but regardless of who you are or what the situation, it's just bad form to act that way in front of someone's ex."

Especially when they've only been officially broken up for a month and a half, and the guy and his ex were finally having their first relatively nice conversation. Well, at least their first relatively nice conversation after the very nice conversation that almost led to a kiss. Hasn't Anna read the rule book?

I knew that Will's involvement with Anna shouldn't alter my intent to follow my mom's advice. I still needed to talk to him, apologize for my part of the wrongdoings, forgive him, and figure out a way to clear the air so that I could move forward.

Admittedly, seeing him with Anna had made me slightly less confident that forgiveness was the final step to placing Will firmly in my past and moving on to a bright, sunny future.

Tears brimmed my eyes and I buried my face in my hands in an attempt to hide my sadness.

I'm pretty sure my forlorn posture and suddenly incessant sniffing still gave it away.

"What's wrong?" Darby asked as she jumped down from her stool and wrapped her arms around me.

Even in front of Darby, I'd done a pretty good job of remaining stoic, I thought. Sure, we'd talked about every last detail of my relationship with Will and pored over and scrutinized the minutia of the breakup, but through it all I'd been resolute that ending things had been for the best. That hadn't changed, but *something* had.

I continued sniffing and raised my head. "I'm sorry. I shouldn't—"

"Yes, you *should*," Larinda insisted. "Honey, get it out. If you stifle it and bury it long enough, you'll wake up one day and realize there's nothing that *needs* to get out."

That sounded nice. "Isn't that a good thing?"

Larinda placed her hand on mine and shook her head. "Doesn't mean anything's healed. It just means it's become a part of you."

Admittedly, that sounded less nice.

"I just miss him," I uttered softly.

I felt them both gawking at what I imagine was a declaration they weren't expecting, and I wanted to take it back. Actually, I wanted to take it back for a myriad of reasons, but I couldn't. It was true.

I didn't miss everything, of course. If I had the

option to go right back where we were at the end and not break up with him, I wouldn't change a thing. Leaving him was the right decision. But oh my goodness, I missed him. At first, I thought I missed having *someone*. Even in our worst times he was there for me. *With* me.

My inner contrarian began debating. *Except he was always working. He was always late. He was distracted. He was distant.* All of those things were true at the end, which is how I knew I didn't just miss *someone*. I missed Will.

I'd been missing him for a very long time.

I raised my head to look at my friends and was greeted by attention on their faces and compassion in their eyes. "When I ran into him in the lobby, there was something different. *He* was different."

"How so?" Larinda asked.

"He was so complimentary. So attentive. He . . . I don't know how to explain it, really. He was a little bit flirty, but not casually so. You know what I mean? Maybe flirty isn't a good word for it. More . . . I don't know . . . " I was afraid to say the thought aloud, uncertain as to whether acknowledging it would dilute its power or just embolden it further in my memory.

"Spit it out," Darby insisted with a knowing smile.

I bit my lip and prepared for the onslaught of romantic overanalyzation that I knew awaited me.

"It's just that all the things he spent weeks doing, attempting to get me back . . . it wasn't that. This wasn't part of a plan. This time it was just Will. It was like he couldn't *help* but look at me like I was . . ."

My voice trailed off and I began blushing at the memory of him taking in the sight of me, head to toe and back again before locking in on my eyes, as if they contained what he found most appealing.

"What?" Darby and Larinda asked in unison.

I couldn't stop the corner of my mouth from turning upward as I said the word. "His."

All of that had been difficult enough to put into words, but finding an adequate way to express the rest of the thought would be impossible. He hadn't just looked at me like I was his—he had also looked at me like he was mine. I'd seen something in his eyes that I hadn't seen in a very long time. Maybe I'd never seen it.

"Here's the thing." I stood from the stool and began walking around the massive kitchen as I allowed the thoughts that had been mingling and battling in my mind for hours to be spoken aloud. "I know he thought I looked pretty good tonight, but I don't think it was *just* because I looked pretty good. He was totally into *me,* you know? Does that make sense?"

Larinda laughed warmly. "Of course that makes sense! That man has always been into you."

"Even if that's true, I can't remember the last time he looked at me like he did tonight."

Like he was in love with me. Like he had always been in love with me, and always would be. Maybe even like he loved me enough.

I groaned and rubbed my eyes in an attempt to sort out the clutter and decide what I could say aloud and what I needed to pretend I'd never thought, even for a moment.

"And there was this brief moment when I thought . . ." *Ugh. Don't go there, Cadie.* "Never mind." I shook my head and laughed as I returned to my seat at the island.

Darby grabbed my arm and squeezed gently. "No! You don't get to do that. There was a brief moment when you thought *what?*"

Getting everything out was one thing, but indulging in fruitless fantasy was another thing entirely.

"Seriously, never mind. It's not worth—"

"There was a brief moment when you thought there was a chance for the two of you?" Darby asked, completely ignoring my too-little-too-late diversion tactics. "When you thought that maybe losing you was all it had taken for him to realize he would do whatever it would take to hold on to you?"

I wanted to laugh. I wanted to make fun of her for getting caught up in impossible romantic scenarios that only occur in John Cusack movies.

I wanted to tell her she had completely misunderstood where I was heading with the conversation. But I couldn't laugh, and I couldn't make fun of her. She'd understood perfectly.

"See?" I asked, throwing my arms into the air. "It's the same old thing. I'm never going to be happy unless John Cusack is running around Manhattan with his one cashmere glove, searching used bookstores for my phone number."

I thought back to my thirtieth birthday, when I decided that my romantic standards were too high. I had given up on ever finding Cary Grant, and then Will Whitaker walked into my life and I got more carried away by the fantasy than ever. And look where it had gotten us. It wasn't Will's fault that life was not a John Cusack movie any more than it was my fault that I wished it were.

Darby leaned in and got her face inches from mine, forcing me to look at her. "And that's what he's been trying to give you. Yes, he's been doing it badly, but he's trying. Maybe if you would just talk to him—"

"I tried, Darby!" I sat back down on the stool and buried my head in my arms on the island as my tears began their torrential downpour. "That's what I was doing. What I was starting to do, anyway. And then . . . Anna."

Darby placed her hand on mine and softly said, "I'm sorry, sweetie."

We sat in silence for a moment, apart from

my sobs and sniffs, until Larinda said, "Who's Anna?"

I lifted my head slightly, so my voice wouldn't be as muffled. "She's the girl I was talking about. She works in accounting and—"

She shook her head. "No, I mean, if Will's looking at you like you're his, why are we worried about this Anna? This clearly isn't a matter of it being too late, and it sure doesn't seem like it's a matter of him not being in love with you. From what I can tell, it's simply a matter of you deciding whether or not you want to spend your life with this man—and what it might take to do that."

We sat wallowing in my sad silence for several moments until we heard footsteps approaching the kitchen. "That's strange," Larinda whispered as she stood from her seat and walked to the door. "Honey? Is that you?" she called out as she walked.

"Oh, sorry, babe," he said from outside the door. "I was upstairs and didn't hear you come in." Darby and I looked at each other and smiled at their sweetness as we heard them kiss in greeting. "How was the concert?"

"Great. That man can still put on a show."

I giggled softly at Darby, who was nodding enthusiastically at Larinda's statement. I had created a Manilow monster.

Larinda continued as they entered the

kitchen. "I didn't think you'd be home for hours."

Kevin looked positively shocked to see us. Panicked, almost. He looked straight at me and said, "You're *here*. What in the world are you doing here?"

"Um . . . is that okay?" I asked nervously, though I had no idea why I should feel nervous.

"Of course that's okay, Cadie," Larinda answered, no doubt as surprised by his reaction as I was—but handling it in a decidedly more no-nonsense way. "I ran into them at the concert and we decided to come back for some coffee and girl talk."

Kevin chuckled and looked around the room. I'd never before seen him appear at such a complete loss. "I'm sorry." He spotted and quickly grabbed a permanent marker from the kitchen counter and stuffed it in the pocket of his pants. "I must just be tired."

Larinda placed her hands on her hips and cocked her head to one side. "Have you been drinking? What are you doing with that marker?"

He chuckled again as he pulled out his phone, appeared to send a quick text, and then put it away once more. "Nope. No drinking. I just . . . I'm sorry, McCaffrey. I just really didn't expect you to be *here*."

It was my turn to cock my head and furrow my brow.

"Why? Where *should* I be?"

21

At the End of the Day

Will was beginning to feel like he should've thought things through a bit more. As he left Kevin's house almost an hour earlier, he'd been fueled by love and enthusiasm, and quite possibly the fumes from the markers they'd been using. They'd all been so certain that the one-two romance punch he was packing would do the trick that he'd taken off running, unintentionally throwing a little *When Harry Met Sally* into the mix. After all, once you figure out you want to spend forever with someone, you get going right away. Or whatever Billy Crystal said to Meg Ryan at the end of that movie.

Running through the streets of Manhattan, from Tribeca to the West Village, had seemed very romantic and not at all daunting. It was only about a mile, door to door, and he'd have spent more time boarding trains or waiting for cabs. But as he ran down Greenwich St., and the December air off the Hudson River mixed with the more-than-usual exertion to make him feel as if he'd swallowed an entire tank of helium, the doubts began creeping in.

For one thing, Billy Crystal hadn't run through the city with poster board under his arm and a gigantic eighties-era boom box in his hand.

But still, he'd run. It would be worth it, he knew, to see the look on Cadie's face when she appeared at her window. It wasn't as if he expected her to be immediately won over, of course. Thus, the one-two punch. And *still* it might not be easy. But he would get her to open the door, and he would get her to talk to him. He would get her to listen.

If she ever got home.

He didn't get Kevin's text that Cadie was at his house until he rounded the corner onto Bleecker Street. After telling Kevin to text him the moment she headed home, he turned around and walked a couple blocks to a Starbucks that, ridiculously, closed at 8:00. He made his way into a pizzeria that stayed open late, but he quickly remembered that he had no money with him, and most trendy West Village hot spots didn't look too kindly on patrons ordering water and taking up desperately needed tables.

He'd wandered around the Village, keeping moving so as not to turn into an icicle, until Kevin finally texted. He computed the amount of time it would take her to get there, via car or train, and then gave her fifteen additional minutes, just in case she missed a stop or got caught in traffic.

But now, after all of that, he had been outside her apartment for twenty minutes—alternating between the middle of the street where he knew she'd be able to see him best, and the sidewalk, where there was less chance of him being run over by a car. He'd lost most of the feeling in his fingers, but thankfully the boom box seemed to be frozen to him, so it wasn't going anywhere. It was four degrees in the Big Apple, and Will was increasingly convinced there was no way Lloyd Dobler in *Say Anything* had held the boom box over his head for as long as Will had. In the movie, you get the impression that one performance of Peter Gabriel's "In Your Eyes" had been enough, but Will had now heard it four times, which felt like forty.

At least Cadie's neighbors seemed to think it was romantic. A crowd had been gathering for a while—New Yorkers who were surprised by nothing but who had the opportunity to see a real, live romantic comedy moment play out right before their eyes. A few of them had shouted out lines from the movie or begun singing along. A couple of men recognized him from ASN, a couple of women said things like, "If she doesn't show up, call me."

He'd borrowed a tan overcoat from Kevin. It didn't *exactly* complete the Dobler trench coat look—it was Hugo Boss wool and dwarfed Will like a little boy playing dress-up—but it was close enough to convey the idea. And it was warm, thankfully. Not warm enough to keep him from getting hypothermia, of course, but beggars can't be choosers.

He held the poster board between his knees and balanced the boom box on his shoulder so that he could look at his watch. It was nearly midnight. He wasn't sure how much longer he could stay out there.

Lloyd Dobler hadn't been acknowledged by the object of his affection either, he remembered, but Lloyd had attempted his serenade on an unusually sunny day in Seattle, during summer vacation. And the only thing Lloyd had to do the next day was practice his kickboxing.

It was time to execute the second part of the plan.

Will pulled out his phone and turned off the Peter Gabriel song—Sam had managed to track down a boom box, but a working one would have been too much to hope for on short notice in the 21st century—and clicked on the MP3 of Christmas carols.

"Okay, Rick. Let's do this."

He couldn't remember the character's name in *Love Actually* and hadn't really tried to remember it. There were so many characters in that movie that he didn't know how anyone was supposed to remember *any* of their names. But he did know that he was played by the same guy who played Rick Grimes on *The Walking Dead*, so nothing else mattered.

Once he was certain that his pieces of poster board were in the right order, he rang Cadie's doorbell and felt his heart race when a light turned on inside. He had to admit to himself that he hadn't even considered the possibility that she'd slept through his *Say Anything* homage. If so, that was a serious bummer. *Can it work in reverse if I need to repeat Dobler?* he asked himself. He was pretty sure it could. Lloyd was supposed to be the appetizer and Rick was the main course, but maybe he hadn't thought it through properly. In the end, maybe Billy running through Manhattan was actually the appetizer—even though Cadie wouldn't know about that until later. Rick was still the main course—obviously—and Lloyd would be dessert. It would work.

It had to work.

He heard the lock grind and the doorknob begin to turn, and he took one last look at his sign to make sure it wasn't upside down.

"You're perfect to me too, Will," a droll and unexpected—and far too masculine—voice greeted him after reading his sign.

His eyes flashed upward in a hurry and were met by an apparently amused Oliver McCaffrey.

"Oli—" he began, but that felt too informal, though it never had before. "Mr. McCaffrey.

Sir. I'm sorry . . . I thought . . . I mean, I was just . . ." He stopped and exhaled. He was pretty sure it couldn't get any worse, but he didn't see any reason to tempt fate. "Is Cadie available?"

Oliver crossed his arms and feigned disappointment. "You mean this isn't for me?"

Will wasn't going to do it. He *couldn't* do it. He had never wanted to see Oliver McCaffrey again, and on the night when he was determined to do whatever he had to do to convince Cadie to give him another chance, he wouldn't allow her father to stand in the way. Not again.

"Cadie!" he yelled into the apartment, and Oliver looked startled. Will didn't care. "Cadie, I need to talk to you. Just give me five minutes, okay? That's all I—"

"Will, stop!" Oliver placed his hands on Will's shoulders with force, most likely in an attempt to stop him from barging in. "She's not here, but the cops probably will be soon if you keep this up."

"Oliver? What's going on?" Nessa appeared from the bathroom. Great. "Will? What in the world are you doing?"

"She's really not here?" Will muttered, his romantic fervor quickly giving way to embarrassment.

"She's really not," Oliver confirmed. "I don't know when to expect her." He took a deep breath and then asked bluntly, "Do you think it's best that you're here when she gets home? I'm happy to call you a cab."

Will's eyes began to burn with indignation. "I know you've never liked me. I know you never thought I was good enough for her. But don't you think she needs a chance to make that decision for herself?"

Nessa appeared behind her husband. "That's not true, Will. We've always liked you."

He laughed bitterly. "I'd hate to see how you treat the boyfriends you *don't* like, then."

Oliver cleared his throat. "I think you need to calm down—"

"Twice I asked for your blessing to marry her, and *twice* you told me no!" he shouted. He couldn't remember ever being as angry or as cold in his life, and he wasn't sure which was causing him to shake. "Now I've lost her, and all I want is a chance to convince her that we're supposed to be together. So, *yes.* I think I should be here when she gets home. I'm just not sure *you* should be."

Oliver and Nessa looked at each other. There were tears in Nessa's eyes, and Will was immediately filled with regret. He didn't regret a single word, but appearing erratic wasn't going to do him any favors. He didn't care what they thought of him, but he knew that Cadie did.

Otherwise, he never would have bothered to seek their blessing to begin with.

"Why don't you come in?" Nessa asked kindly, taking him off guard.

"Okay," he replied, partially because he didn't know what else to say, but primarily because his hot head wasn't thawing the rest of his body out quickly enough.

It felt strange walking back into Cadie's apartment, and even more strange to be there with her parents. The bed in the middle of the room taunted him, a reminder of things gone wrong. He set Rick and Lloyd's props down beside the wall and sat on the couch at Oliver's urging. Oliver grabbed two chairs from the kitchen table and placed them across from Will.

As he and Nessa sat in the chairs, Oliver began speaking. "Will, I think we owe you—"

"Do you have any idea how much I love your daughter?" he asked, overwhelmingly aware that he had some things he had to say before he could possibly be ready to listen. "All I've ever wanted to do is protect her and love her and care for her. And I know that I can't give her the type of life that you've given her, but I don't think you realize that she doesn't *want* that type of life anymore. Sometimes I'm not even sure that *she* realizes it. You got in her head." He scoffed and looked down at his feet, ashamed of himself. "Just like you got in my head, I guess."

Even in the heat of the apartment he was too cold—and too irritated—to sit. He stood from the couch and began pacing the length of the space, as he'd done on occasion and seen Cadie do so many more times.

"If I'd asked her to marry me a year ago, *more* than a year ago, when I first planned to, I think she would have said yes." Self-doubt filled him as it always did when he thought of the reality of Cadie actually choosing to spend her life with him, but this time he shook it off. At the time, he'd known the moment had been right—and he knew it still. No matter how much effort he'd gone to in order to try and convince himself otherwise. "Do you know how stupid I felt, giving her a box as a gift?"

Oliver and Nessa looked at each other questioningly, seemingly unsure how to answer that.

"I'm sorry," Nessa spoke up. "What box?"

"I was going to propose on her birthday. Our anniversary. But then when you wouldn't give us your blessing—" He threw his hands up in the air. "Never mind. That one's on me."

"Well, like I was saying, I think we owe you—"

Will growled to keep himself from hearing whatever Oliver was saying and couldn't help but wonder if there was a romance movie in which the hero goes completely off the deep end in front of his love's parents.

"Sorry," he said with a groan as he noticed how taken aback they appeared. "Really. I haven't lost my mind. But I think you're about to apologize for something and I'll probably appreciate it, and it might make me not able to say some things that I really need to say. Please just let me say them."

They both nodded, and Nessa wiped away tears as Will continued.

"Last year, you weren't wrong. Not entirely. I wasn't very driven and I wasn't focused on moving ahead in my career. I was making enough money to live, and I loved my job. I guess it hadn't really occurred to me that I needed to at least have the beginnings of a plan for the future. Cadie deserved for me to have a plan. She deserved to know that life would be good and safe and that she wouldn't have to worry. I know that's what you've always wanted for her." He stopped pacing and stood in front of them. "But you were wrong for believing that just because I didn't have a 401(k) or a house on Oyster Bay, I wasn't the one to give her a life that's good and safe." He collapsed back onto the couch. "And I knew that. Even then. But I also knew how important your approval was to her." He looked back down at his shoes, where his toes were now finally getting feeling back into them, and added softly, "No matter how archaic I think it is to ask for permission, your approval was important to me too."

"I appreciate you telling us that, Will," Oliver said, no doubt sincerely.

Truthfully, Will had always liked Cadie's dad.

Her mom too . . . in a more intimidating sort of way. But he'd looked up to Oliver and enjoyed spending time with him. Their relationship didn't quite fill the void left by his own dad's passing, but it had been important to him nonetheless.

"The first time you told me no," Will continued, "I got it. I was disappointed—kind of furious, actually—but I got it. I knew you were looking out for her and, I thought, looking out for me too. I'd already bought the ring, and I almost went ahead and proposed. That night . . . I still considered doing it. But you'd gotten in my head. You were right. She deserved more."

Nessa leaned in. "So you gave her a box?"

Will smiled sadly. Regardless of the mood in the room, he understood why that piece of information required some follow-up.

"The ring box. After you guys said no, I came up with this whole plan that I really thought she was going to love. I found out all this interesting history about the box, but most of all it was an important nod to something special in *our* history. The two of us. And I was going to bring it all full circle and propose in a few months, after I'd gotten some things squared away. But I couldn't do it."

"Couldn't do what?" Oliver asked.

"I couldn't get ahead. Not quickly enough, anyway. I looked at other jobs, but I couldn't stand the thought of leaving that place I loved

355

and not being in the same building with her every day. So I just worked . . . *more*." He rubbed his eyes as they began to burn again. "I never should have let you get in my head."

Will watched as Nessa reached out and grabbed Oliver's hand. Oliver took a deep breath and said, "You need to let me say something now. Okay?" Will nodded—hesitant and exhausted. "You've been like a son to us, and we never doubted for a moment that you were right for Cadie and she was right for you. No parents could hope for better for their daughter, Will. I hope you know that." Oliver leaned toward the couch. "We never meant it to be a refusal. Truly. Only a 'not yet.' But looking back now, we can see that was a mistake, and we are very sorry that we said no that first time."

Will jumped from the couch in a flash of anger. "You're sorry you said no the first time? The *first* time? What about the second time, Oliver? I mean, I asked her anyway, but—"

Nessa stood. "I think it was all about the timing, Will."

"You said no because of the timing?" He threw his arms in the air again and said, "Clearly it didn't make any difference anyway. She turned me down. Obviously."

He was just so very tired—of the conversation, of the day, of not having Cadie by his side.

"I waited too long," Will continued. "I . . . I

shouldn't have. . . ." He had to be careful. It wasn't for him to tell her parents that he and Cadie had slept together. "Maybe it wasn't the right timing, and that just makes me mad at myself. The right timing had been a year earlier, or a year before that, or a year before that, or any other countless number of chances. And maybe if I hadn't cared so much about what you thought—"

Oliver sighed heavily. "Will, we would have said yes the second time, but it seemed to us that you and Cadie weren't as close as you had been."

"So you tried to make her decision for her? You had no right to do that!"

"No," Oliver replied, carefully, it seemed. "We called her."

Will looked from Oliver to Nessa and back again. "What are you talking about?"

"While you and I talked, Nessa went in the other room and called Cadie."

"And . . . what?" The room seemed to be spinning. "Told her not to marry me?"

Nessa sniffed and looked as if she wanted to reach out to Will, but she probably knew that her touch would not be welcome. Instead, her hands were left fidgeting.

"No, Will. I just asked her if she was happy with you. I asked her . . ." She sniffed again, and Oliver held her fidgeting hands. "I asked her if she wanted to spend her life with you."

It didn't make sense. Nothing about any of it made sense.

Will crossed his arms because, probably much like Nessa, he didn't know what else to do with his hands. "Are you saying she said no?"

He'd messed up. A million times he'd messed up. He knew that. He knew he would have to make a lot of things right. He knew that she hadn't forgiven him yet, and he knew that they would need time to heal.

And he knew what she'd said to him when he finally asked her to marry him. That she didn't love him anymore. It had never really occurred to him that she meant it.

"You can understand why we couldn't give you our blessing," Nessa whispered. "I'm sorry, Will."

The end of the day looked very different than anything he had imagined.

22

Forever . . . In Spite of It All

I'd been a good girl who had never broken curfew. As such, I wasn't quite sure how to react, as an independent adult, upon walking into my apartment and finding my parents sitting there with serious expressions on their faces.

"Hi, sweetheart. We need to talk," my dad said.

They'd texted me a couple hours earlier to let me know they had early meetings in the city and had decided it would be easier for them to crash on my sofa bed, if I was okay with that. Of course I was okay with that, but I also didn't believe a word of it. My mother had no intention of spending a night on a sofa bed. I had no doubt that she was counting on me being the polite, considerate daughter I had always been who would willingly sacrifice her warm, comfortable bed.

The way I was feeling, after the emotionally exhausting day I'd had, I was tempted to pull out the couch, throw them some sheets, and wish them luck on ignoring the intrusive metal bar in the middle of the mattress. The problem—

besides the fact that I couldn't imagine ever actually going through with a jerk move like that—was that there was another aspect of their story I wasn't buying. I suspected they were there because they didn't want me to be alone, after my emotional breakdown earlier in the day which, thankfully, was the only one of my emotional breakdowns of which they were aware. And while I found the hovering incredibly annoying, I also loved them for it.

"Is everything okay?" I asked in reaction to the loving but sad expression on my dad's face.

"Will was here," he responded. As if that said it all, when it actually took away any semblance of clarity.

"He was here?" I asked, a little more shakily than I would care to admit. I sat down on the edge of my bed. "Why?"

For almost a month after we broke up I had kept working with him—on the same floor of the same office building—and I had hardly seen him, heard him, or even talked about him at all. That was followed by three weeks during which the overpopulation of the tiny island we lived on kept us as isolated as if we lived on separate continents. But then, for the last twelve hours or so, he had seemed to be the only topic of conversation.

"He was looking for you," my mom spoke for the first time. "He showed up at the door playing

Christmas carols, holding up a handwritten sign about you being perfect."

My cluelessness mirrored my mother's for a moment, and then a smile overtook my face. It was a smile caused largely by confusion, but it was a smile nonetheless.

"You're kidding," I whispered. "Did he . . . did he say anything?"

My dad sighed. "Like I said, we need to talk."

About six minutes later, my brief period of stunned silence was coming to an end.

"I—I—I don't understand," I stammered. "He wanted to marry me a *year* ago? Why would you have told him no?" Tears ran down my cheeks, and I just let them flow. "The second time I understand. Then, you were going off what I said. But the *first* time?"

"It was wrong of us, Cadie," my dad said. "We thought we were doing what was best for you, but—"

"And you just held on to all of this information? Dad, I sat at lunch with you that day and cried about how Will had never asked me to marry him because he didn't love me enough! And today, Mom? It never occurred to you that any of this might be good for me to know?"

My dad hung his head. "I know," he whispered. "At lunch, I wasn't sure what to do, but then your mother and I talked about it and we thought it only stood to hurt you. We misread the situation.

We were wrong and we're sorry. You have every right to be angry—"

"You *bet* I'm angry!" I shouted as I sprang from the couch. "I spent a year—starting *that* night, when he gave me the ring box—convincing myself he didn't love me enough. Convincing myself he would *never* love me enough—not like I loved him. And all along . . ." I sank back onto the couch as painful realization dawned. It was almost more than I could comprehend. "It was that year of thinking he didn't love me enough that drove us apart."

My mom stood and walked over to join me on the edge of the bed. She took one of my hands in both of hers and said, "We're so sorry, sweetie. We really are."

Sobs overtook me and she immediately pulled me into her arms for the second time that day.

The next thing I knew, sunlight was peeking through the blinds and illuminating a folded sheet and a couple of pillows sitting on the couch. I was in my bed, and the smell of bacon filled my apartment.

"There's my girl," my dad said as I sat up. "I hope we weren't making too much noise in here. Are you hungry?"

I had no memory of falling asleep, or even of climbing under the covers, but I was keenly aware of a night full of dreams about Will.

"No thanks," I replied, shaking my head and stretching my arms over my head. "What time is it?"

"A little after nine," answered my mom. I watched her flip the bacon in the pan and I felt anger and sadness welling up inside of me as the memory of all I had learned the night before came rushing back to me. "Sure you don't want something to eat?"

I looked down to see what I was wearing and rolled my eyes as I realized I was still in the same blasted dress. "I said I'm not hungry." I hurried to my closet, pulled off the dress and—finally—the pantyhose, and threw on a pair of jeans and a sweatshirt. Socks and sneakers quickly followed and then I headed toward the door. "I'm going for a walk," I announced, paying them a courtesy I wasn't sure they deserved. The fact was, I wasn't quite sure I was ready to be in the same room with them. I grabbed my coat and opened the door.

I don't know who was more surprised—my parents, to whom I had probably never been so rude in my life, or the guy standing on the other side of the door, holding a bouquet of daisies, his hand preparing to knock on the suddenly wide-open door.

"Oh!" I exclaimed. "Sorry."

Mr. Daisy Man had no sense of humor—or manners, I suppose—whatsoever, and simply asked, "Are you Cadie McCaffrey?"

"I am."

"Here ya go."

He handed me the daisies and an envelope, and then he was gone. I couldn't blame him, really. In the past twelve hours a cold front had blown in, and someone would have had to be pretty dedicated to stand still out there any longer than absolutely necessary.

"What have you got there?" my dad asked, coming up behind me, and I was so curious myself that I momentarily forgot how mad I was at him.

"I don't know."

"They're daisies, dear," my mom called out from the kitchen, and I rolled my eyes again.

"Yes, I know they're daisies. I just don't know why I have them."

I looked down at the envelope in my hands, and my breath caught in my throat as I saw my name written on the front in familiar handwriting. After everything? After all he said and all he heard? After all the times I wouldn't listen? My hand began trembling, and I felt hope rise up in my chest.

Hope? Where had *that* come from?

I turned around and looked up at my dad, and as I raised my eyes, the tears broke free from the invisible shield that had been holding them in place.

My dad smiled. "Do you want some privacy while you read whatever's in that envelope?"

I nodded. "Thanks."

I saw my mom look around my open floor plan as she placed eggs and bacon on two plates. "Are we supposed to eat in the bathroom?"

Giggling at the thought through my tears, I said, "You guys stay here," and then I took my daisies and my envelope into my walk-in closet. I closed the door, kicked my dress and pantyhose out of the way, and sat on the floor to begin reading.

Dear Cadie,

I don't know that I've ever written a letter to you before, and for that I'm sorry. Notes? Sure. Emails? Endlessly. But not an actual letter. The truth is, I just never thought of it. I never realized that maybe you would view it as romantic. In all fairness, until very recently I had never seen P. S. I Love You. If I had realized that Gerard Butler wrote letters, I would have gotten to it sooner.

There are some things you need to know, and I'm fully aware that there's a chance you could stop reading at any time, so let's just dive right in to the most important.

I'm sorry.

I'm sorry that I gave in and that we made love. Okay . . . I'm already seeing why people don't write letters much anymore.

I wish I could hit backspace and rephrase that. (I probably should have written out a rough draft or something . . .) "I'm sorry that I gave in" and "I'm sorry that we made love" are two very different apologies, and they both feel very complicated. Also, if I'm being honest, I think "made love" is a ridiculous phrase, but any other way of saying it sounds crude and cold. But "made love"? What is that even supposed to mean?

"I'm sorry that I gave in" makes it sound like I was resistant and you convinced me, but what I actually mean is I'm sorry that I gave in to my desire to be with you at that time—the wrong time for us. I am. The desire was always there, and it was always a battle not to give in, and that night I guess I was tired of fighting. I wish I had a better excuse than that, but the truth is I wanted you, just like I've always wanted you, and on that one night I made the wrong choice.

You talked about whether or not I had asked God for forgiveness. The truth is I hadn't thought about it. As much as I hate to admit it, I hadn't thought about anything other than you. I don't want to be someone who doesn't think about it. If you were to ask me that question again, I would honestly say that I have asked for forgiveness and I believe God gave it to me. And somehow, I think he's used all of this to pull me closer to him. I realize now that somewhere along the line I started putting him on the back burner—in my own life and in our relationship. I really am so sorry, Cadie.

I need to address the second part of the statement too. "I'm sorry that we made love." Just saying that doesn't feel adequate, though. It needs all sorts of qualifiers. I'm sorry that it happened when it did. I'm sorry we weren't married. I'm sorry your first time will always be something you wish hadn't happened. I'm sorry that I wasn't more understanding and sensitive to what it was like for you.

I'm sorry I look so irresistible in that suit. It wasn't fair to tempt you that way.

The tears fell harder than ever as I simultaneously laughed so hard I snorted.

"You okay?" my dad asked from the other side of the door—a little too close to the other side of the door, actually.

"Can you throw me a tissue or something?"

Seconds later the door creaked open a few inches and a roll of toilet paper flew into the closet.

"Thanks." I tore off a few squares and blew my

nose. "Now can you please not stand right by the door?"

I heard frantic footsteps—more than one set, if I wasn't mistaken—and then his more distant voice called out, "We're not."

The truth is, all of this has made me realize that maybe you and I haven't been on the same page for a while now. Look, I don't really understand all of this romance movie stuff. To me, a big, bold declaration of love involving a marching band and a stadium sound system isn't as romantic as the way you used to ask me about my day and then genuinely listen as I prattled on about a thousand sports details you didn't care about.

The daisies in You've Got Mail I could get behind. That was just a simple matter of him listening to her—although when he brought her the daisies he was in the midst of a stalker-ish kind of con, but I'm willing to overlook most of that. (Side note: I didn't have daisies delivered to you because they were Meg Ryan's favorite. I chose daisies because I know they're your favorite. Sometimes I actually paid attention.)

What matters, though, isn't that I don't want that stuff. What matters is that I think you do. Or I thought you did. I don't know. Honestly, as I write this, I'm not too sure about anything.

Did your parents tell you about our lovely chat? Yeah . . . that was fun. It was great to catch up. (How did people survive before emojis? I wish I could insert the eye roll one there.) Just in case they didn't fill you in, I'll just tell you that I made a fool of myself. I don't know what I was expecting. For it to play out like Love Actually? Maybe. (Although maybe not like that storyline of Love Actually, since that would involve you running in to your husband/my best friend before he grew suspicious that there hadn't, in fact, been carolers at the door.) But I wasn't expecting your parents at the door, and I sure wasn't expecting to find out you hadn't been happy. That you hadn't wanted to spend your life with me. That you meant it when you said you weren't in love with me.

That changes things, doesn't it?

"No!" I shouted to the defenseless papers in my hands. "No, no, no, no, no." I stood and began pacing around the tiny space, the hope slipping away as quickly and unexpectedly as it had first appeared.

"Cadie?" my mom called from the other room. "Do you want me to come in there?"

"Do you need anything?" my dad asked, once again too close to the door. "There's plenty of bacon left—"

I shushed them. "I'm still reading. Can you guys *please* stop listening?"

I'm sorry I kept pushing. Somehow I got it in my head that, at the end of the day, it would be you and me. I'm so disappointed in myself that I got so side-tracked, so disconnected, that I didn't even realize I was losing you until it was too late. I promise you, I never wanted this. I never wanted to lose you.

On top of a very long list of regrets is the fact that I took your love for granted. I'm so sorry, Cadie.

I probably shouldn't have shown up at your apartment last night. I guess I just never have known when enough is enough. I had nothing planned the night we went to Staten Island—I was just thrilled to be able to spend some time with you. When things began taking the turn they began to take, I assure you I wasn't thinking, "Everything's going according to plan." No . . . all I could think was, "How did I ever get lucky enough to love her?"

After that, I couldn't imagine ever watching you walk away again, so that was that. I really didn't know how weak I was. I didn't know that all it would take would be the sight of you for me to get right back in the fight.

But I guess all it took was understanding that your picture of forever doesn't include me for me to finally be strong enough to admit defeat.

So, I'm done. I need you to know that. If you and I somehow end up at the top of the Empire State Building together, or having a fight in the rain, or if we're forced to be partners in a dance contest, or you wake up to "I've Got You, Babe" and you're forced to relive the same day until you get it right . . . just know that it wasn't my doing.

But also know that if I thought it was what you wanted, I'd climb however many flights of stairs I had to climb, watch The Weather Channel obsessively and pick fights with you as necessary, learn how to tango, and change every calendar to February 2nd for the rest of my life.

Yours forever . . .
in spite of it all,
Will

Tired of pulling off squares of toilet paper, I resorted to dabbing my eyes with what was left of the roll. I stuffed the letter back into the envelope and pulled my phone from my pocket.

"Pick up, pick up, pick up," I muttered as it rang.

"ASN, this is Anna Alvarez."

Seriously? "Anna, it's Cadie. Did I call the accounting line by mistake? I meant to call Darby's direct line . . ."

There was a long pause, and when her voice returned, her tone made it clear we were no longer on friendly terms—though I thought we had been as recently as the evening before.

"She has your old number now, remember?"

I slapped my forehead. "Sorry. Old habits die hard. Would you mind transferring—"

"She's not here."

I waited for her to give me a little more to work with, but that was all I was going to get. I could call Darby's cell, but if she wasn't at ASN, that wouldn't do much good . . .

"Is there anything else?" she asked.

Yikes. I understood why I wasn't an Anna fan, but I couldn't imagine what had changed for *her* since yesterday evening.

"I guess not. Actually, hang on! Could you please transfer me to Kevin?"

"You know we don't just transfer calls to—"

"Okay then." I was out of patience. "I'll call

him on his cell and explain that you wouldn't put me through."

She sighed. "Please hold."

"Kevin Lamont," he answered three seconds later.

"It's Cadie."

"Hey, kid! You doing okay?"

"I need a favor. Can you tell me if Will is there? Or, more accurately, I need to know if he'll be there in about . . ." I looked at my watch and did a quick computation of traffic and rail schedules. "An hour or so."

"McCaffrey," he growled. "No more. I want out. You want to avoid him, he wants to make an idiot of himself for you, and I just want to go back to being the happy, successful man I was before the two of you turned my life into this depressing reality show version of itself."

I smiled. "Actually, I'm hoping to make an idiot of myself for him this time."

There was another growl, softer this time, and then a slow exhale of breath. "He's in pretty rough shape today, Cadie. Unless you're completely sure about this—"

"I'm sure. I've never been so sure about anything in my entire life." I wiped away a renegade tear. "You don't think I'm too late, do you?"

"I'm pretty sure that when it comes to you, there's no such thing for him. But he won't be here in an hour. He's taking some time off."

"Is he leaving town, or—"

"Here's a thought. Rather than ask me these questions, why don't you two talk to each other for a change?"

"I'm trying, Kev. I promise I'm trying."

He grumbled some indecipherable words of frustration and then sighed heavily. "I convinced him to take a few days and go up to the cabin in the Poconos."

Oh, the blasted Poconos. How they vex me!

"Has he already left?"

"A car's supposed to pick him up in a few hours—"

I pulled my phone away from my ear and looked at the time. "Okay, please, do me one last favor and then, if all goes well, the reality show will be over. Please?" I begged.

He grumbled and groaned but finally said, "Fine. But I'm not watching any more movies."

"No more movies," I agreed and then cleared my throat. "I just need you to help me get Will to the top of the Empire State Building."

Five minutes later I was running toward the door. I grabbed my coat from the hook and said, "I'm going to try and get Will back, you guys. Pray I'm not too late."

My mother stopped me before I could walk outside. "Cadie, honey, I think that before you go—"

"There's nothing else you can say, Mom. It doesn't matter, and I've wasted enough time."

"I was just going to say you might want to clean your face."

I looked in the mirror on the wall and had never been so grateful that my mother had always been just a little bit vain. Twenty-four hours of Syosset, Brooklyn, and at least three independent emotional breakdowns were written all over my face—mostly in mascara and eyeliner.

I kicked off my shoes. "Time?"

"Just past ten!" my dad replied, his urgency equaling my own.

I had to be at the top of the Empire State Building at 12:00, and in Manhattan midday traffic, I knew that if I took too much time I would be pushing it. But I also knew that I couldn't show up looking like Cruella De Vil and Norma Desmond had begun giving makeovers at Sephora.

By 11:15 I was in a cab on Sixth Avenue heading toward Midtown, looking and feeling much better than I had before my quick shower. I had been so tempted to put yesterday's dress back on—since I would be willing to do just about anything to have him look at me that same way again, now that everything had changed—but I had a sneaking suspicion it didn't really matter what I wore. Also, sleeping in the dress all night had resulted in some creases nearly as set in as those under my eyes from all the crying. I had time for concealer, but I most assuredly did not have time to iron.

By 11:50 I was looking at the sheer magnitude of cars outside my window, not moving, and wondering at what point I needed to be like Meg Ryan in *Sleepless in Seattle*, jump out of the cab, and make a run for it. Why had my romantic, impulsive self insisted on taking a taxi? If I'd taken the subway, I would have already been at the top, enjoying the view and probably a cappuccino, which I could have bought with all the extra time I would have had. Instead I'd chosen relative comfort and solitude, both of which should have gone against my best Manhattanite instincts.

"Did you know that Sixth Avenue is officially named Avenue of the Americas?" my driver asked.

"Yep," I replied dismissively as I mentally calculated how many blocks there were to go.

"This very avenue is the inspiration for the song '6th Avenue Heartache' by the midnineties rock band the Wallflowers."

I looked at him, confused. I couldn't remember the last time a taxi driver had spoken to me beyond asking, "Where to?"

"Why are you telling me this?"

He shrugged. "Interesting tourist tidbits."

"Well, thanks, but I'm a New Yorker."

"Sorry," he said. "Locals don't usually have that sort of wonder and merriment in their eyes on the way to the Empire State Building."

"It's a romance movie thing," I said with a sheepish grin.

"Ah." He nodded knowingly. "I don't see as many of you in the winter. Traffic's been backed up all day because of some construction up near Bryant Park. What time are you supposed to be there?"

"Noon." I looked at my watch. Eight minutes to go.

He sighed. "I hate to say it, but I think you need to pull a Meg Ryan."

My eyes flew open. "I was just thinking that! Thanks." I handed him my money and took off running.

I felt so victorious as I ran into the lobby at 11:58, but I had completely forgotten the reality of the Empire State Building. Of course locals don't have wonder and merriment. It's a total tourist trap, with lines for days. I pulled out my phone and found the website to buy a VIP Express Pass so I could skip the line.

"Are you kidding me?" I grumbled as I paid the $65.00 fee. Did Meg and Tom have to pay $65.00? What about when Tom had to go *back* up because his son forgot his backpack? Romance was simpler then, I guess.

"Will's up there, Will's up there, Will's up

377

there," I repeated to myself as I hurried to the elevator.

I took a deep breath as I stepped off at the 86th floor and braced myself—for what, I wasn't quite sure. At the very least, breathtaking views of my favorite city in the world. Also likely: a passionate kiss or two.

And, of course, the wind.

My super cute hat went flying—it was probably to Jersey by the time I turned around—and I was fairly certain that what my mother had been telling me my entire life was actually true. If you go out with wet hair, you'll catch your death of cold. I reached up and covered my damp head with my hands to prevent icicles from forming. Will had gone to a lot of trouble to recreate romantic movie scenes, and I was going to be very disappointed in myself if the best *I* could pull off was Jack and Rose's goodbye in *Titanic*.

I hurried around the observation deck, expecting every man to be him. Every corner was my last obstacle to seeing him, I knew. I looked in front of me and behind me, knowing he was there. I was absolutely certain.

But I walked the entire deck and didn't see him.

I was torn between standing by the door, so I didn't miss him, and making another lap, convinced I had *already* missed him, but suddenly I was too scared to move. Not scared that I'd miss him, but scared that he wasn't there. I looked at my watch—12:10. He wouldn't have left. That wasn't even a possibility. The plan Kevin and I concocted was foolproof. Or at least it was Whitaker-proof. And he wouldn't have been late. Kevin would have called me back if for some reason the time wasn't going to work out. So there was only one other explanation.

He got there, saw me, and walked away. Probably *ran,* more like.

"Cadie?"

I gasped at the sound of his voice behind me and turned to face him. I grew weak and yet empowered at the sight of him. "Hi."

Our eyes met for a brief moment and then he began looking at anything else—*everything else*—besides me. "I'm . . . I promise I didn't arrange this. I'm meeting someone. For work. It's um . . . you haven't seen Hank Aaron and Willie Mays around here, have you?"

Yep. Absolutely Whitaker-proof.

I smiled, enchanted by him. "Yeah, sorry . . . that was me."

He looked confused for a moment and then he shook his head and looked down at his feet. "What do you mean, it was you?"

"I needed to see you. I'm sorry I blurred the lines and used a work thing to get you here. Believe me, I know how ironic that is. But I just didn't know how else to make it happen." Wow, the expression on his face made me feel guilty.

I guess in my head I'd thought he'd be happy to see me, and all would be forgiven. I guess I hadn't really considered how excited he'd be at the thought of meeting two of his heroes. "I'm sorry if you're disappointed . . ."

"It's not that. I admit, it seemed a little fishy that two octogenarian baseball legends, one of whom lives in Atlanta, the other somewhere in California, I think, happened to be passing through Manhattan together, and really wanted to meet me. Here. In December." He looked around and took in the view and the crowd. "I've never been here before."

"You've never been—"

"Never saw the point, really. So when everybody talks about 'the top of the Empire State Building,' I thought they meant the *top*."

"Oh! You mean—"

"I've been waiting for Hank Aaron and Willie Mays on the 102nd floor. Yeah. So, um . . . what's up?"

A smile overtook my lips. "I got your letter."

"Look, Cadie . . . I can't . . . I mean, I said all I needed to say, and I really can't . . . I don't know if I can . . ."

I took a step toward him and grabbed his hands, and I think every muscle in his body froze. But his eyes met mine.

"Will, I need a chance to say some things now. Is that okay?"

He pulled his hands away and lifted the collar of his coat to pull it around his jaw as a gust of wind blew past. "Did you know the 102nd floor is enclosed? Want to go up there instead?"

"Seriously?" I laughed—though the sting of his hands abruptly fleeing from mine certainly clouded the humor. "After I paid $65.00 to get to the 86th?"

"Why in the world did you pay $65.00?"

I shrugged. "I was running late. They sure make it all look easier in the movies, don't they?"

"You're telling me. Do you have any idea how difficult it is to pull off a *Say Anything* moment in West Village traffic? Not to mention tracking down a boom box . . ."

I thought about the words he was saying and tried to make sense of them, but I had nothing. "What are you talking about?"

"Your parents didn't tell you about that?"

"No. It's safe to say they didn't."

"Eh, well."

"Will, I owe you an apology." I stuffed my hands in my pockets and stepped closer to him. "Actually, I owe you a few apologies. My parents told me—"

"You know, at one point I was considering doing something from *The Lake House*," he said, completely disregarding my attempt to make amends. "I thought about mailing you letters from the future, or the past. Whichever."

I shook my head. "I don't think I know that one."

His eyebrows shot up in surprise. "Really? It's pretty good. There's this magic mailbox, or something. I don't know. I didn't fully understand it."

"When I read your letter, I—"

"Are you sure you don't want to go inside?"

"Will, stop!" I shouted as I grabbed his arms. "What are you doing? Why won't you let me talk?"

A sharp intake of breath was followed by, "Because I don't know what you're going to say."

I couldn't help but wonder if my face conveyed all of the sadness I was feeling. How much pain had we inflicted on each other?

"My parents told me. About you going to Syosset. Twice," I added sheepishly. "I had no idea. I promise I didn't know. And I know they told you why they said no the second time. I can't even imagine how that made you feel. I'm so sorry." I shivered, and he led me closer to the building, out of the wind somewhat. "It's like, for a long time, I think I was looking at everything through this lens of what I thought was missing, and what I assumed you were feeling."

He smiled sadly. "Just think of what might have happened if we'd actually talked."

"You sound like Darby. And Kevin. And my mother, actually—"

"Your mother?" He sneered, presumably at the assertion that he was in any way like my mother.

"She was the one who finally got through to me, if you can believe that. Yesterday. She made me realize I needed to talk to you, and forgive you. And that I needed to forgive myself."

He stared at me intently for a moment before repeating, "Your *mother?*"

"And she made me realize that it really was so wrong of me to pile all of my spiritual baggage on top of what you were dealing with. I had no right to try and tell you how you needed to handle your relationship with God. I'm sorry, Will."

He shook his head and laughed gently. "Seriously. *Your* mother?"

I laughed with him, but our laughter faded as I inched closer to him. "I *love* that you did all of those romance movie things for me. Now that I *get* it, I love it. But when I was running down Sixth Avenue, racing to get here, I wasn't thinking about acting out some romantic scene. I was thinking about *you.* I was thinking about your laugh. The way your eyes crinkle up and kind of disappear. Of how secure I always felt when you were holding my hand. And I was thinking about how you used to walk over to The Bench, just to see if I needed anything from the break room. You could have called. It would have been so much easier. But you wanted to see me. I always knew that."

"Cadie—"

I blinked away the tears and put my hands up to stop him from interrupting me. There were still so many things I hadn't said, and if I didn't say them right then, I wasn't sure I would ever get the chance.

"That night last year, when you gave me the ring box and I reacted like a crazy lady . . . I thought that was the beginning of the end. We were different after that. You pulled away from me, and I thought you didn't see us going anywhere. That you didn't love me—at least not like I loved you. But I wanted to marry you a year ago, and I've wanted to marry you every single day since. And when I told my mom you didn't make me happy . . . well, I *wasn't* happy. Not right then. I was so caught up in the guilt and regret, and that was on top of the million ways my brain had run away with itself for a year. I mean, if you weren't interested in marrying me, what were we even supposed to be building toward?"

A smile appeared on his face as he said, "I was always looking toward forever."

"I know that now, and I'm sorry, Will. I really am. For so many things. But in spite of it all, I realize now that I'm *still* looking toward forever. In fact, I can't even imagine a version of forever that doesn't have you in it. And I know that you said you're done, but I don't think I'll ever be done. So I'm ready to fight for you, if that's what it takes."

"I'm *never* going to stop fighting for *you*," he whispered as he closed the gap between us.

Before I even had a chance to store up my breath, the palm of his hand was on my jaw, and his fingers were grasping the back of my neck to pull my lips to his. All thoughts of the frigid Eastern wind were forgotten as that same hand got tangled in my hair and his other arm wrapped around my shoulders, pulling me so close that tourists passing by wouldn't have been able to tell where I ended and he began.

I rested my hands on his chest—no longer noticing the cold wind but in desperate need of the warmth of his arms around me. I wanted to feel the stubble on his face and run my fingers through that floppy head of hair that I had loved from the very first moment I saw him, but he was holding me so tightly, and my hands weren't willing to disrupt his embrace in order to make their way to his hair.

We paused to breathe and I slid my arms around his neck and held his face the way I'd wanted to for so long. My fingers weaved into his windblown hair and tugged the back of his head, pulling his lips toward mine once more. There would be time for breathing later.

"I love you," I whispered when our lips finally parted. "The biggest lie I ever told was telling you I didn't. And if I *ever* claim you're not romantic, please remind me of the time we were 1,200 feet in the air in December and I needed to fan myself." I saw a smile overtake his eyes and felt it overtake his mouth. "I mean, seriously, Will," I said, my breath still coming back to me.

He pulled away, which was the last thing I wanted, and laughed. "But I'm also just a boy, standing in front of a girl—"

I threw my head back in joyous laughter. "You don't have to ask me to love you, Whitaker. It's done."

"Actually . . ." He kissed my hand and lowered onto one knee. "I was going to say 'asking her to marry him.' " The hand that wasn't linked with mine was holding a beautiful emerald cut diamond ring. "Sorry there's not a box," he said with a wink.

My breath caught in my throat. "But, how did you . . . why do you . . ."

"Sorry, but Kevin's on my team. I claimed him pretty early. And he understands, in a way you still don't seem to, that not even Willie Mays and Hank Aaron could provide me with the motivation that you could. Besides, McCaffrey, even *I'm* not stupid enough to fall for that ridiculous plan you hatched." His smile grew wider and he kissed my hand once more. "But I just like that you try."

I leaned down to kiss him. Tears flooded my cheeks, but still I said nothing.

"You're killing me here. And frankly, I'm not sure how long my knee can stay on this cold concrete." He smiled and asked, "Will you marry me or not?"

I sniffed. "Have you asked my father's permission?"

I began laughing as he jumped up to face me. "Oh, you think that's funny, do you?"

"Too soon?"

He captured my mouth once again, and I threw my arms around his neck before pulling away from his kiss, just long enough to whisper, "My answer is yes." I smiled against his lips and added, "I really thought you'd never ask."

As we continued kissing on the top (but not the very top) of the Empire State Building, I had two very important realizations.

1) My previous ideas of "romance" weren't going to make me truly happy or fulfilled.

2) Spending forever with Will Whitaker, I was going to be swept off my feet on a regular basis, whether I needed to be or not.

Epilogue

After the First Four Years
of Forever

O kay, this may sound strange," Will said as he turned his body in the passenger seat to face her. "But this, right now, this whole thing, is probably the sexiest thing I've ever seen in my entire life."

Cadie threw her head back and laughed. "Oh, really? What in the world could I possibly find strange about that?"

As dependent as she had always been on Manhattan's public transportation, he'd never expected to see her behind the wheel. Much less behind the wheel of a beat-up 1975 Chevy truck. Driving down an Iowa dirt road. Wearing overalls, no less.

In response to the click she heard, she looked down at his hand, and then back up at him in mock horror. "What are you doing? You get that seat belt back on, mister."

"Oh, come on," he whispered as he scooted closer to her. "You can't tell me that's not what these old leather bench seats are made for." He leaned his head over, nuzzled his face in her hair, and kissed her neck.

"You're not setting a very good example," she said with a giggle.

He looked behind him and then resumed kissing her, undeterred. "The car's about a mile back. And her seat is rear-facing!"

"Okay. Fine. But when she's sixteen and learning to drive, and your little girl looks up at you—her *hero*—and says, 'You always wear *your* seat belt, right, Daddy?'. . ."

Will sighed. "You play dirty." He scooted back over to his side and rebuckled.

She reached over and placed her hand on his leg. "But I do agree these seats are pretty nice."

"Maybe we can properly explore their benefits once the vehicle has come to a full and complete stop."

"As lovely as that sounds, I'm barely fitting behind the steering wheel here. Any additional activities or, you know, movement at all will probably require some wide open spaces for the next month or so."

Every single day he fell more in love with her, and every single day she became more and more beautiful. But he knew she wasn't feeling that way.

Will reached over and placed his hand on her stomach. "Has he been moving a lot today?"

"Since we got in the truck he hasn't stopped.

Maybe he's a country boy." Her eyes flew open and she glanced over at him. "Maybe we should move to Iowa!" She winked and then turned her attention back to the gravel road in front of her.

"This from the woman who told me the day we moved to Connecticut it felt like admitting defeat."

"And I meant that!" She laughed as she turned left down a side road that seemed to be leading to more vast Iowa nothingness. "But I admit. I like having a bedroom door."

"Yes . . . that's been a very nice feature of suburban life." Just like that, his seat belt was off again, and he was scooting as close to her as he could get.

"Not this again," she said, playfully slapping his hands away.

He laughed and grabbed her free hand and held it. "I'm sorry you have to do all the driving. I had no idea my license had expired."

Cadie shrugged. "It's kind of fun, actually. I'll happily haul camera equipment all around the Iowa countryside in this potentially labor-inducing heap of disco-era metal any day, in exchange for a little time alone with you."

He kissed her on the cheek. "That part is nice. I am sorry I have to work on our anniversary, though."

"Are you kidding? For Darby's first piece as a segment producer? What choice was there? I'm just glad you guys are letting Gracie and me tag along."

Will scooted back to his side so he could see her better. "This is Darby we're talking about. You and Grace are the talent, and she's letting *me* tag along."

She shook her head and laughed. "I think that false humility stuff stopped working for you about two Emmys ago, Will."

He chuckled and took a quick peek behind them to make sure their daughter was still visible. They may have been about a mile apart, but he had no trouble spotting them across the flat farmland.

"I'm happy to be on camera and interview this guy for her, if that will help get her piece some attention, but honestly I hope it doesn't take too long. Since I'm not really getting paid for this, maybe she'll at least babysit tonight and we can go out on the town."

"Definitely. Although I'm not sure I brought anything fancy enough to wear to the place I really want to go. You know, that Dirty Ernie's we passed about twelve miles back? With the billiards and the propane station?" She glanced at him and winked.

"You, Cadie Whitaker, are a snob," he laughed.

Suddenly, the truck began slowing down and he looked around to see if they had arrived. If they *had* arrived, it sure didn't look like it. There was nothing but green for days. At least, that's all he could see out of the window on Cadie's side of the truck. It didn't occur to him to look away from her until she pointed past him, and then he finally turned. That direction told a very different story.

A familiar white farmhouse stood out amongst all the green, but not as much as the baseball diamond did. *No. It can't be.* But once he saw the cornfield, there could be no question.

He jumped out of the truck before she put it into park. "Are you kidding me?" he shouted as he took it all in. "This is the *Field of Dreams* house! Cadie, come look at this!"

Her joyous laughter filled the air, and he realized he'd run off and left his very pregnant wife to fend for herself getting out of a massive truck. He ran back to help her, but she'd already stepped out.

"What are you doing? Don't wait for me. Go," she insisted. "Darby's pulling in. I'll wait for her and Grace, and we'll be right there."

He looked down toward the field and then back at Cadie. "Who are all those other people?"

Kevin and Ellis came up from behind Will. "We couldn't get Shoeless Joe, since he's been dead since the 1950s and all," Ellis said, "but I think Cadie and Swoosh pulled together a pretty good team. Barry Bonds, Johnny Bench, Sandy Koufax, A-Rod, Derek Jeter . . . oh, and Hank Aaron's here."

Will scoffed in disbelief. "I've heard that one before."

Cadie smiled at him. "Go see for yourself."

Once again, he looked toward the baseball diamond, where under the lights some of the greatest ball players of all time were warming up on the set of one of his favorite movies of all time. But, as always, nothing could steal his attention away from her for very long.

"This was *you?*" he asked, the emotion over-taking his voice. He wrapped his arms around her and whispered in her ear, "How in the world did you pull this off?"

Throwing her arms around his neck, she replied, "Well, you *are* working. That part's true. It's an ASN special. And Darby's producing. The rest? Well, let's just say there are a few people in this business who think you're an okay guy."

Their embrace was interrupted by two-year-old Grace running to them and grabbing on to their legs. Will bent down and scooped her into his arms and kissed her on the cheek, before leaning in and kissing his wife on the lips.

"Do you have any idea how madly in love with you I am?"

She cupped his face in her hands and pressed her body as close to him as she possibly could, their two children between them. "I have a pretty good idea. Now, go. Seriously. Life is passing you by."

"Dance with me," he said, and he began swaying his family to music only he could hear.

"What? You're crazy." She laughed and rested her forehead against Grace's. "Daddy's silly, isn't he?"

Will continued swaying, and Cadie followed his lead as he called out, much to her delight, "The *Field of Dreams* house and the state of Iowa wish to extend a very special welcome to Will and Cadie Whitaker of Stamford, Connecticut, who met as young ladder-climbers at American Sports Network, eight years ago, and tonight are celebrating their fourth wedding anniversary— along with their two children, one football legend, one basketball legend, and half the living members of the Baseball Hall of Fame."

"Ahem . . . what about me?" Darby called out.

"And Darby," Will amended. "And a film crew, apparently? And who's that guy? Are you the owner of the house?" The man nodded that he was, and Will added, "And the owner of the house!"

He set Grace down, and she took off running toward the field. "That's my girl," he laughed as Ellis took off following after her. Cadie squealed at his attempts to dip her, but her laughter subsided as he took her in his arms once again, unobstructed by a toddler, and silenced her with a kiss that put every single romance movie to shame.

Acknowledgments

There are so many people who came along with me on the journey as I prepared to introduce Cadie and Will to you all, and I am going to do my best to thank as many of them as possible. But first and foremost, I owe thanks to the Lord, who introduced *me* to Cadie and Will, not to mention this love of story that springs from him.

I'm so grateful to my church family at Rock Springs. You guys have been so supportive, and I can't even tell you how much that has meant. One of the greatest gifts God has given me is allowing me to worship and serve alongside you.

Secily, Jacob, David, LeeAnn . . . you guys ride with me on my emotional rollercoaster more than just about anyone else. Thanks for splurging on the Unlimited Rides pass. Jenny, as always, I'm desperately hoping you think this one lives up to our standard. Zaida, Kaari, Kristi, Kristen, Tonya, Donna . . . thanks.

I have the best street team in the world. Most of the members of the "See Bethany Launch" team have been with me since before *The Secret Life of*

Sarah Hollenbeck released, and I am so grateful for each and every one of you!

Which brings me to all the readers who have embraced me and embraced the stories I write. I'm so grateful for all of you, but especially those of you who follow along on social media, send me encouraging notes, take part in the FB chats, and especially the members of The Book Club Closest to My House. You have become my community, and my affection for you goes even beyond books.

The team I get to work with at Revell is simply the best. Karen and Michele, working with you is such a joy! Hannah, no one has to field more of my questions and ideas than you, but you welcome each one with patience and enthusiasm. Thanks for dreaming with me. Kristin, thank you for challenging me and helping me think new thoughts.

Kelsey Bowen, in every single way, this story is being told because of you. You are a treasured friend and a brilliant editor, and I'll never stop thanking God for bringing us together.

Jessica Kirkland, I hope you're even half as happy to be working with me as I am to be working with you, because you're stuck with me, my friend.

Sarah Monzon, not only did you make my writing stronger, you also kept me going when I was not feeling the love for this story *at all.*

Melissa Ferguson, you crack me up. Always. Thanks for being #TeamJoe. Nicole Deese, I'm really not sure how I made it through as much life as I did before I had you as my co-host. Annaliese Flautt and Maureen Drake, I'll always go back to that first day as one of the absolute best. Mikal Hermanns and Carol Moncado, I can barely remember a time before MiBeCa. #MiBeCaIsEternalYo

Colleen Coble, Irene Hannon, Kristin Billerbeck, Becky Wade, Liz Johnson, Rachel McMillan, Melissa Parcel, Rel Mollet. You have each encouraged me at a time when I desperately needed it—and you probably didn't even realize it. You were just being the wonderful, supportive people that you are. But trust me. You made a difference.

Thanks to my parents for instilling a love of pop culture and supporting it through various crazy, obsessive phases. And my sister may not read my books (don't get me started . . .) but she's gotten pretty good at acting like she has, so she never misses a moment!

Ethan and Noah, the way you believe in me and encourage me to keep at it, even when it means you don't have clean laundry, fills my heart to overflowing.

Kelly Turner, you're still my favorite, and I'm pretty sure I'm *your* favorite. That overwhelms me. Being your favorite's favorite? Yeah . . . a girl can't do any better than that.

About the Author

B ethany Turner is the award-winning author of *The Secret Life of Sarah Hollenbeck*, which was a finalist for the Christy Award. When she's not writing (and even when she is), she serves as the director of administration for Rock Springs Church in southwest Colorado. A former bank executive and a three-time cancer survivor (all before she turned thirty-five), Bethany knows that when God has plans for your life, it doesn't matter what anyone else has to say. Because of that, she's chosen to follow his call to write. She lives with her husband and their two sons in Colorado, where she writes for a new generation of readers who crave fiction that tackles the thorny issues of life with humor and insight.

Books are produced in the United States using U.S.-based materials

Books are printed using a revolutionary new process called THINKtech™ that lowers energy usage by 70% and increases overall quality

Books are durable and flexible because of Smyth-sewing

Paper is sourced using environmentally responsible foresting methods and the paper is acid-free

Center Point Large Print

600 Brooks Road / PO Box 1
Thorndike, ME 04986-0001 USA

(207) 568-3717

US & Canada:
1 800 929-9108
www.centerpointlargeprint.com